Gib

A Contemporary Western

D1706510

Gib: A Contemporary Western

by Jon R. Horton

JR Horton

SUNLIGHT
PUBLISHING

Acknowledgments

Thanks to Stormy and the crew at Sunlight:
Aysha, Margaret, Fred — even Goldie helped.
This is a beautiful book.

Special thanks to Jim Bama, world-class artist,
husband, father, neighbor, gentleman.

SUNLIGHT PUBLISHING, INC
Colorado Springs, Colorado 80920 USA

Published 1998. First Edition
Printed in the United States of America
ISBN 0-9643978-3-8

Cover art by James Bama
"Cal Todd – A Cowboy"
Watercolor

For Ariel, who made all the difference.

You may have been born elsewhere,
but God gave you a heart for the West.

Prologue

The first cold front of autumn has passed through the Yellowstone Park country. What was rain in the valleys became snow on the high mountain plateau of the Absaroka mountains. The peaks are frosted with a few inches of ephemeral white, which will be mostly gone by the end of this day. A warming sun is dropping its early light down into the valleys west of the mountains, etching away at the shadows below. It washes the yellow-splashed and rust-tinged lowland vegetation and pokes its fingers into the dark swaths of pine trees which lie at the feet of the rocky heights far above.

Where this valley meets those trees, a huge, black bull moose stands belly-deep in a dead meander, now a beaver pond, of a lost creek in Yellowstone. The animal's hump is more than six feet from the bottom of the pond and the palms of its enormous antlers are white in the morning light. A brain the size of a fist clicks insides its skull, for this is a living fossil. The oldest and the most primitive of the deer family, it is a relic of the pleistocene age whose ice floes, more than half a mile thick, ground much of western Wyoming to powder twenty thousand years ago.

The bull is grazing on the bottom of the beaver pond in early morning light and frost is thick on the long, bent grasses at the edge of the bright water. Pink light glistens on the rime of frost on the willow leaves and the Absaroka mountains are perfectly imaged in the pond.

Suddenly, a beaver's tail slaps the water and the moose lifts its wet face. Water cascades from the majestic rack of horns. Dripping aquatic vegetation hangs from its mouth. The large, delicate nostrils open and the small pig-like eyes blink to clear its sight because it knows well enough to heed the wary beaver's alarm.

The rank smell of rotten flesh drifts to the moose on the air and an explosion of breath balloons in a rainbow mist around the shovels of his antlers. A tall ridge of black guard hairs erects along his neck and hump. Adrenaline floods his muscles as his eyes pick out another beast standing in the willows only twenty-five yards away. It is a bear. A griz.

The cold, painful night has crept deep into the grizzly's spine and stiffened his damaged hip. He is making his way down to the water for a drink, joints burning with a fire that had robbed his rest. But now the pain and weariness leave him as he stares at the black hulk in the water. He is flooded with rage because the big bull is shaking his antlers, snorting, and even now is taking a couple of menacing steps through the water. Enough!

The bear dives into the water. A large wave hurries to bases of the willows, and frost falls from the leaves when the wave surges against the bank. A howl breaks from the bear's chest as he lunges through the water. The moose comes to meet him.

Both are shaken by the impact. The shock of their enormous bodies meeting hangs in the air. Birds scatter from trees a hundred yards away.

To his astonishment the bear feels himself thrown into the air and then water closes over his head. He feels a moment's panic, but rights himself and then bounds toward the bank of the pond. He shakes the water from his eyes and coughs to clear his lungs. Glancing at the bull, the bear feels a surge, for the moose is shaken and wobbling.

The bear roars and the bull turns again, lowers its massive shovels and charges a few feet, blasting the surface of the pond with his nostrils.

The bear needs better footing. Here the bottom of the pond is a rich, gooey black clay and silt. He knows that the upstream part of the beaver pond has a firm bottom so he quickly circles. The moose spins to follow the enemy with its antlers. But the moose also chooses to begin a cautious retreat—but it is a mistake, for that means backing through deeper water.

The bear feels gravel under his feet and he digs his claws into it and begins a swooping charge straight down the gravel bar, digging powerfully into the firm footing. He sees the bull drop its head and brace to meet the charge head-on.

But at the last moment the bear sidesteps, slips his left arm under the moose's right antler, thrusts his right forearm against the left shovel and

2

powers the moose onto its side and under the dark water. The bear feels the moose's face roll up under his chest, and he lays his seven hundred pounds down on it.

He feels the bull's frantic efforts to get its hooves into the pond's bottom, feels them dig into the goo and slip. This animal is the strongest he has ever tested and he knows he cannot let it gain its feet. For the first time in his life the bear feels the limit of his strength. A muscle spasm cramps his shoulder.

He relaxes the edge of the right antler, which allows the moose's head to swivel. As he sees the moose's nose start toward the surface, the bear drives his own face, jaws agape, down to meet it.

A foot below the surface of the pond he bites through the bull's soft muzzle and feels the delicate nose bones break between his teeth The crunching sound runs up his jaws and fills his ears. He feels the big animal stiffen in shock and air from the moose's lungs shoots out the sides of the bear's mouth. The moose's legs straighten out and a monstrous shiver shakes both the animals.

When he runs out of his own breath, the bear looses his bite, throws his head out of the water and draws in a vast draft of air. He gasps, then groans, begins to relax his grip.

But the moose gives a strong shudder and digs a hind hoof into the pond bottom. The bear quickly shifts his weight back and bears down. The hump on his back bulges and the muscles stand out in relief. The sunlight shoots off the silver hairs on his massive back. He looks as if he's been electrified.

The surface of the pond slowly stills back to a mirror. Reflections of the snow-capped mountains, the willows and the pines reappear in it. A squirrel chatters maniacally in a nearby tree. Another joins his frantic voice and they scamper to shelter, causing pine needles to rain down on the forest floor.

Finally, the bear moves slowly and releases an arm. He pulls a leg loose and rests for a moment. He moves again and stands, blows water from his nostrils. He sneezes and shakes his enormous head. Then he wades slowly to the bank and moves through the willows. A wave of damp foliage marks his slow progress and he emerges into the sun. He steps over a dead log and limps to the trees. The thick scar tissue of the ancient bullet wound is burning again.

He reaches the edge of the tree line and pauses because it is chilly in the shade. He turns back into the warm morning sun and lies down, straightening his bad leg. Then he stretches out his arms and puts his massive face between them. He blinks, groans, blinks again. A great breath escapes the great bear and he closes his eyes.

He will need to rest for the long walk that still lies ahead, the one which had been interrupted by the challenge of the now-dead bull. Today he will begin his trek over the mountains and back into the territory of the ancient enemy, of the man who wounded him and handed him his one defeat. Long ago when he was young. And strong.

Chapter 1

When the first white men came to the mountains of northwest Wyoming they met a mountain tribe of Indians who described an enormous black bird which had spanned the skies above the mountains when they first arrived from the north, in the first days of the people. Not a raven, they said to the strangers, bigger. No, not an eagle — much, much bigger. Huge. They called it the absaroka, and the trappers had pinned the name on the tribe. Eventually, they used it to name the tribe's home mountain range as well. Later the name of the tribe would would devolve to the "Crow" Indians but the mountains kept the original appellation. Only the native people knew the bird for what it had been — before the white men came, because it was long gone when they arrived.

Jack Scott is thinking about the story as he drives below Carter Mountain. It is magnificent in the morning sun and the largest single feature of the Absaroka mountain range. The south fork of the Shoshone River shaped it from the ancient Absaroka volcanic plateau and its sheer face rises almost two-thousand feet above the rubble hills at its base. Its long, banded gray face gradually disappears upriver, and as Jack drives he visualizes every mile of the long river valley. Jack, as well as his father, grandfather and great-grandfather, spent their whole lives beneath Carter Mountain and its sisters across the river. The Scotts have been on this ranch, the Hoodoo, over a hundred years.

I wonder what the absaroka was, really? He thinks it plausible a species of condor might have been native to the area when the glaciers were retreating and the American continent had a population of animals which would have shamed the plains of Africa. A scavenger of that size would have had a natural niche, especially during the slaughter that followed the arrival of a people who had been starving in an ice and snow environment for generations. Personally, he liked the idea of some great relic of a fossil age gliding above these mountains, impressing the new human arrivals with his enormity.

But the whites had not been completely insensible to all the myths. They had chosen to give the name hoodoos to the resistant volcanic rock pillars that were common to the Absaroka country skyline. Jack's great-grandfather had chosen to name his ranch after those stone watchers because he had been another disenfranchised veteran of the Civil War and knew the legends of the African Americans in which voodoos rose from the dead and hoodoos waited to snatch unwary folks, especially children. Jack had passed on those Southern stories to his son and seen the goose flesh raise on JC's thin arms, the same reaction he'd had when he was boy.

Jack slows down when he sees the flag up on the mail box. He removes the wad of mail inside, shoves the door shut and sorts through the bundle of agricultural magazines, bills and business mail until he comes to something that gives him a twinge in his chest. It is a postcard with a picture of a gaudy neon casino on it. "*ELKO!*" is gashed in subscript across the bottom of the card. He turns it over quickly. It is addressed to "Anisa Scott and Kids" and the text says:

> Heard you was looking for me don't wory.
> I am doing all rite.
> > Gib

Jack's name has been left off altogether and the omission causes a painful twinge in his chest. The twinge turns into an ache as he drives toward the ranch house. The truck tires thump over the rocky road and Paul Harvey's voice fades on the radio as Jack's memory goes back almost three years.

In his mind's eye he sees Gib's broad back in the doorway of the foreman's house, one boot bracing the screen door open as he heaves his duffel out onto the porch with a thud. Jack remembers vividly the pain he experienced as he realized that Gib was leaving. Really leaving. But that's the way the old man does things: Get 'er over with and make it stick.

The feeling of abandonment comes back, fresh as ever, when he reaches the very same crest over which Gib's truck had disappeared. If he'd topped the river bluff and found the ranch burned to the ground, it would have been little different. An enormous part of the family's lives, their emotional landscape, had gone. It had been as if Carter Mountain itself was missing.

"Lord," Jack whispers. A large lump fills his throat.

Jack had needed a long time to come to terms with the loss of the man who had raised him since he was a small boy. Until the previous winter, to be exact. He remembers walking down the street in Cody with his son, JC, who was wearing a new coat Jack had bought him. The coat was too big and he realized JC had not had the nerve to tell him. The boy was walking with his head down, the cold wind blowing his hair around. He was miserable and Jack realized the boy looked that way a lot of the time. Ever since Gib had left. Jack knew then it was his own emotional state being reflected in his son.

That boy needs a full time father, Jack had thought. Memories of his own boyhood had washed over him and the emotion of the moment inspired him to stop on the windy, snowy street and hug the boy. He had known exactly how JC felt. A boy needs his dad one hundred percent of the time. Fatherhood is no part-time deal.

Jack's painful reverie ends. But, we've come a ways since then, he thinks. It's a fact that without Gib the ranch is in tough financial shape.

"But we've still got a shot," he says aloud and glances down at the truck seat to make sure that the envelope with the legal papers is still there.

After crossing the river bridge, Jack drives down the ranch lane. He sees his son and the dogs running up to road to greet him. The weight of his worries eases. On this old ranch among the cottonwoods and next to the river, he is home, he is loved, and he feels strong.

❄ ❄ ❄

Three hundred miles to the south, in the town of Evanston, Maggie Scott is entering the front door of the Wyoming State Hospital. It is the home of the human flotsam and jetsam which has found no other place to lodge itself. Maggie is Jack's sister and a medical doctor. As she enters the building she is thinking that the name of the place is as homely and unpretentious as the state itself — just call it the way it is. The Wyoming State Hospital.

The hallway is dark. Dark wood and a burgundy and white checkerboard flooring swallows light, except for streaks and blotches where the light from windows smears itself down the long corridor.

Maggie reaches a Dutch door and places her purse on its gouged little shelf. "Hello," she says to the secretary, a woman with silver-shot dark hair and half-glasses who is working at a computer. She looks up and quickly notes the other woman's expensive purse and suit. She stands and, approaching the door, sticks out her hand, a ready smile on her face. They shake hands and Maggie retrieves her purse.

"You must be Doctor Scott. Congratulations on getting the position. I was rooting for you, personally. I'm Patty Potter, Doctor Hillyard's secretary."

Maggie steps back as Patty opens the door. "Doctor H. is busy at the moment. He said to make you feel at home, so I thought I'd show you your office. The carpet was late getting laid, the paint is still drying, and they're not going to be able to hang the drapes until tomorrow. But it is going to look grand when it's done."

They turn down another, better lighted, corridor. A door at the end stands open, exhaling the smell of fresh paint. They step through the door and stop in the middle of the room.

"Isn't this nice?"

"Yes, it is. I like it very much."

"Make yourself comfortable, I've got to get back to the phone. I'll be back in a minute or two, the doctor shouldn't be too much longer."

"Fine. Thank you."

Maggie looks around the room and does a quick inventory of her art print collection, trying to come up with something which she might hang. But nothing comes to mind which would be comfortable here. Puzzled, she takes another look. The paint scheme is a very light beige with pale lemon trim. Odd choice, she thinks, though the unusual combination appeals. Then it strikes her. The state university's colors are the autumn colors brown and gold and the painter has chosen that palette, though a muted version of it. She smiles — there is something endearing about the sentimentality. Again, the lack of sophistication and pretension strikes a positive note. It is good to be home again.

Still smiling, she steps to the office window and looks out across the drive and the lawns.

A tall man is standing about twenty-five yards away, leaning with his back against one of the big shade trees. He wears a western-cut suit and a soft, white Stetson. He appears to be waiting for someone inside, not having been able to summon the nerve to enter the institution and confront what, or who, waits inside.

Maggie moves closer to the glass, the better to examine the man's wind burned face. There is something very familiar about the stance, and the attitude. He has one hand in his pants pocket and the other hand at his mouth as he draws on a cigarette. She watches the thick hand come down, the thumb nick the filter to scatter the ashes. The gesture freezes her. Suddenly, the room is full of the smell of bay rum, cigarette breath, and a working man's body odor.

It is the essence of Gib. Maggie closes her eyes and feels a welling of emotion deep inside her. Memories push themselves out of neglected corners and she imagines wind on her face, sun on her head, the smell of meadow hay and sagebrush crushed beneath horse hooves.

When she opens her eyes the man is gone. She takes a deep breath and the smell of fresh paint brings her back to the hospital office.

"Doctor Hillyard is ready to see you now." The secretary is standing in the door. When Maggie starts toward her, Patty points, "Your eye makeup is running."

Startled, Maggie reaches up and touches one cheek and then the other. Her face is wet with tears.

Gib poises his pickup on the battered edge of the arroyo and eases the transmission into "grandma." The old Jimmy pickup growls slowly down into the dry watercourse, then up the other side. It rolls to a stop and the man shifts from the compound gear into low and starts down the track scratched along the foot of a Nevada mountain range known only to map makers, geologists and cow men. It is only 8 o'clock in the morning, but the temperature is already working its way rapidly up through the nineties.

"Them two pups had better have everything ready to go," he mutters as he upshifts and glances in the rear view mirror at the boil of dust rising behind him. It is roundup time and the men from the widely scattered ranches will be showing up for the spring gathering of cows which have wintered on the mountains' sides.

The man is hauling the last of the groceries to the cow camp where the cowboys will leave on horseback to gather the loose cattle into bunches and then one large herd for counting, branding and doctoring.

In the fall the area ranchers push their cows onto their government leases. Because there are no fences and cows are herd animals, they inevitably mingle. Springtime means that they have to be sorted out and each rancher take charge of his property. In a perfect world each of the cows will have a calf by her side. But this is not a perfect world and this is the time for the hard realities of a hard life to be toted up, chewed on and swallowed.

It is a neighborly time of year, and the only one where most everyone can be found in the same place. It is a time for hard work, rough play, yarning, drinking for the drinkers and singing for the singers. And the perfect time to cuss about the government and everyone else who appears to be trying to grub out the cow culture which they represent.

This roundup is one of several going on in the valley, an area of almost three hundred square miles, and Gib is "repping" it and, by God, it is going to be the quickest and most efficient of them all, even if it kills him doing it.

"And it just might," he says aloud. His back is bothering him again and both his hernias are tingling from the rough ride.

Gib is looking down the barrel of his seventieth year, though he doesn't look it when he is on horseback and has his hat on. Once he is back down on the ground his crooked ankles and swaled knees help give his age away. Then he moves with the stilted, awkward movements of a sand hill crane.

"Where the hell's that beer?" he growls to himself, and rummages through the plunder on the truck seat. He finally comes up with a hot can of Coors. Steering the truck with his forearms, he holds it toward the open window and pulls the tab. A plume of hot liquid sprays the truck's door and dash, as well as the man's gnarled hands and weathered face.

"Damn!" He shakes his wet hand, wipes it on his Wranglers. He pushes back his hat and wipes his wet, sticky face, then tilts his head back and pours the half can of hot bubbles down his throat. The beer has been skunked by the heat and the taste lies somewhere between paint thinner and Perrier. He grimaces.

"Boy, does that taste good," he says, ironically. He is thankful, though, for the way the beer almost instantly eases his Jim Beam headache.

He pulls his hat back down to the line of his rancher tan and looks across the valley to the distant mountains in the west, twins to the range whose feet he is crossing.

"Damn corduroy state. Everything runs north and south; mountains then desert, mountains then desert for four hundred miles," he gripes, "and all of it hot as the hinges on the door to hell." The miserable combination of the heat and his hangover is making him homesick for the green and cool Absaroka country with its alpine plateaus and their pleasant breezes.

Trying to ignore the dust and heat, he drives until his eyes pick out a scrawny string of cottonwood trees marking the meager stream which trickles out of the cow camp canyon. In a few moments he is close enough to see that all the horses are in the corral, but no men in sight.

"Them two are shaded up, wouldn't ya know. Where have all the real cowboys gone, anyway? Neither of one of 'em has enough sense to pick a giraffe out of a herd of sheep." He shakes his head in disgust when he sees his cowhands saunter off the cabin and onto the porch. Obviously, they'd heard him coming.

Becoming a good cowboy means being born for it; you have to care about the life like a musician born to make music. These two didn't have a heart for it, though he had to admit that the one, Chris, tried hard enough.

As he approaches the cabin, his thoughts go back to Wyoming. And Jack. Gib had tried to raise him to work hard from the time he was a tyke. He had not wanted any man to fault the boy and he had been willing enough — most of the time. But, he had a dreamy side to him that took over. You could see in his handiwork where his mind had veered off onto something else and his imagination took over. The first six tiers of his haystack would be tied tight as a drum, the next two tiers would be a mess. From then on one could see where he'd had to fight like hell to get it back into shape, so it wouldn't fall over.

"Oh God," Gib muttered, and threw the beer can out of the window.

How could Jack feel what wasn't in him? Blood ran true. Jack was never going to be anything more than what he was right now — little more than a working stiff with only a partial understanding of what made fortune smile on men like Judge Scott, and his father before him. He would probably amount to no more than Gib himself had, run over boots, bad back and all. The thought brings bile up into the big man's throat. He hocks and spits out into the hot day and the dry little wind that was lifting the truck's dust high into the blistered sky.

He rolls the pickup to a stop in front of the shack. The two cowboys come over to meet him.

"Morning," Chris says.

11

"Mornin," Gib replies and gets out. He strides to the tailgate and drops it with a bang. "Let's get this stuff inside. You two unload 'er. I'm gonna take me a look around." He heads for the corrals, suspicious that the water trough might be dry. As he drove up he'd seen the horses standing around it, patiently waiting for someone to run them some water.

As the old man disappears behind the cabin, Chris smiles and says, "Friendly ol fart, ain't he?"

"Who does that old bastard think he is, anyway?" the younger cowboy asks as he slides a case of canned peaches onto the tailgate of the pickup.

"Gibson. He's from Wyoming. I heard that him and the Old Man were in the army together. He knows just about all the old timers in the business, I guess. Old rodeo champ."

"Well, he don't show me shit. I don't like anything about 'im."

"How come?"

"Oh, the way he give you that disgusted look, and shakes his head, every time you make a little mistake."

"All them old timers is like that."

"Not like him. He makes you feel like you're an inch tall."

"He's a hard teacher, sure. But that's what I like about him — a man might learn a little something from him. He damn sure knows his business. Can't take that away from him." Chris grabs a case of pork and beans and puts it on his shoulder.

"Maybe so. I just hate it when he gets down on you for the little things, things that don't mean a pinch of shit anywhere but on this alkali patch." He picks up a sack of flour and grimaces at the big smudge of white that covers his front. He follows Chris.

"I'll agree there. This ain't the prettiest place that anyone ever ran cows on."

"Hell, a man couldn't raise a good hard-on here, let alone good beef. I never heard of a place that wasn't fenced before. What kind of a ranch is it where all they do is put up a north-south drift fence to keep the cows from walking clean into Utah?"

"Well, they got water in Utah, and cows do get thirsty. Utah musta traded Nevada straight across: Water for all the sun and snakes in the world. Those Mormons are good businessmen." Chris puts his load down on the counter and walks back to the truck. He stacks a case of Spam on top of a case of cream corn.

"Hell, let's take a break," says the young cowboy.

"Better not. He ain't but just around back."

"Hell, as old and stove-up as he is, it'll take 'im an hour to walk the hundred yards back from the corral. I'm gonna roll me one."

"If you get caught smokin' that shit, he'll run you off so fast you'll get picked up for speeding in Las Vegas."

"Who's gonna tell…you?"

"Nope. None of my business what you do. Just givin' you a little advice, that's all." He lifts two more cases and starts for the shack.

"Suckass," the younger one mutters. He reaches into his shirt pick, pulls out a tin and some papers then squats down in the shade of the pickup to roll a pin joint. He lights it, takes a deep drag. He snorts a bit of smoke out his nose and holds the remainder deep in his lungs.

This is some righteous shit, he says to himself as he looks out over the desert toward the distant mountains. How in the pluperfect hell did I ever wind up with this nickel-dime outfit, anyway?

He takes off his hat and wipes his forehead on his sleeve as the smoke expels from his lungs. Suddenly, he is aware of a pair of boots with patches on both sides. He doesn't have to look up to know who is in them. Kee-rist, he thinks.

"You ain't gettin' paid to sit out here in the shade with your finger in your ass and your mind in Arkansas. Get movin'." The boots disappear.

"You prick," the young man mutters as he stands.

"What did you say?" Gib is standing on the other side of the pickup bed, reaching for a box of groceries. His voice isn't angry or loud, is even a little amused. But the eyes under the hat glitter.

"I said, 'I'm sick.' Little too much sun, I guess."

"You're a liar, son," Gib says quietly. He picks up the groceries and shuffles toward the cabin.

In cow country, where a man's word is his proudest possession, being called a liar is a deadly insult. And it is an unmistakable challenge.

The young man feels sick to his stomach. He feels stripped of everything he holds important, of that which he has come West to find — self-respect. He slides a case of chili onto the tailgate and stands there for a moment. What am I going to do? he thinks.

But, burning with pain, there is only one thing he can think to do. He starts quickly toward the cabin.

Inside, Gib puts the box of groceries on the table. "Does that kid smoke what I think he smokes?"

Chris stops a dipper full of water half way to his mouth. "Dunno," he says and takes a drink. As he puts the dipper back in the bucket he looks out the door, and says, "What the hell is wrong with him?"

Gib follows his glance and looks around the room. He grabs a large butcher knife from the counter top and quickly tosses it behind the stove. Then he stands in the center of the room, ready for the young man with the red face.

But the youngster dashes by him, kicking the wooden box with the checkerboard on it across the room. He jerks his bedroll to the floor as Chris shouts a warning and throws himself onto the floor. "Gun!" he hollers and puts his hands over his ears.

The young cowboy grabs his pistol from its place and, thumbing back the hammer, is drawing down on the old man when the water bucket hits him. The window over the sink explodes and the muzzle blast rocks the room with its force and noise.

Knocked to the floor by the thrown bucket, the man wipes his face and re-cocks the revolver. A box of salt hits him over his left eye, snapping his head around as he grunts with pain, drops the gun and falls back against a bunk.

Chris scrambles to his feet but Gib's hand pushes him out of the way. While catching his balance, he sees Gib's boot come up and catch the sitting man under the chin. There is a loud "pop" as teeth slam together. Hands and feet jerk convulsively from the floor where the man is sitting and Chris sees a large piece of his partner's tongue fall from his mouth, then flop slowly down the front of his dusty shirt.

Chapter 2

"Good morning, Doctor Scott. I'm Bud Hillyard, please come in and sit down." Maggie follows the bobbing pink scalp, the pinky ring and the powder-blue western suit into the overstuffed office. Dr. Hillyard drops into his large chair where, with his round face and blue shoe-button eyes, he looks like a Cabbage Patch Kid. On the wall behind his desk, a James Bama print of a rugged working cowboy is a study in contrast. Maggie smiles. The little man makes a tent in front of his face with his fingers and smiles over the top of it. The expensive brass and rosewood name plate introduces him as:

Dr. M. 'Bud' Hillyard
Ed.D., M.S., B.S.

Perfect, Maggie thinks.

"Dr. Scott, I understand that you were born here in Wyoming."

"Yes, I was. On a ranch near Cody."

"I've never been up there, sorry to say. I find myself mostly in Jackson Hole, Cheyenne and Laramie, when I'm not tied down here. All in all, it's a lot of responsibility. I'm on the Board of Governors of the University, you know."

"No, I didn't know."

"Yes, yes, yes. I'm originally from Utah, but it didn't take long for me to make myself at home here in Wyoming."

"I'll bet it didn't," Maggie said.

Dr. Hillyard pulls open a desk drawer and retrieves a file. He holds it in front of him, reading. A few moments of silence pass, then he lays the file on the desk, still reading. Another moment passes before he begins to summarize the file.

"Smith College, uh hm, Georgetown University, Johns Hopkins, Brigham Women's…" He pauses. "Veteran's Administration hospitals from 1982 through 1987…" His voice trails off as he turns to the next page. "In 1992 you helped to open a clinic devoted to poor black women in Washington, D.C.. Very admirable. Very." Dr. Hillyard leans back slowly into his big chair and re-erects the tent in front of his sharp gaze.

"Dr. Scott," his voice is quiet, neutral, "just what are you doing here in Evanston, Wyoming?"

Maggie is not surprised at the question, but her mind goes momentarily blank. It could not cope instantly with Hillyard's metamorphosis. His appearance obviously belies a very shrewd man. She has misjudged him completely.

He goes on. "Dr. Scott, your credentials and professional history qualify you for a staff position at some place like the Neuropsychiatric Institute at UCLA, Menningers, or another institution of that order." He pauses. "Doctor, this is a public institution in the least populous, and one of the most economically strapped, states in the country. If it weren't for me, and a handful of others, the legislature would just as likely let this place be sold for the used brick." He sighs. "This is the ranking institution only because it was the first one built, plus the fact that alcoholism and drug abuse are epidemic in this state. Otherwise, it would have been torn down long ago, and the residents left to cope on their own."

Maggie replies, " You paint a very distressing picture, but I suspect that it is not in a complete state of crisis, no more so than any other institution dedicated to the same kind of work in other places." She gives Hillyard a sharp look of her own, and says, "Dr. Hillyard, are you trying to talk me out of accepting the position as head of your geriatric program?"

"No, I'm not. I am delighted, in a way, to have someone as eminently qualified as you are. I simply do not understand why someone like yourself would come to Wyoming and choose to work in a state institution for comparatively low pay, rather than start a private practice, for instance."

"Doctor, if you look carefully at my file again, you will see that for the last six years I have specialized in geriatrics. And, inasmuch as I have been hired by the board, unanimously I might add, the question should be what do you expect of me…and when do I start?"

Hillyard takes a deep breath, puts his hands on the desk. "I'm going to be flat honest with you."

"Please do."

"My fear is that you are going to come here, set up a brilliant program, make me and the institution look like a million dollars by using your connections to bring in a lot of expertise and foundation money, and then take a hike on us. And I will end up hiring a comparative mediocrity like myself to replace you — someone you would expect to be applying at a hospital like this." He waves his hand at the window and the buildings visible through it. "And I will feel very disappointed, abandoned and eventually look like hell in comparison with what you've accomplished during your tenure."

He leans back in his chair. "I'm being selfish. I have to be. This job isn't easy, and I care about this place a lot. We try hard and we have to, given what we have to work with."

He smiles, but the sharp look remains. "If you've come home to Wyoming to do something special for your own gratification — something to make you feel better — I would prefer that you didn't do it here. Please, spare me that."

Maggie feels a real respect for the man because of his frankness. "Doctor Hillyard, all I can promise you is that I will do my very best while I'm here. Promising anything more would be dishonest. Let's just take it as it comes." She pauses. "And I honestly don't know why I have come back to Wyoming — I just knew that I had to."

Hillyard purses his lips, shrugs, and finally smiles. "I can't ask any more than that, I guess."

He stands. "Let's go over to the ward and I'll introduce you to the staff. They are looking forward to meeting you."

❋ ❋ ❋

"Get yerself a cup of coffee, Gib."

Old George sits at the kitchen table with a coffee cup, an overfull ashtray and a greasy white envelope in front of him. The remains of breakfast cover the rest of the table. It bears witness to the lack of any feminine influence, the oil cloth dirty and worn by the domestic traffic of too many men.

The usual buzzing of flies in the room is absent, most of them busy at the leftover syrup and breakfast leavings on the plates.

Old George massages his weather-ravaged eyes with his thick fingers, then looks at Gib as his friend sits down.

"There's yer pay," he says and nods at the thick envelope. Gib glances at the envelope as he slurps hot coffee from the mug, knowing the contents are made up of fives, tens, and twenties.

"Ya know I gotta let you go," the old man says.

Gib nods and looks up from under his hat brim as his boss, and old friend, reaches into a shirt pocket with thumb and index finger and comes out with a single Pall Mall. Gib watches him straighten out a leg and dig into his faded jeans for the ancient lighter. It comes out and there is the distinctive Zippo click as the top flips open.

George lays it down on the table. A worn brass nub on the side of the lighter is all that is left of the insignia of their old Army division. Fifty years before.

"Gib?"

"Yeah."

"What the hell has happened to you?"

"Dunno what you mean."

"You've changed. A lot."

"How so?"

"You know what I mean."

Gib crosses his arms and looks out the window toward the sun-battered barn.

"Whatcha gettin at?"

Old George puts both of his elbows on the table and grasps one hand with the other. He pulls the clump of twisted fingers to his mouth and takes a drag from the cigarette. Then he lowers his head and stares at the oil cloth.

"Old son, you've gotten meaner than hell since I last saw ya. You drink too damn much — though I guess I'm no one to be preachin about that. But it's gotten so that whiskey just turns inta poison when you do. You don't drink laughin whiskey anymore. You drink that damn fightin whiskey."

"George…"

"Huh?"

Gib is still staring out the window. "Where did it all go?"

"Where did what go?"

"Everything. The fun, the money, the friends, the… Everything," he adds quietly.

George shrugs. "It just went."

"Well, I miss it."

The two old men stare out the same window. The sun is just starting to really bear down. The little pockets and nooks of cool morning shade are evaporating.

Old George takes another deep drag and lets the smoke ease from his nose. "We done it to ourselves, really. With a lot of help from the goverment, of course. And the banks."

Gib nods, toys with the thick porcelain mug in his hands.

George continues. "When we took our first dime from the goverment it was all over but the pissin and the moanin. The way Young George tells it, price supports is nothing more than welfare and the banks was loanin us money against our welfare checks.

"The first time he told me it that way, I almost knocked him down and stomped a mud hole in his ass. I never thought I ever got somethin for nothin, but I guess I did."

He stares at the smoke coming off the end of his cigarette and smiles wryly. "I was right down there at the welfare trough with all the rest of 'em." He is quiet for a moment and then says, "God damn but it hurts to say that."

Gib nods. "Well, maybe that was the way of it. I dunno. Just some more tough times is the way that some see it, but I don't. Hell, I don't mind things sorting themselves out so's a man has to get right down, dig in, and start over. That's the way it's always been in this business." He finishes his coffee and sets the mug down emphatically.

"It's just that this time around they are takin a whole way of life with 'em — lawyers, banks, developers, damn sagebrush huggers. A whole damn world is goin down the drain — a way of living that everyone in the world admired and looked to as an example of the last honest way to go. It's disappearing right in front of us, and I can't see the good in one pinch of it!"

The house fills up with silence, underlined by the twittering of a desert wren outside in the heat.

Gib goes on. "In the old days, you could look to being kept on til she was over for ya. You could sit on the chopping block, look out over the place and see what you'd done, could see the work of yer hands as plain as if you'd been building ships in bottles and set 'em all over the place. The owners'd keep you on, even if ya weren't worth a cup fulla cold piss to anyone, including yourself. And then they'd find a place in the corner of the family cemetery for ya. There was enough heart around so's a man could rest easy his last days."

Gib raps the table and juts his chin. "George, I can see the end of my life as plain as I can see that barn out there…" There is a haunted note in Gib's voice, "And I got nothing saved and nowhere to go."

"This just don't sound like you. But if yer just lookin' for a place to give up and die, we're not short on room here, God knows — I got almost two hundred square miles of heartache out there."

Gib puts up a hand and waves it. "Oh, hell no. I guess I'm just feeling sorry for myself. I still got a coupla good years left in me. Sump'n will turn up, it always has." He pauses. "Looks like Young George is coming in." He nods at a pale rooster tail that is making its way toward the house.

"What about Jack Scott?"

"Jack? Nope. He got inta bed with a lawyer who's got more crooks in him than that gully out there. Jack'll be damn lucky, with a partner like that, if he ends up with as much as I got."

He stands up. "Well, old friend, I guess I better get to gittin." He picks up the envelope from the table.

"Where you headed, Gib?"

"Dunno. Right now, over to Pioche and have myself a cold beer. It's gettin hot and thirsty."

Old George stands up and follows Gib to the porch. They take each other's worn and crusty hand. They shake and George holds his friend's hand longer than customary.

"Sorry about that kid," Gib offers, breaking the grip.

"He'll be fine. He's young and tough. They got him sewed up like new and put in some new teeth. Don't worry about 'im. Maybe he learned something about guns and who not to pull 'em on."

"How in the hell did them dope heads ever find their way out here, anyway?"

"Times've changed. Everything's changed."

Gib clumps down the steps and walks to his truck.

"Let me hear from you sometime!" George shouts. But he knows he never will.

Gib waves a hand over the cab of the truck and slides in. The old Jimmy's engine turns over and a spurt of dirt comes out from under a rear tire.

The truck runs across the yard, finds the road, rackets over the cattle guard and disappears. Old George watches as the line of dust from Gib's outfit meets the line of dust from his son's truck. He hears a distant, unanswered, beep from Young George's horn.

The sound strikes him as the saddest thing he has ever heard, in what has been a long, tough life.

❄ ❄ ❄

Maggie's first staff meeting went well. The atmosphere was positive. When she had asked the people to be forthcoming about problems that should be addressed, they all responded in a frank, but positive, way. The group did not appear to have any malcontents and she was relieved at that. The work ethic seemed to still be alive and well in Wyoming.

The ranking staff nurse was only an LPN, a Licensed Practical Nurse, but she had been on the unit forever and her experience more than made up for advanced course work. She was large, a bit disheveled, and her polyester pants and blouse had obviously been in her wardrobe for years and years. She bagged and sagged, wrinkled and rolled. However, she was shrewd, experienced, authoritative and organized. Her reports were models of concision and her suggestions were short and directly to the point. Her name was Roberta Evans, but the staff called her Bertie.

The chief aide, Dewey, was a bit different. He was slightly cynical, fey, and his wit had an edge to it that left little sparks in the room when he exercised it. He had opened the meeting with a joke: "Why was Elton John invited to sing at Princess Diana's funeral? Because he was the only old queen who cared!"

Maggie wondered how he fit into the picture. After all, this was redneck country, not New York, San Francisco or even Salt Lake City, for that matter.

But it was the recreation director who really caught Maggie's attention. Lorna Bildmacher is in her early fifties and dressed in a long skirt, a batik blouse, rings, beads, and bracelets — a style strongly suggestive of the '60s. She is funny, vivacious, articulate, opinionated — liberated in the best sense of the word. She had countered Dewey's mordant thrust with a joke of her own, about a gay Wyoming cowboy and a California congressman. It had collapsed everyone in the room. She and Maggie were going to get along.

At the moment, though, Maggie is being shown around the unit by Bertie.

"That's the recreation wing, Doctor," Bertie says. "As you can see, we have the basics here on the unit — ceramics and painting studio, sewing room, board games and card room. Over in the main building we have wood shop, leather working, and the main ceramics studio. We also have a nice greenhouse. That's where the more socialized ones go."

"What about the sewing group? They seem like a tight-knit bunch."

Bertie grins at the pun. "Yes, those gals stick pretty much together. Most of them came from ranches or farms, and they have tried to maintain that lifestyle as much as possible. The county fair is held here in Evanston, and they have common projects as well as individual ones which always place high."

Maggie nods in approval.

"Now, this is the men's wing…"

As they enter the corridor, a small commotion can be heard in one of the rooms. They walk down and see a male aide standing over an old man lying in bed. The aide is trying to pull a sheet from the clutches of the old man.

"Dammit, Dan, it's way past time to get up. You can't spend the rest of your life in bed."

"It's my life, get the hell outta here and lemme be," the man in the bed growls.

Maggie looks at Bertie, whose face has taken on a long-suffering look. She sighs and says, "Dan Williams. He's impossible lately."

She strides into the middle of the room, puts her hands on her hips and barks, "Dan Williams, get your ass out of that bed this very minute!"

He looks at her. His grey, whiskered face is crowned with tufts and strings of colorless hair.

"You lemme be too, Nurse Ratchett!"

Bertie grins. "You've never read a book in your life — you got that from someone who has. Get your scrawny butt out of that bed, right now. This is the new unit director and I want to you try to make a good impression on her…if it's not too late already."

Maggie steps to the foot of the bed. "Is this his name?"

"Yes ma'am."

Maggie reads, "Daniel Williams…Cody, Wyoming." She walks to the old man's bedside. "Dan?" she says, "don't you know me?"

"Nope. Should I?"

"I'm Maggie Scott…from the Hoodoo. You used to work our ranch, when I was young."

Dan blinks, stares at Maggie for a moment. "Well yes, now that I take a good look. You look just like your mom…and I'd know her ashes in a windstorm." He looks embarrassed. "What're you doing here?"

"I'm working here now. I'm a doctor."

Dan smiles, showing his toothless upper gums. "I did hear that you was a doc, back East."

"Well, I'm back here now. Back home, almost."

"And I wish ta hell I was back up in the Cody country, steada down here in this place."

"Tell you what, get out of that bed and get cleaned up. We'll meet in the cafeteria and I'll buy the coffee."

"No, by golly! I'm buyin'."

An hour later she enters the dining room. Dan is waiting for her, clean shaven and dressed neatly. He smiles as she enters the room and Maggie sees that he has his teeth in. This was an occasion. He put in his uppers only when eating or for something special. He had worn them at her mother's table, when invited on occasions like his birthday, or Christmas.

"Now, that's much better," she says as she approaches the table.

"Siddown, I'll get yer coffee for ya." Dan leaves to return with a cup of coffee. He holds it in both hands and Maggie notices that they tremor a bit. She makes a mental note to order a neurological workup.

Then she smiles as she looks into the cup. Nostalgia floods over her as she sees that he has made her cowboy dessert coffee. Gooseflesh runs lightly across her shoulders as she remembers that the coffee will be laced liberally with condensed milk, and at least two heaping teaspoons of sugar. Her teeth fur over at the thought. But she bravely raises the cup and drinks.

She runs her tongue over her teeth, and asks, "How long have you been here, Dan?"

"Oh, only about five minutes or so."

"No," she laughs. "I mean here at the hospital."

He frowns. "Lemme see. Two, maybe three years, I guess."

"You don't know for sure?"

"Well, time kinda slips by when you get my age."

"How old are you?"

"Seventy two, seventy three, maybe." He looks every pale day of it.

"Let's see if we can figure out exactly how long you've been here. What time of year was it when you came?" Maggie has looked up the exact date, but she wants to get Dan back on real time.

"Well, it was in winter, I remember. A blue norther had blew in and she stormed for days. Seemed like a week, maybe. I don't know exactly. Anyway, it was a long time 'cause I run outta food and the stove went out — fuel line froze up." He stopped and a quizzical look came over his face. He'd run out of memory.

"You don't remember anything more about it? Can't remember how long you were snowed in?"

"Nope. But it musta been quite a while. Musta been, 'cause my dog froze to death." Tears brim in his washed out eyes. "I really hated to lose her," he says softly.

"Oh, Dan." There is a sudden lump in Maggie's throat, she reaches over and puts her hand on one of his bony ones.

Dan had always had a dog, and he'd been completely devoted to the ones she'd known. They had been Border Collie-Australian Blue crosses whose tails he had bobbed. Cow dogs. He'd named them both Queenie, she remembers.

"Oh, I remember now," he says. "It was Bode Crawford found me. I remember them saying something about Bode busting the road open and bringing me out to the county hospital. I never did get a chance to thank him."

"I suppose it was the county that sent you here."

"Could be. For all I know, Maggie...or do I call you Doctor?"

"Maggie's fine.

"Little Maggie." He smiles again. "You sure were a tyke — cuter than mouse ears. Say, how's your brother doing? And Gib?"

"Jack is doing OK. He and the family are getting by all right, but I don't know about Gib. He and Jack had a falling out a couple of years ago, and Gib left the place. The last time I talked to Anisa, they didn't know where he was. Some said he was in Utah. Some said Arizona." The lump comes back to her throat, her mind flashing back to the scene in her unfinished office two days earlier. The man leaning against the tree outside her office window! That wind-burned man in the hat had reminded her of Gib.

"What'd Jack and Gib fall out over? Those two were like father and son, almost. It musta been somethin bad to split them two up."

Maggie raises her eyebrows and says, "Oh, the family law firm took on a new partner from California, and he came out with all kinds of new ideas for making money, trying to get the cash flow going again. Beef and hay just weren't paying the bills.

"The Hoodoo's business was assigned to this new fellow, and he and Jack got to be pretty friendly. He seemed nice, at the time, and he and his family spent a lot of time at the ranch. They boarded their horses there, and whatnot.

"It all started when Jack sold him the Trout Creek cow camp and 160 acres, for a real good price. Plus an easement to the place. At the time it seemed like a good idea — the ranch needed some cash. I went along with it." She shrugs.

"Then, later, when Jack cut back on the number of cows he was running, he let the lawyer talk him into going into partnership on some of the low-use range. The lawyer needed a tax shelter and Jack couldn't see the harm. He took the money, sold the cows and went into the purebred bull business. He figured he could make the same kind of money with fewer animals, even though Gib was against it from the beginning. He wanted to wait for the market to cycle, rather than getting into a whole new business that neither of them had much experience in.

"Before we knew it, Villel, the lawyer, got around the county laws by subdividing the cow camp drainage into 35-acre lots instead of the usual 40-acres. Then he subdivided again and sold the lots. He made a killing, and the traffic through the ranch on the easement has been hard to take for everybody. When Gib found out about the subdividing, he blew up and left.

"Anisa told me that when Villel asked to buy the cow camp, Gib had warned Jack against it. The upshot is, Villel now effectively has his hands on a quarter of the ranch, has made a hundred times the money that Jack has, and has none of the liabilities that go with ranching."

Dan grimaces and says, "That's always the way she goes; the rich get richer and the poor get babies."

Maggie stands, hoping that Dan won't notice that the coffee cup is almost as full as when he brought it to the table. "I've got to get going." She reaches down and puts her hand on his arm. "You start taking better care of yourself."

"I will," Dan says, with a smile.

"I'm here to make sure that you do."

"Yes'm. I won't mind a bit. I guess I do need a kick in the slats sometimes."

"Just like everyone else. I'll see you."

Dan levers himself up from the table, takes out his uppers and puts them in his shirt pocket. Store teeth are expensive and having them busted by some iron mouthed colt can set a working man back a big chunk of pay.

He buttons the shirt pocket and plans the rest of his morning. He has to go make his bed, then see if anyone has any black boot polish he can borrow.

Chapter 3

"Hi, Gib. What are you doing back in the country?" The bartender reaches down into his cooler, takes out a Bud and puts it in front of Gib as he sits down on a stool.

"I dunno, to tell ya the truth, Scotty." Gib pushes a wad of dollar bills across the bar.

"Nah, lemme get this one." The bartender helps a thick leg up and places his boot on a crate. He glances at the clock, which says 10:38AM. "Maybe I'll just join ya." He takes a bottle of Dickel out of the bar well and pours himself a shot. Then pours one for Gib. "Here's how," he says and pops the whiskey back.

Gib raises his glass and drinks the smooth whisky away. Scotty rummages to the bottom of the cooler for the coldest beer he can find.

"You been gone for quite a while."

"Yup." Gib offers nothing more.

"Where'd you go? Anyplace interesting?"

"Nah. Just bounced from place to place, some of 'em good and some not so good."

"Work pretty scarce, huh?"

"Yeah. The older ya git, the harder ya gotta scratch."

Scotty shook his head. "Hell, you're one of the best ranch managers there ever was. What is wrong with people anymore?"

"Too old. It makes sense, really. Who wants to hire someone with one foot in the grave and the other on a moving train? I wouldn't hire me either." Gib tilts his head back, drains his beer and stands up. "Gotta go." He untangles two dollar bills from the wad and lays it on the bar.

Scotty pushes it back at him. "It was good to see you again. I'll catch you next time."

Gib picks up the wad and puts it in his shirt pocket. "Thanks, Pard." He turns toward the door then stops. "Oh, if you hear of anyone needing any help, let me know."

"Where you gonna be?"

"The Bunkhouse, probably."

"I'll do 'er. Take it easy, Gib." He watches as the big man shoulders his way out of the door. He squints as the bright shaft of light falls across his pale face. When the dark returns, he reaches again for the bottle of Dickel. "Damn shame," he says, as he pours himself another one.

As Gib pulls out of town, everyone he meets raises a hand in a sign of recognition, or good will. As he drives past the fields and ranches, everything is as it should be. There is no alkali or dust in sight, everything is green or harvest gold.

Ollie is baling on his riverside fields. Gib can see from the big wind rows of hay that summer had been good to the country. Being beneath the Absaroka mountains means that rain showers, when they come, join with the plentiful sunshine and the irrigation water to make excellent high-protein hay.

As he tops the grade north of Meeteetse, Franc's Peak, JoJo Peak, and Carter Mountain gathered off to the west seem like white-headed old friends welcoming him home. He has run cows on the sides of every one of them, summer after summer for many of the years he's cowboyed the Cody country.

Gib eases back in his seat and relaxes. He steers with his right hand as the wind flutters and pops the shirt sleeve of his other arm. He sticks his big hand into the wind and lets it test his strength. The aroma of the hot, green country fill the cab of the truck. There are cows out there; he can smell them. He also catches the whiff of freshly-mown hay, lying in meadows out of sight from the highway. A small herd of antelope, barely visible, graze on a distant hillside in the golden afternoon grass.

"Damn, but it's good to be home," he says, and inhales deeply. Each breath is like inhaling the steam of hot herbal tea laced with honey.

The familiar voice of Jeff Moroz warbles from the AM band, naming off the country-western songs and calling every single one his favorite.

"I wonder if that guy ever had a bad day in his life?" Gib muses. He moves his gaze from the long straight stretch of highway and looks over at Carter Mountain, thinking of the Hoodoo.

I wonder how the kids are doing?

❄ ❄ ❄

At the Hoodoo ranch house, Jack, Anisa and JC are sitting at the kitchen table. Family conference.

"You are going to have to phone her, Jack," Anisa is saying.

"I can't. I just can't."

"Look, Maggie has as much an interest in keeping this place going as you do. She'll understand that this is what's going to have to be done if we are going to keep Villel, or someone just like him, from ending up with the whole ranch."

Jack slams his hand down on the table, making his wife and son jump. "Now don't go throwing that son-of-a-bitch up in my face again!"

Anisa turns to their son and says, "JC, go find something to do. Please."

The boy looks at his parents, his face neutral.

"Yes'm," he says, stands to pick up his hat and leaves. He has his mother's quiet way, and walk.

"I didn't mean to swear in front of the boy, but I don't want to hear Jerry Villel's name, unless it has to do with business. Period." Jack's face is red, even under the weathered tan.

"Jack, we are stretched as far as we can be stretched on our credit. Buying Crider's hunting camp was the smart thing to do. Why, Pete's widow practically gave it to us. But we've got to have enough money to get the things we have to have. You can't go into the mountains and plan on feeding your hunters elk liver three times a day."

"Anisa, I'm not simple. Please don't tell me things that I already know." He looks at the stove. "Is that meat loaf I smell?"

Anisa takes his hand in both of hers. "Don't change the subject. All you need is five thousand dollars and you can go to the mountains with everything you need, and not have to worry."

"I could do it on two thousand."

"A new generator is going to cost you that much!"

"I can fix the old one."

"It's completely worn out — and if it quits you are going to have to ride out forty miles for a new one, and wind up spending the money anyway, besides losing two days in camp with your clients.

"Honey, hunters aren't going to want to come back the next year to an outfitter that doesn't have what he needs for a good camp. You know that's true, don't you?"

Jack leans back, toys with a spoon, spinning it on the table top with his free hand. Anisa goes on.

"Look, the first two hunts are booked completely and we're booked seventy percent for the rest of the season. The deposits are going to be…"

Jacks raises his hand, stopping her in mid-sentence.

Anisa pulls his hand down. "Jack, please hear me out!"

"I am not going to Maggie for any more money, and that's all there is to it."

"It's only five thousand dollars! Our first hunt will bring in twice that for the first ten days. We can pay the loan back right then. She'll have her money and interest as soon as the hunters pay the last of their fees." She appeals, "Honey, please listen to me. Please."

"And what if she doesn't have it to lend? Did you ever think about that?"

"She has the money." Anisa is staring at her husband. She knows that when Jack intends to play the jackass he will not be moved, no matter how much she goads him with reason. She knows that he is now due to fly off on a tangent, avoiding her logic.

"And how do you know? I don't think she's even straight with the IRS yet. That fancy "Flying Doc" ex-husband of hers is still trying to dance his way out of that one, and I know she hasn't gotten all her settlement. I never did like the flaky little bastard and the way he looked down on us. He wasn't the only one, either."

Anisa's voice dropped. "Jack, Maggie never, ever, looked down on us."

"It damn sure seemed like it to me."

"That is ridiculous, it's just…"

"Well, those step kids of hers damn sure did, just like their dad."

"It may be true, but they were raised in Virginia, and all those people back there think they are special."

"It was more than that. I can still see them getting out of that Suburban and looking around the place with their lips curled up, going 'P-heww'!"

"This is a ranch, Jack. It smells to city people."

"It wasn't just the cow shit they were turning their noses up at! Maggie took one look at those princesses and started apologizing for Wyoming, apologizing for us! Why, that snotty bunch of ba…"

"Stop it! Stop it, Jack. Calm down, and sit down."

He realizes he has risen from his chair. "I'm sorry. I'm sorry, it's just that I can't go to her again, with my hat in one hand and the other one stuck out for money." He sits down. "She's done too much already, and it makes me feel guilty as hell…and incompetent. I owe her too much as it is already."

"Jack, phone your sister." Anisa's voice is soft, and has a gently pleading note.

He pushes himself away from the table and stands up. "There's gotta be another way to go." He starts to leave the room, but is stopped by his wife's voice.

"There isn't," she says as she stares at her husband's back in the doorway. She watches him hunch his shoulders and lower his head, like one of their bulls. He strides from the room, banging his bootheels against the worn wood flooring.

Anisa picks up the now-cold coffee. "Oh, Jack," she says softly, and finishes her cup of bitter brew.

Outside on the porch, JC waits for his dad. When Jack comes out of the house, the boy says, "Dad, when you go up to set up the hunting camp, can I come with you?"

"Depends on school, Son."

"I never have school work on weekends. I get it done Friday night, so I can work around here. Helping you."

Jack smiles inside. This is a good kid. "Well, it's way too early to be setting up the tents. Elk season doesn't open until the middle of October. You know that." Jack puts on his hat and stares at the mountains, thinking. The cottonwood in the yard and the ones along the river are turning yellow. Though it is still warm during the day, the nights are cold enough to make the trees drowsy, to ready themselves for the long Wyoming mountain winter that is just around the corner.

"I tell you what, JC. I've got to ride up and make sure that the stove and the tent floors are in good shape. You can come with me. We'll go this weekend. How's that?"

The boy's face takes on a cautious look. "Just you and me, Dad?"

"Yes. Just you and me." Jack smiles and reaches over to tug the boy's hat down to the bridge of his nose. JC pushes his hat back up to reveal a smile bright as the sunlight bouncing off the river. He turns and runs into the house.

"Gotta tell his mom," Jack thinks. Tomorrow I better go to town and see if my outfitter and hunting camp permits are getting processed at the Forest Service office.

"Anisa!" he hollers through the screen door, "When's lunch going to be ready?"

No answer. Jack's stomach sours.

❄ ❄ ❄

In Cody, Gib folds the receipt for a week's rent and adds it to the clump of paper in his shirt pocket. He then strides out to his truck and reaches into its bed. He grabs his army duffel bag, scattering the beer cans that litter the box.

"Gonna have to do something about them cans, and the rest of that junk," he mutters, then shoulders the duffel and walks to a door of the long, wooden frame building. He opens the door and a plank of stale heat falls out into the cooling day.

"Good Grief," he says, and enters the room. "Just a little bit of Nevada, in case I'd forgot."

Inside, there is a cot, a dresser, a sink, and a hot plate on the counter. He throws the duffel onto the bed, opens the room's single window. He props it open with the stick that waits inside the screen.

"I think I'll go get a beer and let this stink hole air out."

Chapter 4

As they let their horses blow, Jack and JC are looking back down the Ishawooa trail, toward the ranch from Overlook Mountain. All around them, in every direction, the summits of the Absaroka range are spread out before them. At 10,000 feet, the air here is as pure as it's possible to be, and today it's aromatic with the hysop mint which the horses have crushed beneath their hooves.

Jack's attention is drawn by Cloud's Home Peak. He wonders who gave the mountain its name. Mountains in the Rockies were usually named for federal bureaucrats or something just as mundane. However, this mountain had been set above other mountains by the poetic vision of some mostly forgotten person. The name had probably outlived the poet, and would last until all maps were ash or ice, and names no longer applied. Which suited Jack just fine.

Once, as a boy, Jack had been leafing through a National Geographic magazine and came across a picture of a road winding, in multiple switch backs, up a mountain's side. In bold type under the picture the words had read "Going-to-the-Sun Highway." There, in his quiet room, a resonance of some kind set up in his soul. Going-to-the-Sun; hearing or seeing the words "Cloud's Home Peak" never failed to recall that same resonance.

"That's Cloud's Home over there, JC," he points out. "And that's Kingfisher Peak, that's Yellow Mountain over there. And Chaos, then Battlement…"

"And those are Ptarmigan and The Citadel…the one behind our place, " JC finished for him.

"That's right. Y'know, you're a pretty smart kid, for a kid." Jack enjoys his son's proud smile at the left-handed compliment. "Let's get going, if we want to get there before dark."

Jack dallies the pack horse's lead rope around the saddle horn and kicks his mount into motion. He hears JC's horse's iron shoes fall into cadence behind him, and Jack's eyes automatically begin a nonstop scan of trail, trees, rock and skyline. He has inherited a set of "hunter's eyes" from his father. Very little moves without him picking it out from its background. His eyes also acutely decipher faint animal sign in the rocky trail. A few scattered pellets of elk dung pull his eyes to the left and right, where he picks out faint tracings in the high altitude dwarf vegetation. It is sign left from a small herd of elk returning from water. Fifteen head or so. The sign is only a couple of hours old and the animals are probably lying up on Smoky Ridge, chewing their cud, at this very moment.

In his mind's eye he can see the calves dozing at their mothers' sides, flicking their ears at the occasional bee as it forages among the remnant flowers. A big barren cow, the "watch cow," will be standing sentry for the rest.

"Son," Jack hollers back, "come up and take the lead!"

He hears JC's horse snort in surprise as JC digs him in the ribs. Quick hoof beats in the grass announce JC's pleasure at his reassignment. He falls in front of Jack and the pack mare.

When his son and his horse settle down, Jack says, "Son, did you know that there used to be elk all the way back to Virginia, in Sir Walter Raleigh's day?"

"Ah, c'mon Dad."

"No, there really was. And buffalo, too. Buffalo and elk are like cows, they're also ruminants; they live mostly on grass. Anyway, the buffalo and the elk used to range together, in the woodlands of the east and then on the plains, as civilization pushed them further and further west. Everyone knows about the slaughter of the great buffalo herds, but few people know that the elk were reduced almost as drastically."

Jack's eyes roam the mountain meadows, studying the last range of the majestic elk. He then goes on. "There's a couple of herds still living on the plains north and south of Rock Springs. But, mostly, the elk and buffalo were finally pushed into the mountains. The buffalo reached the end of the country they could live in at about 8,000 feet. The elk adapted a survival technique of following the melting snows, almost to the tops of the mountains, and staying there all summer. Then, when the weather turns cold in the fall, they learned to migrate down to the foothills and plains for the winter."

"I guess that we're kind of like the elk, then. Huh, Dad?" JC says over his shoulder.

"I guess we are, Son," Jack answers. " More than you could possibly guess. The world is filling up, right to the brim, and we are like the elk — pushed right up against the mountains, in an effort to save our culture and ourselves. And more pressure coming all the time."

They ride down the trail that snakes across the high alpine plateau, toward the drainage where their new hunting camp is.

Jack tightens the pack horse's lead rope on his saddle horn and says, "I'll take the lead now, Son. The trail peters out up ahead." He pops his chaps with the end of his reins and the two horses step out smartly in unison. "Yellowstone Park is just on the other side of that little range of mountains, JC."

"All right! We're clear up on top of the world!"

❄ ❄ ❄

Gib wakes to pounding on the door of his room. He parts his dry eyelids and looks at the face of his landlord, who is peering through the window screen, shading his eyes. The screen and the whiskey haze in Gib's brain make the man's face blurry, as if it were under water.

"Mr. Gibson, I know you're in there. I need you to come out here and move your truck. It's using up three spaces and the others can't get in."

Gib turns over and falls back into his alcohol-drugged and dreamless sleep, ignoring the man in the window.

"I know you're in there," the man says, lamely, and leaves.

It is full dark when he wakes again, this time to the sound of a cricket filling the room with its resiny arpeggios. Gib lies there for a minute, aware of the body smell that exudes from his undershirt and the twisted sheets. In disgust, he realizes that the odor is the smell of an old man. A drunken old man.

He rises quickly and finds his clothes in the dark. He puts them on, then slips quietly out of his room and into the night.

He walks down the chill autumn street, under the dark shade trees which are tentatively dropping their nipped leaves onto the sidewalks. At a corner, he breaks out into the light of a street lamp and turns left, heading for the Buffalo Bill Bar. Half the places in Cody have been named after the town's founder.

He enters the place and finds himself a stool near the end of the bar. Both pool tables are busy and the bartender, a busty woman named Kim, is doing middling business for a Saturday night. He glances up at the big clock set between two trophy elk heads. Only 9:30, he notes with satisfaction. Plenty of time to get comfortable before the 2:00 AM closing time.

"Tab?" asks Kim, as she sets two short glasses in front of Gib, filling one with water and the other with three fingers of whisky. Gib nods, ignoring the extra question in her voice.

Don't worry, he says to himself, you'll get yer damn money.

He turns on his stool to watch the pool games, as she makes her way back down the bar, razzing the patrons in a friendly, yet obscene, manner. She is one of the most popular bartenders in town, and she treats everyone the same, whether they sell real estate or marijuana for a living.

A tall fellow in a hard hat moves to the bar, pool cue in hand, and hollers over the jukebox, "Say Kim, is that pizza about done?"

"Ah, keep your fucking pants on. I'll give you what you want when it's good and hot!"

The man shakes his head and looks at Gib. He drawls, "Down home the women don't talk thatta way." Oklahoma is splashed all over him.

"Yep," Gib agreed. "When she says 'shit' you can almost taste it."

The man howls with delight at the remark and goes back to his game, where he repeats it to his partners. They all laugh and pound the butts of their cues on the floor in appreciation. One fellow raises his beer in salute to Gib's wit. Gib returns the gesture in the mirror.

Fifteen minutes later, Kim sets the pizza down at Gib's elbow. His stomach clenches and saliva fills his mouth.

Kim hollers, "Hey Fred, here's yer fucking pizza. Come and get it before I give a piece to every guy in the bar and it's too sloppy to eat."

Gib looks down at the hot food. Each slice seems to jump up at him. He tries to remember when he ate last and he can't remember. He swallows the remainder of his whiskey and puts the glass down in front of Kim. She fills both glasses without looking at him, then walks down to the cash register to add the drink to his account. Fred comes over, pulls a slice from the pizza and goes back to his game. Gib turns his back to the aromatic food. He tries to concentrate instead on the game that is going on at the far table.

❄ ❄ ❄

Up in the mountains, Jack sits bolt upright, before he is even properly awake. His senses are being overwhelmed by the combination of the black night, his horses screaming in terror, and the sound of their hooves pounding the ground, wood splintering, then the sound of the picket rope snapping. Then he hears the pounding of their fading hoof beats.

He is aware of JC's clawing hands as he struggles to get out of his sleeping bag. Halfway out of the bag, he is paralyzed by a nearby roar that makes his body vibrate and sends a pain through his chest.

The man and boy hear the sound of a splintering board. Dry pine needles rain down as a heavy body throws itself against a close pine. A piece of board whoops over their heads, then thumps down on the ground beside them.

After a moment's silence, huffing, grunting, licking sounds come, then the rush of a huge bulk not ten feet from them. A metallic crash follows and Jack knows it is the big wood stove.

The crash is followed by the sound of the stove being torn apart. Ten pound stove lids whiz and thump as the heavy stove is heaved through the air and crashes to the ground. Sheet metal screams as bolts and rivets are twisted and broken. A stove pipe woofs and crunches as it is bitten through. An invisible cloud of suffocating soot flies onto the terrified father and son. Some remnant of the stove crashes as it is swatted against a tree. Then a lull.

Great slobbering breaths are heard for a few moments, followed by a grinding of teeth and a deep, asthmatic chuffing. The smell of rotten meat, and an animal's hot body permeates the panting darkness. Then a bounding crash and the sound of scrub pine being roughly parted. Then silence.

❄ ❄ ❄

The back door of the Buffalo Bill Bar opens to flood the alley with the music of a jukebox and the sound of loud voices. The door spring makes a resonant thrumming as it is stretched as far as it will go. Gib steps carefully out, then lets the door slam, chopping off the sounds inside.

He walks slowly to a row of garbage cans, moving out of the cone of light that falls down from a single bulb mounted over a Coors beer sign. Some scamp editor with a pistol has changed the company slogan to read, "Made from Pure Rocky MountaiOring Water."

"Heh, heh, I bet that brought the cops running," Gib says, then opens his fly and throws his grizzled face thrown toward the moonless sky. He teeters for a long moment and then, finally, hears the sound of his piss hitting an empty garbage can. The tinny splashing goes on and on.

Finally, he drops his head and listens carefully. He hears nothing more, so he goes about putting himself in order. A couple of warm drops run down his leg.

"Damn," he says.

Taking a deep breath and letting out a sigh, he makes his way down the alley. As he passes the back door of the all-night cafe, the smell of frying steaks almost overwhelms him. He is hungry. He stands at the door for a moment, trying to remember if he has enough money to buy a hot meal. He does not. He begins to shamble again, heading for his room.

"Hi!" he says to a lilac bush in front of a white house where a sprinkler is whizzing gaily around and around. Gib puts a hand on the picket fence, watching the sprinkler wetting down the lawn and the bush. He feels absolutely wonderful about the happy busyness, the splashing and tinkling.

"Tinkle, tinkle, tinkle," Gib says, amusing his happy self.

"Tinkle, tinkle, tinkle," comes an echo.

The biggest Rottweiler he has ever seen is coming full bore down the side of the house. "Tinkle, tinkle, tinkle," goes the dog's tags as it makes its grim, muscular, and silent way across the lawn and through the water spray.

Gib's elastic youth returns to him instantly. He sprints at full speed, one hand clamped to his cowboy hat as his other arm pumps in perfect rhythm with his long strides. His heels make a sturdy tattoo as he rounds the corner and disappears noisily into the dark of a shady side street.

He is still trying to calm his pounding heart when he enters the 24-hour IGA store, across the street from his bunkhouse room.

"Damn Rottweilers, they oughta take every damn one of 'em out in a gully and put a bullet in their heads," he mutters.

He sees that there is only one checker. She is busy with a customer. Otherwise, the place appears deserted. He walks to the meat department, not noticing two night stock boys who are standing behind the doors to the stock-room.

One of them nods through the glass and says, "There's a shoplifter if I ever saw one."

"Who?"

"That big old fart who needs a shave. What do you want to bet?"

"A Pepsi."

"Uh, uh, you lose. Look — a pound of wienies…"

The other clerk joins the count. "And a package of baloney. This guy's no connoisseur."

"Cheese, cheese, you old cuss, don't forget the cheese."

"Man, you do know your shoplifters."

"Now he'll put the meat and cheese in his coat while he's in the bread aisle. Let's go!" The clerk takes off his apron and opens the door. He grabs a head of lettuce and falls in at a discreet distance behind Gib, who has picked up a small loaf of Wonder Bread.

I coulda guessed that one, the clerk says to himself.

"Good evening," the checker says, looking over her glasses at the disheveled cowboy.

"How much for the bread?"

"One dollar and nineteen cents, plus seven for the governor."

"How much is that, all tolled?"

"A dollar twenty-six, please."

Gib weaves a bit as he fumbles out the correct amount. The cashier steps back a bit from the smell of his whisky breath. She puts the money in the cash drawer, then tears off the register tape. But, Gib is already heading for the doors.

"Got a live one," the clerk says to the checker, as he follows the big old man outside.

Gib is just rounding the corner of the store when the clerk catches up to him.

"Hey, old timer!" he says, and Gib stops to turn around.

"Whatcha want?"

"You got anything that don't belong to you?"

Gib gives him a baleful stare, and notes another kid coming out of the store to join the first.

"Why don' you just go on back inside and mind your own business?"

"I am minding my business. You have some meat and cheese that you didn't pay for. That's my business."

The second clerk joins them and said, "You're under arrest for shoplifting, mister. Now c'mon back in the store because we're gonna call the cops."

"Now, son, you don't want to go and do that. Believe me."

"Look, you old fart, you're coming back into that store whether you like it or not." He has his eyes squinted, his hands on his hips.

"Old fart, huh? OK," Gib says, and holds the loaf of bread out to the kid, who reaches out with both hands to accept the bread. Gib flattens him with a quick left, then speeds down the sidewalk and out of sight.

❊   ❊   ❊

Jack and JC stand next to a small fire, where an enamel coffee pot is beginning to steam. The father looks down at his son, noting the dark circles under the boy's eyes.

"You gonna be OK?"

The boy nods, then puts his head against his dad's side.

The morning sun is coloring the rim of the basin with a wash of pink and lavender light. The dawn light allows them to survey the destruction around them.

The flooring for the cook tent had been ripped up, broken and scattered. The stove was smashed and pulled apart. The stovepipe sections were flattened, bent, or bitten through. Only the cast iron top remained intact.

The only other thing destroyed by the beast was the old high-backed saddle Gib had ridden for years. It had been bitten through, the saddle tree broken, collapsed at the middle. Enormous teeth had punctured the leather and wood, mighty jaws had shattered the thing beyond repair. It lies limp as a gutted fish, its skirts flattened against one another. The ruined saddle has been left, almost like a signature, on top of the broken and twisted stove.

A shiver runs through Jack. He hunches down to warm himself by the flames and JC mimics his actions. He closes his eyes in thanks that his son is whole.

He opens his eyes and looks again at the high rock walls across the rolling alpine meadow. The reflected light now has a pink hue because it is gaining strength. Suddenly, his eyes pick out three dark shapes about a quarter mile away. He stands and steps away from the fire for a better look. It is his horses.

"Thank God," he says aloud.

The animals are placidly grazing on the frost rimed grasses, as if they were in the river pasture at the ranch. He had worried all night about how he was going to get JC home, knowing that there was no way the boy could walk the almost thirty miles back. And he could never have left him at the camp alone. But it looked as if their luck had turned.

"C'mon, JC." He picks up their bridles, hands one to the boy, and they start out through the lemon-colored light toward the distant horses.

❄ ❄ ❄

Two police patrol cars are parked next to the curb, in front of The Bunkhouse. Their lights are flashing, bathing the side of The Bunkhouse in washes of bright yellow and red.

"Yeah, he's in there," says a young cop with a brown beard.

"Well, let's go shake him loose," the rotund sergeant replies. They walk up to the door of Gib's room and position themselves on either side of the door. The sergeant reaches around and pounds on the door with the side of his fist.

"Mr. Gibson! Police! Wake up!"

Inside, Gib rolls over and sits up. Swaths of red light jerk across the wall of the dark room. His whiskery face is vacant, then he tries to blink himself awake. Suddenly, the events of the early morning come back and panic washes over him. It has been a very long time since the law has come looking for him, but the fear is as strong as it was all those years ago, in Cheyenne.

"Go away!" he shouts.

"Mr. Gibson, I want you to open the door slowly, and then put both your hands outside where we can see them. Come out slowly, and when you're outside I want you to put both hands on top of your head."

"I said, go away!"

"Mr. Gibson, don't make this hard. Just come on out…make it easy for all of us."

"You get the hell outta here, and lemme alone!"

"Too late for that. Now come on out and let's get it over with," the sergeant says, and gives the bearded patrolman a worried glance. "We don't want to have to come in there and get you," he adds.

"I tell you what," Gib shouts from inside. "I got a .44 in here, and if you don't get the hell away from that door, I'm gonna start smoking the place up! Now get the hell outta here, like I said!"

The two cops draw their pistols and begin to retreat down the side of the building, away from the door. The sergeant takes the radio from his belt and speaks rapidly into it. "Cody, this is Cody-Six."

"Come in, Six."

"We have a possible 10-32 at The Bunkhouse. Dispatch all available officers immediately."

Inside, Gib hears the crackling of radios and the shouts of the officers to a passerby, ordering him to clear the area. He reaches over and pulls down the shade of the window, throwing the room into complete darkness.

He stumbles over the duffle and falls to his hands and knees. He tries to right himself, but loses his balance again. He grabs the foot rail of his bunk and begins to pull himself upright. Like lightning, an excruciating pain in his chest drives the breath from him, and then explodes in his eyes and ears. An involuntary shriek is the last thing that he hears, before he blacks out and falls to the rough wooden floor.

Chapter 5

Maggie enters her office and turns on the lights, juggling her cup of coffee and two thick files. She puts them down on her desk and crosses the room to open the blinds. The sun has melted the light rime on the lawns and turned it to sparkling dew. Another beautiful autumn day.

She returns to the desk, sits and opens a file to where she had marked it the night before.

It was a bitter night in the winter of 1942. Joe Echeverria was in his sheep camp on the Red Desert of southern Wyoming and urgent voices had awakened him. The voices insisted that the man sleeping in the bunk next to him was going to kill Joe. In reality, the man was the company camp jack, the man who supplied the distant sheep camps scattered over the enormous salt sage wintering grounds.

A ground blizzard had stranded the supplier. He planned to wake in the morning and depart for Rock Springs, if the wind had stopped blowing. But before that morning came Joe had cut his throat and dragged him out onto the snowy ground for the coyote, the eagle, and the magpie. Then the big, gentle Basque had gone back to the loving business of caring for his sheep, soothed by the voices and the stark beauty of the landscape.

Southern Wyoming in winter is no place for a man used to comfort. It is no place for someone who likes being with people. The weather races down from the mountains, picking up speed as it reaches the high desert. Over the eons, every geological formation which has stood against the winter weather has been rounded, pedestaled, and finally felled by the abrasion of windblown sand and gritty snow.

December brings purple clouds which hurry over the high winter desert and wring the light from the sky, casting the land in greys and other dead man hues. Native animals bear it by having been exposed to the weather for eons. Very much a newcomer to this landscape, man does not do so well here. The winters are long. Their stark beauty demands a minimalist eye, and heart, to appreciate it. Only the marginal and the mad can love it. And somewhere along the line, since emigrating from the green land of northern Spain, Joe Echeverria had gone completely mad.

The record of Joe's long institutionalization made a very thick file. Through forty-odd years, the pages recorded the history of different regimes at the institution, as well as the changes in the treatment for the insane. A veteran of the barred cells and physical restraints of the past, he was now almost normal, thanks to psychotropic medicines. And Joe had found his place in life — the bench in front of the geriatric unit. He sat there summer and winter, for hours each day, gazing out over the sere sagebrush hills. Joe was a sensitive, and sentimental, man. He was also rich.

Maggie takes a sip of her morning coffee and turns another page of Joe's thick file. Her professional curiosity is piqued. She had finished the other file, the one for Mr. Herbert Silver, the night before, and it had also been fascinating. But Echeverria's story is peculiar to a state with a ranching culture and, as she teases the thread of his life out of the clinical record, she finds Joe's history fascinating reading.

As a young man fresh from Spain, Echeverria had been given the option of payment for his labor in either money or lambs. Luckily, Joe had opted for lambs.

Joe's boss kept a true accounting of Joe's share in the ranching operation, and the wars in Europe and Korea created a large demand for wool and meat which had founded Joe's fortune. When Joe killed the camp jack, and entered the institution, the sheep man sold Joe's sheep and invested the money in blue chip stocks. Then he turned over the management of the man's money to the local bank in Evanston. Time and the stock market had done the rest.

The president of the bank personally managed Joe's account. The balance astounded Maggie. Mr. Echeverria could call himself a millionaire, and then some. And he knew it. But he was content to sit placidly on his bench and look out over a corner of the great American sheep country as his money accumulated. The money meant very little. Everything that he needed, he had right here at the hospital. And more. He finally had a friend.

At this very moment his friend, Herb Silver, is sitting on the wooden bench beside the big Basco. Joe is one of his favorite people, too, because Joe is a world-class listener. As a matter of fact, Joe has probably said no more than a couple of hundred words in the many years that they have known one another. That is in stark contrast to the sea of words with which Herb has inundated Joe. Herb is a little crazy, of course, and he is a talker; he is a raconteur. Herb is a bullshitter par excellence and Joe loves it, now that the voices inside his head have faded. He loves listening to the little madman. It is familiar and comforting.

The two are a natural contrast. Joe is a stump of a man no more than 5 feet 8 inches tall and over two hundred pounds. He is meticulously neat, and combs his well-trimmed, oiled hair straight back. His large black eyes lend his head the look of an animated, and very intense, bowling ball that swivels on an invisible neck.

Herb is a disheveled and animated little man who chain smokes Camel straights, living in a rain of smoke and ash. He never combs his hair. His untidy pants, jacket and a food-spattered tie hang loosely askew on his small frame and are the despair of the staff. And that is exactly why he sports them the way he does.

Joe had been a good boxer in his youth, and had fought for the Spanish national light-heavyweight championship. Herb had a doctorate in philosophy and had fought for The One Big Union. He, like Joe, was seriously overmatched in the end. But the one thing that they shared was that they had both been Communists in their youth, though of different sorts. Joe was a guerrilla in Spain's civil war, fighting against the monarchists and fascists. Herb had been a guerrilla in the battle between the American Communist Party and capitalist society at large. Both had fought like good soldiers. Both had been defeated. Now they found themselves old veterans segregated from society in a far place which had become their final home.

Even as Maggie reads, the two old comrades sit on a lawn bench and Herb is talking. And, as usual, he is engaged in subverting the powers that be. Joe is listening to Herb's instructions, while also engaged in watching the great Wyoming sky. In his years alone, in the mountains and on the desert, he had developed an intimate interest in the sky.

"Joe," Herb says, "I need you to do something, an assignment of sorts. It must, as usual, be handled discreetly and with the greatest secrecy. You are, of course, going to the leather shop at 1400 hours, as is your habit. There will be a young man there shortly after that hour, a young man with long hair and small earrings in one ear. His name is Ace. Now, Joe, do not be put off by his appearance, because he is not a real hippie, per se. I know that you do not like hippies, and do not approve of their informal and casual attitudes. This man is, in fact, working in disguise and has infiltrated this institution. I cannot reveal his mission, but you may trust me when I say that it is of the utmost importance."

Joe loves it when Herb is in his conspiratorial mode, talking without moving his lips. He waits for his friend to finish lighting a Camel stud from the glowing butt of another.

Herb continues, "When I get up and leave, I am going to leave this newspaper on the bench. Inside the newspaper is an envelope, an ordinary envelope, and it contains material that is crucial to the mission that Ace has been sent here to accomplish. Do you understand me?"

Joe maintains his wordless observation of the progress of the great fleecy cumulus clouds trooping slowly out of the west. A great grin animates his face.

"Excellent," Herb says. "Mr. Ace will sit down one chair away from you, and you will place the newspaper on the intervening chair. He will ask, 'Are you through with this?' He will then leave with the materials. Excellent. Excellent.

"And, of course, you will be rewarded as usual. I can not, can not, overemphasize the delicacy and importance of this assignment. To demonstrate that fact, you will be paid with two, rather than one, boxes of chocolate-covered almonds."

Herb stands up abruptly. "Good luck," he says, and scuttles toward the cafeteria.

Joe watches as the little man hurries across the lawn, through a flower bed, to the doors of the building. He smiles another great smile, puts his thick hand on the folded newspaper, and goes back to his celestial vigil.

That evening, when Joe goes to his bed and puts his hand under the pillow, the boxes of almonds will be there. He will make himself comfortable and open one box. He will munch the candies, one at a time, enjoying every crunchy, chocolatey bite. And life will be good, the only things missing will be the freedom of the open plain and endless sky, and the knowledge his animals are safe in his loving care. But, instead, he has this one friend. And for that he is very grateful.

A page from the PA system interrupts Maggie's study of Joe's record.

"Doctor Scott, Doctor Margaret Scott, you have a call on line three. Line three, please."

She picks up the phone. "Hello, Doctor Scott here."

"Hello, Maggie, this is Anisa. I'm very sorry to bother you, but this is urgent."

"What's the matter?"

"Gib is in the Cody jail."

"Jail! What is he doing in jail?"

"Public intoxication, shoplifting, assault, resisting arrest, destruction of property. You name it."

"What is going on?"

"We don't know, for sure. He showed up in town a few days ago, I guess, and started drinking. Pretty heavily."

"But Gib is no drinker. He might have a few beers, but he's not a drunk."

"It looks like he's changed since he left."

"What can I do? Do you want me to come up there?"

"No. We've talked to the prosecuting attorney and they are going to ask the judge to send him down to Evanston to dry out. You will probably be seeing him and I just wanted to let you know."

"Of course. Does he have a lawyer?"

"We wanted to get Ernie Stoddard… Well, he has a public defender."

"Wouldn't Ernie take the case?" Maggie asked, indignantly. "He's had the ranch's business ever since he got out of law school…"

"Oh, Maggie," Anisa breaks in, "we just couldn't afford to hire Ernie for a criminal case. We've got cash flow problems, again."

Maggie is silent for a moment. "Do you want to talk to me about it?"

"This time it isn't just some of Jack's blue sky. We had a chance to get a real good deal on a hunting camp. It is a good deal, but it has taken every liquid cent we have."

"How did you get such a good deal?"

"We bought the Crider hunting camp for a song, and on unbelievable terms. Pete's widow is well off, she loves Jack and disliked the hunting, anyway. They had a real good business and this season is almost completely booked. The problem is that we've stretched our credit to the limit but we still need, I figure, five thousand dollars to get the camp in decent shape. Also, a grizzly bear tore the camp to pieces and that's going to take more time, and money."

Maggie runs the figure around in her mind. Five thousand would be almost half her cash, but a phone call would free up something in a day or so. "Anisa, call Ernie and tell him that I, we, are retaining him and to get Gib taken care of. Also, I will send you a check for the five thousand dollars by the end of the week. Just send me a simple receipt from the ranch corporation — capital investment."

"Oh, thank you Maggie! We will have you paid back in full by December first. Even with your loan, we should be able to clear thirty thousand dollars by the end of the season!"

"Well, that is good to hear. I'm glad that the tide has turned. Now, back to Gib."

"I've told you everything I know. He has been less than cooperative with the officers, and he refuses to see anyone. Jack tried." Anisa's voice trembles. "I'm so sorry to bother you like this, but everything seems to have happened at once."

"It always does, it seems. More life."

"Are you going to get a chance to come see us at Christmas? You know, JC was only four the last time you saw him. He's going to be thirteen in November."

"It doesn't seem possible. Yes, Anisa, I promise that I will be up for Christmas."

"That would be wonderful, Christmas will be perfect. I really want to see you again. And maybe we could talk, I don't have anyone since my mom died."

"I was very sorry to hear about that. Yes, it will be good to see everyone again."

"Yes. I'll let you go. And, Maggie?"

"Yes?"

"Thanks again."

"Don't mention it."

"And Maggie…"

"Yes?"

"We love you."

"Goodbye," Maggie says.

"Goodbye."

She puts the receiver down softly and stares at the wall for a moment. Then she picks up her files and leaves the office.

Chapter 6

"Hello, Grace, is my appointment with our prosecutor still good?"
"Good morning, Ernie. Yes it is. Let me tell him that you are here."

The slim secretary disappears around a corner. Ernie looks out of the second floor window of the courthouse. The street teems with traffic. Most of the cars burst at the seams with tourists going to, and coming from, Yellowstone Park, fifty miles up the road from Cody. The first influx of tourists in June is always nice to see. But when the first aspen leaves start to drop, signaling the end of the gawking season, locals like Ernie and the rest of the residents always feel a bit relieved. Having two million people pass through a town of only eight thousand puts a lot of pressure on everyone.

Ernie judges at the Cody night rodeo. Though he loves doing the job, he is looking forward to the end of the season. Semi-retired from his law practice, he now chooses only the clients who interest him. His life is now a little law, a little rodeo, and a little marlin fishing in the winter.

He'd judged almost every champion cowboy from Jim Shoulders and Casey Tibbs down to the current champs. And, once upon a time, he'd had the luck to watch Gib Gibson ride bucking horses from the local rodeo grounds all the way to the world championship.

In the old days, the finals were held in New York City, at Madison Square Garden. He and about a hundred others took the train to watch their local hero become the number one saddle bronc rider in the world. They partied for the whole three days that it took the train to cross the country. The party hadn't stopped all the time they were in the city. But the biggest party of all was after the last go-around when Gib had won 'er all. World Champion Saddle Bronc

Rider. Hell, the whole Wyoming delegation to Washington D.C. had been there that last day.

He remembered Gib after that. The big man with a big smile, whenever he came to town from the Hoodoo, flashing the gold belt buckle studded with diamonds and rubies. He'd been the pride of the town for years, and his name always came up when rodeo was talked about seriously. Even to this day.

Ernie shakes his head. "Villel, you sorry son-of-a-bitch," he mutters, turning away from the window. Splitting off part of the Hoodoo had been a low trick. But forcing Gib Gibson from the ranch, and away from Jack Scott, was a sin appreciated by only a few of the old timers like himself. It was a secret, bad business.

The prosecutor sticks his head out of his office and says, "Hey, Ernie, come on in. Get a cup of coffee."

Stoddard pours a cup and walks into the man's office.

"Sit down, Ernie. I assume you are here on Mr. Gibson's behalf."

"Yes. How are you planning on proceeding against him?"

"The charges against him are several, the most serious being the assault and interference with a police officer."

"But you are considering an involuntary committal to Evanston for detox. His health isn't all that good."

"I'm waiting for the doctor's evaluation. Also, the kid he punched, the officer he assaulted in the jail, and the sheriff are going to have something to say about how we proceed."

"I have written a petition to the judge. I have a copy for you here." He lays a file on the prosecutor's desk.

"Thank you."

"I want to get Gib out of here and in the full time care of a doctor as soon as possible. I have known Gib for a very long time, and this just isn't the man I know. Something is seriously out of whack."

"Well, I can sympathize, but these are not trivial charges. But, let's see what the judge says."

Ernie stood. "Thanks, John, I appreciate your time."

"Not at all. Good luck with the judge."

"How long has Gib been custody?"

The prosecutor looked at his watch. "Well, he was in the hospital for the first 28 hours, so he's been in the county's custody for about 22 hours now. If you are going to request a hearing, you have 14 hours left to get it done. As you know, by statute, involuntary committal proceedings must take place within 36 hours."

"Yes, I know. I'm going to the jail right now, and then to see Doctor Montville. I'll get back to you as soon as I've done that and talked to the judge."

Ernie left the courthouse and walked to the jail. As he waited for a jailer, he pulled out his pipe. Then he remembered the no smoking ordinance and put it back in his jacket pocket. "Too damn many rules, anymore," he gripes, "a man can't do anything anymore."

"Excuse me, are you Gibson's attorney?" A lanky, red-headed sheriff's deputy stands at his elbow.

"Yes, I am. Would you please bring him to the attorney's room, so I can talk to him?"

"I don't know. He's real shaky."

"What do you mean 'shaky'?"

"I mean just that. He's got the shakes."

"Well, can I see him in his cell?"

"Yeah, c'mon back."

Stoddard follows the jailer down a corridor and through a steel door with a no nonsense sign affixed to it:

JAIL
NO ADMITTANCE
NO WEAPONS BEYOND THIS POINT

They go through the door and the booking room, then turn left down another corridor. At the end of that corridor, they enter "A" block. On the left stand a series of tall windows covered with steel mesh. On the other side of the narrow catwalk are five barred doors. They walk to the end of the catwalk. The jailer stops and peers into the cell.

"Mr. Gibson? Mr. Gibson!" There is no answer.

Stoddard moves to where he can see into the cell. Two steel bunks, a toilet and a sink in the cell. Nothing more. A lanky human form lies in a fetal position on the lower bunk, completely covered by a brown wool blanket. The man beneath the blanket is shivering.

"Gib? It's Ernie Stoddard, Gib."

The form's arm makes a tentative movement. Slowly the mass rolls over. A big, grey-veined hand comes out and pulls the blanket down. The stubbly face and the long hair are those of a complete stranger.

"Gib?" Ernie says, a bobble in his voice.

"Yeah?" the apparition croaks.

"Gib, it's Ernie Stoddard. Are you OK?"

"I ain't doing so good, Ernie. I'm sick as hell."

"Look, I've come to see if I can't get you out of this mess. Are you going to be all right?"

"Lord, but I'm sick. Never been so sick in my life. Can you get me outta here?"

"You relax, Gib, I'm going to go see the judge right now. Are you going to be OK til I get back?"

The wraith replies, "I'll hang tough. Just get me out of this hole."

Stoddard spins on his heel and strides to the booking room in a fury. "Why isn't that man in the hospital? He has no business being here in that shape! He needs medical attention!"

"Hold on, Mister. In the first place, he raised so much hell over at the hospital that they gave up on him. In the second place, the doctor comes over here to check on him three times a day. In the third place the ornery SOB won't take the medication the doctor left for him. He says he doesn't give a damn whether he lives or dies. We're trying our level best to see that he gets what he needs but he has fought us every inch of the way, and we've just run plumb out of patience and ideas. So if you have any to spare, then just hop right in."

"I'm going to do just that. I promise you that I'll have him out of here so fast it will make your head swim."

"That suits us just fine. And the sooner the better. But I wouldn't worry about him too much."

"Why is that?"

"Because that old man is too damn mean to die."

Chapter 7

On the substance abuse ward at the state hospital, a voice comes over the PA system.

"Andy, come to the nurse's station. Andy, the nurse's station."

The young male aide appears and asks, "What do you need?"

"Some deputies from Park County are coming in with one. Security says that he will be here in a few minutes to give you a hand."

"Security? Why is he coming over?"

"I guess this guy is combative. We are going to put him in the side room. We'll do the intake after he is calmed down." The nurse walks the short distance to the isolation room and unlocks the door. The small interior holds nothing but a bed, bolted to the floor. Attached to the head and foot of the bed are canvas and leather restraint cuffs.

"We are going to need 24-hour observation, vitals every hour. He has had some DTs, plus an angina attack while in the jail in Cody. We are going to have to be careful with him for a couple of reasons; he got violent when he heard he'd been committed involuntarily. Also, he is almost 70 and is in poor physical condition — we don't want to lose him. Be calm. Be firm. But no unnecessary excitement."

"Yes, ma'am."

"We haven't had one of these since you've worked here, so pay attention to how Security handles it. Here he comes now."

A black man in his forties, Security is 6'3" tall and weighs 210 pounds. He weighed the same as a force recon Marine in Viet Nam. A happy, self-confident man, he is an elder in the new Baptist church and has a wife and three handsome sons. The staff likes him for being double nice. And double tough.

"Hi, Security. What's the story?" Andy asks.

"Oh, I guess we got us a live one. Let's go see what it's all about."

The two men walk to the admissions door, exiting as a sheriff's car swings onto the tree-lined drive. When the car pulls up, they see three men in the back seat — two deputies on each side of a big, silver-haired mess who is almost out of its strait jacket. Both the deputies' shirts are black with sweat. Their faces look as though they just finished running a marathon.

"Have a nice trip?" Security asks the driver as he gets out of his vehicle.

"That ain't even funny," the deputy says, shoving a clip board at Security. Security smiles, signs the papers and returns the board. The deputy tears off a copy of each paper and gives them back.

"He's all yours," he says and opens a back door. A weary deputy gets out, whispering, "Watch 'im."

Gib looks up at Security, turns his head and clenches his jaws.

Security leans down and says, "OK, Pard, you ready to go?"

"I ain't going with no nigger."

Security never even blinks. He straightens up and turns to the aide. "Fine with me. Andy, would you please show this gentleman the way to A-2?"

The embarrassed aide leans into the car and he and the other deputy help Gib out. All five men stand alertly, ready to grapple. Gib looks at them with disdain and turns to Andy.

"I sure could use a drink, Son."

"There's a fountain inside."

"I ain't talkin about water," Gib says, surveying the entrance to the hospital.

"We'll see what we can do about getting you something," Andy says. "Right through that door right there, then hang a left."

"Are you gonna need any help?" offers a deputy.

"No, that's OK. Thanks," says Security. He goes to the door and opens it.

Gib strides defiantly through, saying, "Thanks, but I ain't got no money for a tip."

Andy looks at Security, embarrassed again for the big black man. The man's face wears an absolutely neutral look. He's heard this all before.

When they reach the door to the ward and begin the unlocking process, Gib's head falls until his chin rests on his chest. Andy is surprised to see a large tear drop onto the front of the strait jacket. "The damn Bughouse," he hears the old man whisper hoarsely.

The charge nurse stands in the hall next to the side room door. "In here, please," she says.

"Here, let me get you out of this zoot suit," Security says, and reaches for the belt on the back of the strait jacket.

Gib shrugs his shoulder violently.

Security looks at Andy and nods. Andy unbuckles the belt, takes the device off and hands it to the nurse. Gib massages his arms. He is staring at the bed and the restraints. He begins to shake.

Security steps in a little closer, gesturing with his head for the nurse to stand aside.

"Mr. Gibson," he says, "we need to get you out of those coveralls. Sit on the bed, so the nurse can get your blood pressure; give you a little checking over."

"Nope," he says, simply.

Security waves the nurse through the door and nods at Andy. They both reach out in unison and grab Gib at his elbows and wrists. The flaccid biceps and forearm muscles cord in reflex, and Andy flies against the wall. Hard.

Security changes his grip to Gib's wrist and goes for an arm bar. The old man is quicker than he thought possible. He escapes serious damage to his face only by pure reflex.

Andy comes off the wall and grabs Gib by the waist. He catches an elbow on the forehead that sets him on his butt. He grunts in pain.

Security crouches in an Aikido stance.

The nurse, standing just outside the room, sees what Security sees: Gib's eyes are absolutely vacant. He is focused with total concentration, just as he had done a thousand times as he waited to be vaulted out of the chutes on the back of a fifteen-hundred pound horse mad with rage.

She sees Security step in on Gib and make a move, but Gib's fist intercepts him and Security goes down against the door, slamming the thick metal inches from her face.

She drops the strait jacket and runs for the nurse's station. As she raises the microphone of the PA system, a cry of exultation rises over the banging sound of heavy bodies and the screeching of the metal bed.

"Yeee hawwwwwwwww!"

As Maggie drives into the parking lot of "A" Building it is dark and a fingernail moon is hanging over the hills, limning the autumn clouds' edges with faint filigrees of light. She hears crickets chirring as she gets out of the car.

She takes a deep breath and walks toward the foyer door. Inside, her heels clack on the terrazzo as she makes her way toward the square of lighted glass in the door to ward A2. She peers through the glass and taps with her car keys.

A nurse sitting at a small desk in the corridor looks up and puts down the magazine she has been reading. Maggie steps back and waits until the key clicks the heavy lock open and the door opens half way.

"Hello," Maggie says, "I'm Doctor Scott."

"Yes. Good evening, Doctor."

"How is Mr. Gibson doing?" she asks, shrugging off her coat.

"He's not doing very well at the moment, I'm afraid."

"What's wrong?"

"Delirium tremens. His blood pressure is elevated…"

"Then he should be in the county hospital, shouldn't he?"

"He's too violent. Dr. Reyes is here on the ward, in case something goes wrong, but he is asleep. We are monitoring Mr. Gibson very closely, Doctor."

"May I see him?"

"I can't authorize it myself, and I hate to wake the doctor…"

"Listen, I am a medical doctor myself and I am not going to interfere in your procedures or regimen in any way." Maggie's voice is rigid with measured authority. "Go wake Dr. Reyes and tell him I'm here."

The door closes and is locked. Maggie imagines the nurse muttering "Bitch" as she goes to waken the doctor, but it doesn't matter to her. She has pulled her rank a thousand times when it was necessary. And when it comes to dealing with her "family" she feels the necessity. Gib is family.

As she waits, her coat draped over her arms, she walks slowly back and forth, heels clicking in the darkened and lonely foyer. She makes a dozen trips across the room before she hears the key in the door and hurries to the sound.

"Please come in. Doctor Reyes okayed your visit." She steps aside and lets Maggie in.

As she leads the way down the hall, she says in a low voice, "Mr. Gibson is in the side room. We are taking vitals every thirty minutes and he's on a glucose/Librium drip, at the moment. He has calmed down a bit, but he is still somewhat dehydrated and feverish."

"In here," she says, and stops to point through an open doorway.

Gib is spread-eagled on the bed, each wrist and ankle secured in a leather cuff. A towel covers his pelvis. Other than that, he is naked, shaking, and sweating profusely.

Maggie had seen hundreds of persons in delirium tremens during her years in Washington, D.C. clinics, but she had forgotten how bad they could be. The wrecked body on the bed is in true agony as it trembles, shakes, and goes into occasional brief spasm. Animal moans and lip smackings come from the face that lies in shadow, turned away from her. Suddenly the man's fingers bend into claws, his toes splay, and all four limbs jerk savagely at the restraints.

"OH GOD, DON'T LET HIM GET ME! PLEE—ASE DON'T LET HIM GET ME!"

The voice comes from a throat wrung dry and hoarse. The tongue sticks to the roof of the mouth. Maggie's heart staggers for one beat, and then her medical training takes over.

"Nurse," Maggie says, "get me some cool water, some towels and some oranges."

"I have to get it okayed by Doctor Reyes."

"Of course."

The nurse leaves the room and Maggie moves to Gib's bedside. Her professional discipline wobbles briefly as she gazes at the ravaged face. Deep grooves run from his nose down sides of the stubbled gray face. The forehead wrinkles with pain. The slitted eyelids pulse as the pale blue eyes move spasmodically back and forth, up and down.

Maggie puts her hands gently on his stomach, to palpate the liver. She notices a huge old scar of a crudely done splenectomy. She thought it curious that the man had never mentioned it in all their years together. At that moment it occurs to her that she had never seen Gib with his shirt off before. A typical cowboy.

She lifts the edge of the towel and sees, finally, the raised and twisting, ropy scars left on the body by the great grizzly bear, many years ago. When she was a little girl she had heard the story of those scars many times, though never from Gib himself.

She lowers the towel. Her gaze runs down the skewed legs and scarred shins to a twisted ankle and then thick, unpared toe nails. This was a body that had carried this man through a whole world of physical pain.

She puts her hand on Gib's brow, but her fingers jerk away in reflex at the sudden scream her touch excites.

"HE'S BACK! OH, MOMMA, HELP ME. PLEASE!"

"Doctor?" The nurse has returned with the towels and a basin of water. "I had to send an aide to the kitchen for the oranges, but here are the other things."

"Thank you." Maggie wipes her own face with the towel, then takes the basin and sets it on a chair. She folds the towel into a pad, places it in the cool water and wrings it out. "I can take care of this alone, Nurse."

"Yes ma'am, if you want. I'll be right outside if you need me."

The nurse's eyes are full of sympathy, though she still feels a bit resentful at the imperious way she had been treated half an hour earlier. She wants to help, but she knows that there must be something special about these two people's relationship. Probably family. She backs from the room and closes the door.

Maggie sits down and looks at Gib. He is thin, dehydrated, wasted. The alcohol has desiccated him. She is stunned at the change in the man since she'd last seen him. His sideburns had been white then, and there had been deep crow's feet at the corners of his eyes. But this was the difference between mature life and the rim of death.

What have you done to yourself? She is angry, but unnoticed tears of sorrow run down her face.

How could you do this? How could you let go? Why did you give up?

Maggie puts her face in the towel and sits for a moment, allowing memories of Gib as her childhood hero run through her mind. Then she raises her head, to see Gib looking at her. His face is haunted. Then he smiles with joy, and cries out.

"Laura!"

"Oh, Gib!" Maggie sobs, and tucks herself beside the gray-haired chest, her arms around Gib's neck. And she gives herself permission to feel, then to cry.

The startled nurse, who had come to the door at the shout, looks through the glass. After a moment, she sits down and returns to her vigil, happy. Real love is not often manifested in this house of unfinished, and abandoned, souls.

Chapter 8

It is early morning when the telephone rings. Anisa answers it, then walks to the door. Crossing her arms against the fall chill, she goes to the edge of the porch.

"Jack! Jack!" she hollers down to the corrals and places a clenched hand to her ear.

He drops bale of hay into the horse manger and raises his hand in acknowledgement, then turns to his son. "Thanks for the help. Now let's go to the house and get us some hot chocolate before we take you to the school bus."

The boy puts down the pitch fork, shrugs his collar closer to his hat, to cover his ears. "That sounds really good."

Inside, Anisa returns to the phone. "Hello, Allen. Jack's on his way up to the house. How is Deanna doing? I've been meaning to get over there, but with JC going back to school, and Jack getting the hunting camp ready, I just haven't had the time. How are things upriver, anyway?"

Anisa listens intently until she hears the screen door slam. "Is Eddy OK?" she asks, then nods. "Well, I'm glad for that. Jack's right here, I'll let you talk to him."

She hands her husband the phone, then turns to the boy and says, "Come in the kitchen, JC. I want you to give me a hand."

He looks at his mother, then his father. "What's going on, Mom?"

"Never you mind, we'll let your father handle this."

"But, Mom…"

"Come with me." JC falls obediently in behind his mother and follows her to the kitchen.

"What's the matter, Allen?"

He listens for a minute then says, quietly, "How is Old Eddy doing? Good, I'm glad he didn't get hurt. Now, did you say that he got a look at the bear after it pulled his trailer apart? Uh huh, uh huh. Yep, it's the same bear. I tracked him for half a mile the morning after he trashed my camp, and he's got a slewed back leg that he drags a bit. I told you he was a monster, didn't I?"

Jack turns and steps to the window, clenching the phone between his jaw and shoulder. He throws his hat onto an easy chair. The first rays of the rising sun are breaking through the front window to light up his face. It turns his white forehead pink and rouges the mahogany of his lower face, lights his brilliant blue eyes.

"Allen," he say quietly, so his son in the other room can't hear, "that thing followed us down here to the ranch, I just know it. Ripping the side off Old Eddy's trailer, with him still in it, is just a way of leaving his calling card. He likes to do that." Jack is thinking of Gib's saddle left on top of the wrecked cook stove.

There is an edge to his voice as he looks into the bright kitchen where his son is trying to overhear the conversation. Jack turns around to face the black form of Carter Mountain, silhouetted against the cerulean early morning sky, and whispers. "That bear is headed straight for here. I'd appreciate you and your hands keeping an eye out for him, or his sign. If anyone sees him, kill him and I'll answer to the Game and Fish for it. If anyone cuts his sign, let me know." He pinches at his lip as Allen speaks, then says, "Thanks," and hangs up the phone.

He walks to the kitchen and stands in the door. JC waits for him to speak.

"It doesn't seem possible, after all these years, but it's gotta be," he says to Anisa.

She is surprised at the ashy tinge under her husband's eyes. "What is it, Jack?"

"Gib's bear. He's back."

❄ ❄ ❄

Gib is sitting in the dayroom, looking out onto a small grass courtyard. Two resident alkies are playing croquet in the bright sun. He watches them for a minute, then turns his gaze back into the room, to a muted TV set.

After a week in the hospital, the faces on the screen are familiar to him. A young soap opera couple are walking by a lake, speaking earnestly to one another as swans drift along the shore. Gib recognizes the lake in Central Park. It looks the same as when he had ridden at Madison Square Garden.

I'll bet me and Dan fed those swans' great-great-great-granddaddies, he thinks, and chuckles.

So, Dan is here, too. A man who should be sitting by some good old woman instead of in this hole. Soft-hearted Dan, who gave a dime to every raggedy kid in sight and held other people's babies like they were his own. Most of us were born bachelors, but not him. Damn shame.

Dan had been married once. And Gib was probably the only one that Dan had ever told anything about it.

They had been working outside one winter, mending fence the elk had taken down along the Clark's Fork river south of Billings. One day, after working all damn day long at thirty below zero, they had ridden back at dark. They were colder than a well digger's ass when they got to the bunkhouse. Once inside, they built a fire, sawed up some steaks and put potatoes on to fry. While they waited, they poured a couple of tumblers of whisky to warm up on. The whisky on an empty belly had loosened Dan up.

He told how he had come out of Nebraska as a kid, looking for his older brother, and his first stop was Cheyenne. He needed work, and a guy at the stockyards asked him if he could ride colts. Dan said, "Yeah I can ride colts." Two hours later he was heading for Iron Mountain with eight head of slick-mouthed colts and a saddle horse.

It was a hard working ranch, and Dan was at it every day from dark-o'clock til dark-thirty. Down the way, about twenty miles, was another place with a long-haired blonde cook, and she was a beauty. Dan had seen her a couple of times. One evening he couldn't stand it any longer so he told the foreman that he was going to take the next day off, ride over to the neighbors and visit a spell.

"Yer going over to see that blond aintcha?" the gap-toothed foreman had said. Yeah, Dan said, that's where he was going. "Well, you might as well take one of those new horses we got the other day," the man said.

Dan knew what that meant — the SOB was giving him a horse to break on the long ride to see the girl. So after work he tied up a hind leg on a proud cut bronc, got his saddle on him and when they opened the gate for him was it was just getting dark. But instead of bucking, the big iron-mouthed bay took off running. In the wrong direction.

Dan fought the horse for hours, finally turning him around just as the moon was coming up. But it was a rodeo or a race damn near all night long.

Just at daylight, Dan got to the gate at the ranch. He was worn to a nub when he got down to open the gate. The horse was broke pretty good by now, he figured. But damn if that bronc didn't spin and kick Dan right in the chest with both hind feet. The pretty blonde cook was out getting water from the well, and she saw it happen.

The short of it was that Dan fell in love while she was nursing him out at the bunkhouse. She jumped right on his proposal when he asked her to marry him.

By the time Dan got around to telling Gib that part of the story, he was almost sliding out of his chair from the whisky and the heat from the stove.

He looked up, and Gib could tell that he was still hurting right down deep, where only a woman can hurt you. And he said "Y'know, that woman was the meanest son-of-a-bitch I ever met in my life." And in them days the country was full of mean sonsabitches, so that was saying a bunch.

Suddenly Gib sits up straight and looks around. He hates catching himself day dreaming like some old man. He always prides himself on living in the present. Lately, he had caught himself living more and more in the past. He hated it. He wasn't afraid of anything on God's green earth. Except not having a decent place to die with some dignity — and that had been preying on his mind for a couple of years now.

I wonder what that big nigger is doin', starin' at me through that glass? he asks himself. He had picked out Security and the guy he knew as Dewey, standing at the Nurse's Station. He was the subject of the conversation, he could tell from the way they were looking at him as their mouths moved.

Gib hadn't forgotten how Security had manhandled him; he still had sore places and bruises left over from their wrestling match. But, Gib had gotten in a couple of good ones, he remembered. As a matter of fact, the black man's eyebrow was broken by a shaved patch and highlighted by a couple of butterfly stitches.

He also remembered the names he had called the big man, and he was more than a little ashamed. It simply hadn't been like him, and he had been puzzling over how the recent events had come to pass — the arrest, jail, the judge sending him to the loony bin; or the "gin bin," as the staff called the substance abuse ward.

"How is Gibson's temperature?" Security was asking the Charge Aide from the geriatric unit.

"Gib? He's OK for someone who is supposed to be dead. That was the worst case of DTs I ever saw. He's still a bit disoriented, but improving daily. He walks the corridors and watches TV late at night, and won't take anything to help him sleep."

Security smiles. "He's rough. Those old guys who worked this country before it was all machines and gadgets have got a physical toughness that only a life of hard work can put into a man. But hard work don't make a man mean as that. I wonder what his story is?"

"Hard to tell when they reach his age," Dewey offered. "Could be from having to look at the last of his life."

"Hmm. Could be. You know, he was one of my heroes when I was a kid."

"Gib?"

"Yup. He was a world champ, y'know."

"No, I didn't. Dr. Scott hasn't mentioned it, I'll have to ask her about it."

"Yeah. He looked real good. My dad thought he had more style than any of the rest of the competition cowboys from those days. We saw him ride in Billings more than once, and he always won it all. Best All-Around — saddle bronc, roping, steer wrestling. Not only that, he was the saddle bronc champ of the whole dang world, and that's something."

Dewey smiles. "I just don't see you as a rodeo fan. I mean…being black, and all."

"Why not? My great-grandfather came up to Montana from Texas as a working cowboy on a cattle drive. He finally settled in Great Falls. My grandpa was the first black kid born in the upper Missouri country, and cowboyed around there his whole life. My dad did too, til he got a steady job with the Burlington Northern and married my mom. Our cowboy heritage has always been a matter of pride to my family." He smiles a big, wry smile. "The Crow Indians remembered grandad for being one of the first "white" kids born on Rosebud Creek. We think that's cool, too." The big man grins. "You can go back and tell Doctor Scott that the old guy is doing fine, considering. He's starting to come around."

Security steps away from the Nurse's Station, smooths his shirt over his flat stomach and checks his gig line, an unconscious gesture left over from fifteen years in the military.

He pauses and falls into thought as he stares through the glass at the silver haired old man slumped in the day lounge. He aches to think he may never have this man's respect. And only because of the color of his skin. The old pain comes back.

He had left the Marines because of a conflict with a white officer from Alabama which had resulted in a Captain's Mast for him. He had landed in Los Angeles after his discharge, and landed hard. He ended up laying around South Central, hustling the working girls for their money. He needed to get himself some dream time, to get away from all that "less than."

One night he had OD'd in the ratty rooms of a dime connect. His body roused itself somehow, knowing that it was dying. He had dragged himself to his feet and outside to the street. The red and dying ozone evening had been fading and falling farther away each second.

He heard singing and fell up some steps, thinking in a dim way that he might be on the way to heaven. He crawled through a door, knocking over a water cooler. The cascade of cool water felt hot as blood. As he began to melt, he begged, "God, please save me."

Men from the church burst through the foyer door, raised him in their arms and began to call on Jesus to save him. They carried him to a small room with a rickety cot and began to minister to him. They clasped his feet and head, fell across his body, sang, implored God with their hands and faces raised to the water-blotched, sagging ceiling.

He felt love flowing from their hands, a love that he would come to know as the Holy Ghost, and the peace of God. At that moment he realized that it was not pain that he had felt all his life, it had been fear. Fear because he'd always felt alone in the world, fear because he had always felt "less than." And suddenly, in the arms of his brothers and God, he wasn't alone and he wasn't afraid.

The sweet memory of that first moment's peace returns to Security, and he absently rechecks his gig line as he looks at Gib. He knew and understood cowboys. Men like this had learned to live for years without the touch of another human being, except for the occasional hand shake. It wasn't a good way to live, yet they invariably prided themselves on their isolation.

He must love this man. Just as Security had been saved by the love of his brothers, perhaps this man could learn what he had learned. That he wasn't alone in the world.

But Security doesn't preach. Talking isn't his way. He tries to witness through his conduct. By extending the confident and loving hand of a man who finally knows who he is, and what he was put on this Earth for.

Gib's attention is drawn to the corridor by Security's approach. The man's open face is lit by a glow which touches Gib strangely.

"Mr. Gibson, I'm supposed to escort you over to the charity room, so you can pick out some duds. Let's get you out of that robe and PJs. Besides, you need to get some fresh air."

"Yeah. I do need to get some of the stink blowed off me, I guess."

When they reach the last door, Security pushes the solid metal open. They step outside and Gib stands for a moment with his head thrown back. The fresh air, scented with the spicy smell of fallen cottonwood leaves, caresses his face and neck. He can pick out a half dozen other natural perfumes, including a horse pasture somewhere upwind.

"Lord, that air smells good." A shiver runs over Gib's shoulders, and he wonders at all the richness of life he has been insensitive to for so long. What have I done to myself?

"Security, what month is it?"

"October. October the 12th today."

"October! The last thing I really remember it was summer time, and hot. I was in Nevada."

"Booze will do that to you. And drugs." Security had also lost months on end, when he was using.

They start toward the building where the charity room is located.

"October twelve," Gib mutters.

"Say what?"

Gib looks a bit embarrassed. "Sorry, I got the habit of talkin' to myself out loud — I was just thinkin' about something that happened to me in an October, a long time ago. I been havin' dreams the last coupla nights…"

He stops and looks at the distant Uinta Mountains on the southern skyline. "It happened in the quakies. They was turnin' color, but hadn't started falling yet — we was havin' a late fall like this one.

"Well, this one afternoon late, the light was coming through the leaves and they were all just the right color…you know, like in a kid's story book, or something where there's magic going on." His voice falls off to nothing, then slowly comes back up. "I was riding the mountains above the ranch, lookin' for some cows we were short, and just enjoying the end of the day as I headed back. I was riding down from the sunlit top of the ridge where it was warm, moving into the shade, going downhill where it got darker and darker the further I rode." He puts his chin down and starts to walk again.

"Y'know, sometimes,when it's getting late and the sun drops behind the mountains, a quakie grove can be like it's…an evil place."

The hair on the back of Security's neck prickles at the haunted note in the big old man's voice.

Gib goes on. "When it's getting dark and cold and you ride into one of them groves where there's a water seep, and there's rotten quakie logs laying all over the place, and they're covered with black cow shit from the summer and there's a foot of frosty black goo and dead leaves where the seep oozes up out of the ground…" His voice threads off again, then restarts, "and there's the smell of dead quakie bark and putrid stuff in the deep hoof holes, it's, well, spooky."

He stops and looks up at the mountains again. "But, I guess I got ahead of myself. About five months before this evening in the grove, I'd took a quick shot at a big griz that was eating one of our cows, just as he was about one jump from the timber. I knew I'd hit him, because there was blood and hair plastered to one of the trees.

"Anyways, I went in after him, alone, which was dumb, and the big SOB damn near got me — doubled back and jumped outta some deadfall. If I hadn't had a real good horse under me and he hadn't had a bad leg from the bullet, I'da been a goner.

"So there I am droppin' down into that cesspool in the quakies on the dark side of the mountain," Gib shakes his shoulders to clear the goose bumps, "and he was waitin' for me. Prob'ly been stalkin me for days, mebbe even weeks."

Security waits for a minute, hoping that Gib would go on, but afraid he might. A story like this could keep him up nights, even as old as he is.

"Anyway, my horse knew the griz was there first. But we was heading downhill and in the shit and the sweat before either of us could do much about it. My horse blew up, bucked me off and got outta there." Gib shakes his head and his voice drops to a whisper. "He got me."

Security says softly, "So that's where you got all those scars I saw the day you came in."

They stopped at the door to the building and Gib continues, "I can't seem to forget it lately. It keeps comin' back." He stops for a moment, then adds, "That animal is something unreal. He…he's huge, but that's only a part of it. It's like he's *electric* or something." He stares at the distant hills, silent for a few seconds. "And he smells like a graveyard turned over."

Security pulls the door open and shakes his shoulders. "Man, I wish you hadn't told me that."

He points up a flight of stairs. "Up there, Gib," he says, then looks over his shoulder and pulls the door shut solidly behind them.

They hear women talking and laughing. They climb the steps and walk down a corridor to an open door, where a group of women volunteers are unpacking boxes.

The room is full of tables and racks stacked and hung with clothing. The gabble stops when the two men enter the room. A tall woman with an expensive platinum hairdo glances at her watch and says, "I'm sorry, Gentlemen, but we won't be open for another twenty minutes."

"It's OK, ladies. Mr. Gibson doesn't like crowds."

"Oh," the matron says, and they all arch their eyebrows and scrutinize Gib. Ordinarily, only the dangerous patients are escorted by Mr. Security, as they call him.

"Help yourself, Gib. Take some, leave some. I'm going for a cup of coffee to cut these goose bumps you gave me. Take your time."

Security stops at the door and turns to the huddle of ample floral-print bosoms and says, "Don't worry ladies. Mr. Gibson isn't violent."

The women relax and smile as Security exits. Then his voice floats back into the room from the corridor, saying, "He's a notorious Peeping Tom."

"Thank goodness," says the tall lady. And the group goes back to sorting clothes and visiting.

Gib meanders about the room. The first thing to catch his eye is a heavy wool coat with a fleece collar, good as new. As though he'd found a hundred dollar bill, he feels lucky; something he hasn't felt in a real long time.

He rummages through the shirts and finds three, also like new. A couple of sets of thermal underwear go on the pile. Then, he walks to a rack of sport coats, more out of curiosity than anything else. He'd had only two in his life, both corduroy ones with leather elbow patches. He dressed up only once in a blue moon.

He stops and pulls a soft wool jacket from the rack. It is of such quality even his unsophisticated eye is drawn to it. He runs his fingers down a sleeve, enjoying the touch of the expensive weave. He opens the jacket and looks at the label. The large, silk sewn-in tag reads:

Nelson's Oasis Shop
Palm Springs, California

Palm Springs, California. To a man like Gib those words imply an elegance and a sophistication which outruns his imagining. But, the touch of the expensive material between his calloused fingers inspires him to pass a moment in thought, trying to conjure up an image of what downtown Palm Springs might look like, or how it would feel to stop under the sign "Oasis Shop" and know he could go inside and know exactly what he was doing. The closest he could come were memories of cruising the hock shops in Las Vegas. He hangs the coat up and continues to browse until Security shows up.

Security looks at what Gib has picked out and says, "It's going to be kinda drafty without any pants."

"They don't have any."

Security looks at a pile of trousers and points. "Those have bugs in them?"

Gib answers, "Those are slacks, not pants. I've only had one pair of slacks in my life and they're still good as new. I wear jeans, and that's all I've worn since I was big enough to buy my own clothes."

"Well, until you get some money in your account, it looks like you're going to have to get out of the jeans habit."

Gib goes to a pile and picks out a pair of tan work pants. "Suntans will do for now, I guess."

Security says, "Thank you, Ladies." They pause at their sorting, smile and nod.

"You're very welcome, Mr. Security."

The two men walk down the stairs and return to the sunshine, Gib's arms loaded with clothes.

"Say, what is your real name, anyway?"

" My real name is Lester. Lester the third, no less."

"What's yer last name?"

"Purce."

"Purce. Purce. I should know that name."

"Not too many of us around."

"Yeah, I know."

Security drops his voice into neutral and says, "I meant there aren't too many of us 'Purces' around."

They walk in embarrassed silence for a few steps. Then Gib stops, puts the clothes under his arm and begins to rummage around in the pocket of his hospital robe. His head is cocked, with one eye squinted and his hair hanging to the side. He retrieves a toothpick chewed to a fan on one end. He sticks the unchewed end in his mouth and looks at Security. "I owe you an apology," he says.

"For what?"

"I called you a nigger, and I remember saying it more than once. And for that I offer you my apology. You see, I was real upset 'cause the judge sent me here — I'd rather he'd sent me to hell itself. But, I don't want you thinking that I'd use that for an excuse.

"The fact is that I haven't had much at all to do with colored people since I was a kid in Missouri. Now, my pap was as mean a man as ever walked when it came to you folks, and he raised me up to be the same way. I never had to stop and ask myself if that was excuse enough for me to feel the same way, until a couple of days ago."

Gib looks down at the ground for a moment, then looks up at Security again. "Over the last while I been worrying that question pretty good. And I come to a conclusion about it — I have no excuse whatsoever for behaving the way I did, for saying the things I said. I'm sure it hurt, and you have my apology."

Security sticks out his hand for Gib to grasp. The old man's hand was hard from a lifetime of work, something that helped Security to accept the man's apology with no reservations. He was a man who meant what he said.

"Mr. Gibson, I accept your apology and thank you for offering it."

"Yer welcome. There now, that makes me feel a whole lot better."

They begin their walk back and both men fall into thought.

Security knows terrible things happened between the races in places like Mississippi, Arkansas, Missouri, and there was hate enough to go around on both sides. But the people who Security had trouble accepting were the ones raised in places like Montana and Wyoming who feared and hated other races for no historical reason. It could only be rank, knee-jerk hate. Prejudice seemed to come as naturally to them as breathing, and it tested the bedrock of Security's faith as nothing else in the world.

He takes a breath and says "If you don't mind, I'd like to slide by the softball game. There's someone there that I'd like to check on."

"Lead on," Gib says, and they change direction toward the ball game in the distance. When they reach the noisy field, Security thrusts his chin and says, "See that guy over there?"

"Which one?"

"The one that looks like Albert Einstein with hemorrhoids."

"Yeah, I see him."

"And he sees us, too. Did you see him duck his head and say something to the guy next to him?"

"Musta missed it."

"Well, one of these days I'm gonna lean on him real good."

"How come?"

"I'm positive he's dealing meds. Most of these guys are on dope strong enough to stupefy a buffalo and a lot of the time they hide their medication under their tongues. If the med nurse doesn't catch 'em they trade the meds to Red for cigarettes or candy and he deals them on the junkie ward."

"Naw! He's a dope dealer?"

"Yeah, in a small way. He does it mostly to get under the staff's skin. He's got a real authority problem — an original shit-disturber, for sure."

"Well, if I catch him doing any of that around me, I'll disturb his own shit for him."

Security laughs his big, bass laugh. "I'll just bet you would. But, be careful of him all the same. He doesn't blink when it comes to confrontation, and he's mean enough to make a badger hunt his hole.

"C'mon, let's be getting you back to the ward, it's going to be lunch time pretty quick."

When they reach the door of the ward, Security knocks and they wait for the attendant to unlock the door.

Suddenly, Gib says, "I been putting two an' two together. You say that you're from Montana?"

"Yes, Billings."

"Not Great Falls?"

"Billings."

"I knew of some Purces from Great Falls. They were colored."

"You're thinking of my grandpa."

"He was a rodeo hand, right?"

"You knew about him?"

"Yeah, and he was a helluvva all-around hand. Bucking horses, bulls, roping, dogging. The best. If he'd been white, he'da been famous as hell. Good man."

The door opens and Gib steps inside for the attendant to lock the door behind him.

Security watches through the glass as the tall man walks down the corridor.

Those old guys are getting scarce. It's too damn bad their generation is going. Miss Manners might not think much of them, but it'll be a shame when they're gone.

Chapter 9

Gib returns to the ward after eating lunch. As he walks by the Nurses' Station he hears the ward clerk say, "Mr Gibson, you have some packages to sign for."

"Packages for me?"

"Yes, sign here please."

"Where'd they come from?"

"There were here when I came back from lunch. Someone must like you."

As Gib signs his name he says, "I can't imagine who in the hell that'd be."

He takes the packages, wrapped neatly in brown paper, to his room. At the door he looks around to make sure that no one is watching. He puts the packages down on his bed and starts to open them in private. At Christmas, when he was the nominal head of the Scott family, despite Jack and Maggie's protests to join in, he would watch everyone else open their presents and then take his to his room to open them while alone.

Even as a child he found it impossible to open a gift in front of anyone. He had never felt deserving, and never knew how to thank anyone for being good to him.

As he opens the first package, a note falls on the bed. It reads, "Dear Gib. Here are some things you can probably use." It is signed, "Maggie."

He puts his hand over his eyes for a second, until his stomach turns back over where it was supposed to be. Ever since he'd heard that Maggie was here at the hospital, that she might see him derelict and resource-less, he had been terrified of any contact with her. Now it had happened.

Inside the first package are two pair of Wranglers jeans whose newness had been washed and ironed out of them. They are exactly the right size. He closes his eyes as a small lump works its way up to his throat. He can see Maggie, not even in her teens, standing on a footstool at the folding table, folding a pile of clothes — always so intent on everything she did for her two men. She had started mothering them when she was way, way too young to be without a mother herself.

He swallows the lump and whispers, "Yer a darn good woman, for a kid." The old pet phrase brings the lump back, and chokes him to tears.

❋ ❋ ❋

Maggie is at the door of the ceramics studio, peeking in at Lorna.

"Can you get out of here for a few minutes? I feel a real need to take a walk and vent some stuff. I have picked you as Designated Listener."

Lorna glances up and sees the tension in Maggie's face. "Of course. I was supposed to meet with the new Home Ec person, but I assure you that I'd much rather spend the time with you. I'll phone her and cancel."

Once in front of the building Lorna asks, "Whither?"

"Let's walk down by the river," Maggie says.

The two women move slowly down the hill to where they can see the Bear River, which runs below the hospital. No longer fed by snow melt, the river is shallow and clear as gin. The shore is cobbled with bleached river rock and edged with browning grass. The banks are swathed with green willow turning more yellow and golden as crisp night succeeds crisp night. A flight of geese wings noisily by, flying upriver toward the distant Uinta Mountain range in the south.

"The Wild Swans of Coole," Maggie remarks and raises her face to the sun.

"Swans? Aren't those geese?" Lorna asks.

"Yes, I'm sorry. These peerless autumn days always remind me of my mother. 'The Wild Swans of Coole' was one of her favorite poems. We would sit on the edge of the river that ran by our ranch and she would read Yeats to me, then explain the imagery. Just us two...girls. It was wonderful." Maggie sighs quickly.

Lorna takes Maggie's arm and the two women look out over the river to the dun colored hills beyond.

Maggie finally says, "Lorna, I have known you for only a very short time, but, as the saying goes, I feel as though I've known you all my life. Perhaps even before that." She pats Lorna's comforting hand.

After a moment Maggie goes on. "I'm going to tell you something that I have never told anyone else in my whole life."

"OK," Lorna says, simply.

Maggie looks down at the ground for several moments. Finally she looks up and says, "When I was going through my interview with Doctor Hillyard, he asked me why I had come back to Wyoming after all my successes back East. I told him then that I didn't honestly know what had brought me back.

"His question angered me at the time. It's hard to admit that beneath all the 'successes' was a broken marriage, two stepdaughters feeling emotionally abandoned…" She runs her fingers through the hair at her temples. "In fact, everything that was of real human importance was wrecked. Ruined. Wasted." She laughs ironically. "But I looked wonderful on paper."

Maggie looks around for a moment, then sits down on the grass, carefully pulling her legs under her and arranging her skirt. Lorna lies down on her back and pulls her skirts to mid-thigh to enjoy the sun the more. They both smile at the contrast.

"Go on," Lorna says.

"After my interview, I went to my motel room, mixed myself a double martini, sat down, and asked myself what I was doing — for the first time since I'd packed my apartment in Georgetown. I came up with nothing, really. So, I mixed myself another martini, and asked myself why I had ever left Wyoming, or rather, why I had stayed in the east after finishing my schooling. And then I remembered something that I had stuffed into the darkest corner of my psyche a very long time ago." She stops speaking and carefully watches a honey bee foraging on a dandelion in front of her knees. She pushes her finger toward the flower until the bee lifts off and hums away.

"Lorna, that violent old cowboy who is over on the substance abuse ward, the one I told you about?"

"Yes?"

"He's my brother's father."

Lorna waits a moment, then she quietly offers, "And your mother's lover."

"Yes. My perfect, poetic, mother's lover." She picked a small stick from the grass and scratches at the lawn, frowning.

"I had no idea until Beth the Bitch told me when we were juniors at Smith. She was from Cody, too, and we'd always been rivals. We were competing in a dumb way for this guy named, so help me, Beau. It was over a crummy, innocent date and she had to drop something like that on me, just to get even.

We didn't call her Beth the Bitch for no good reason. We even ended up spelling her name B-e-t-h-e-b-i-t-c-h, as one word."

The two women giggle briefly at the old calumny.

"So, I cried a bunch, denied a lot, cried some more, and then sat down and thought about it. You see, Mother had been dead for almost ten years at this time, two years after Father had been killed. There was no one I could ask about it...except Gib, maybe. And that was impossible for me to do." She heaves another deep sigh.

"But, I began to think about it and saw that Jack had Mother's personality, God knows. He's dreamy, poetic, and has both feet planted firmly in mid-air. And that's not good for someone engaged in a business as volatile as ranching is. Anyway, I could see that he had mother's personality, but when I turned my mind to it, it was obvious that he was Gib's — same eyes, same rangy body, same hand and head gestures. Genes don't lie."

"No," Lorna agrees. "These chubby legs, and the freckles, are my mom's and that's the awful truth."

Maggie smiles. "My father was an excellent businessman, educated at Princeton — very literate, but also a pioneer importer and breeder of exotic European purebred cattle. He was president of the bank and in state politics up to his eyebrows. He defined the Western power broker, from what I learned about him when I got older."

"What happened to him?" Lorna asks.

"Plane wreck. He was out looking for cows on our summer range in the Absarokas and a down draft shoved him into a mountain side. I was eight when it happened."

Lorna glances at Maggie. Her face is serene as she looks out over the river at the distant sandstone and sagebrush hills.

"I remember that I loved him very much, and he loved me the same." She waggles the little stick in her fingers. "He always smelled of pipe smoke when he picked me up and swung me around, then hugged me tight. I used to wait for him at the landing strip next to the ranch house, until that one time...when the plane didn't come, and didn't come...

"I waited until it was dark. Mother couldn't get me to come in until it was dark dark." Her voice trembles.

"Father's face, I remember, was always shaven — smooth, fragrant and generous." She pauses a beat. "Gib's hugs, when you could drag one out of him, were whiskery and...brief." Her voice trails off, then she adds, "But he loved hugs himself, they made him absolutely glow."

Maggie scratches at the lawn again. "Jack was almost two when Father was killed. He never really knew him. He was four when Mother died, so he was raised by Gib." She misses another beat before adding, "but then, I guess I was, too."

"What about your mom?" Lorna rolls over on her stomach to listen, her face pillowed on crossed arms.

"Laura."

"Hmmm?"

"Her name was Laura. I don't know if it's the name itself or because of how I remember her, but the name has some sort of ethereal, other-worldly quality, doesn't it?"

"Mm-hmm. It does," Lorna agrees.

Maggie points. "Here come some more geese."

"I thought they were swans."

"Swans, yes."

The flight calls down to their kind on the river and a clarion chorus rises to invite them down. They flatten their wings and begin a shallow glide. The flight loses altitude and swings down on the autumn air, following the crooked course of the river and the gilded willow. Correcting from side to side, they adjust their glide to match the course of the water. They drop into a great gabble of welcome, offered by the other beautiful birds, and shatter the pristine surface of the Bear River with their silver landing wakes.

"I wonder how many that makes?" Maggie asks.

Lorna lets the question pass and puts her face back down on her freckled arms to listen.

Maggie accepts the invitation and begins again. "Mother was a teacher. She taught 'slow' children, long before it was a major part of the education process. She developed all her own materials…"

"Sounds like you," Lorna remarks.

Maggie's eyes widen and a smile of appreciation turns her mouth up, then moves quickly on with her story.

"She taught for three years and became one of Cody's most popular teachers. She'd started teaching at the one-room school near the ranch, but her interest in the special kids took her to town, 25 miles away, and she stayed there for the school year. Father was really involved in his cattle breeding program, and was spending most of his time at the ranch. It meant that he had to either commute from town or stay at the ranch without Mother.

"It was impossible, I guess, the way he saw it. Anyway, Mother found out that she was pregnant with me and resigned her position immediately, as they did in those days…"

"Doesn't that just chap your buns?! God!" Lorna shouts. "I'm sorry, I forgot my proper female self. Please go on."

Maggie grins. "So, she came back to the ranch, had me, and then decided that she was going back to teaching, when I was a little over a year old. She wanted Father to buy a house in town. But, he was spending everything he had on the cow operation and his investment in the bank.

"That's what he said, anyway. But, looking back, I can see that he could have done it if he'd wanted. He just wanted Mother and me to stay at the ranch near him and his work. And I guess you can't blame him.

"So, Mother stayed. But then something happened. She developed allergies to animals — dogs, horses, cats, cows, anything with hair. It was psychosomatic, of course. But the result was that she retreated to the house and became pretty much house-bound. Effectively, she simply cut herself off from Father's world."

Lorna sits up. "That's some seriously neurotic stuff."

Maggie nods. "It gets even more complicated."

"Gib," Lorna offers.

"For the life of me I cannot decipher how Gib figured in Mother's life. He was the absolute epitome of ranch life, of everything that she seemed to hate. He was a rough, uneducated cowboy. And I mean a cowboy's cowboy. He was a rodeo hero who went to town, got drunk and rode his horse into the bars. He…there was a whole apocrypha built up around the man and the macho things he did!"

Maggie flips the stick across the lawn. "I just don't understand how he fit into the thing. I honestly don't."

Lorna sits up. Her forehead is shiny with little beads of sweat from the heat. "You don't?"

"No, I don't." Maggie looks quizzically at her friend.

"You don't think that it was just a way of getting even with your dad?"

"No," Maggie says emphatically. "She simply wasn't that way — there was never anything dishonest or underhanded about anything she did. And I'm not just saying that because she was my mother. It had to be something else."

"Have you ever thought that it might just have been simple romance?"

"Romance!"

"There is little that is more romantic than the mythic cowboy swain — rough hewn, quiet, strong and independent. For me, it isn't the guy in the French cuffs, Jerry Garcia tie, cigar, and suspenders who makes my little heart go pitty-pat. Gimme a cowboy every time."

Maggie gives a quick, dismissive chuckle. "Not Mother. Surely, not."

Lorna goes on. "The cowboy myth is not some gross fiction that men conspire to pass off on the world. Women have always been full partners in the myth-making process. She could have fallen for it too, in some vulnerable, romantic moment. Who knows — a mountain meadow, or a lazy afternoon with no one around the ranch except the handsome ranch foreman…"

"But the ignorance…"

"Sometimes we call it ignorance when some people refuse to play by the same rules that we choose to live by. Besides, the lack of an education doesn't mean that someone is stupid."

"Lord, I'm not saying that Gib is stupid, far from it. But Mother was about nine cuts above most of the educated people in Cody, let alone ranch hands."

"Maybe you're a bit class-conscious."

"There is no doubt about that. I won't try to deny it. I can be a snob when I want to. I am entrenched in Cody's unacknowledged caste system as deeply as all the rest of the ranching and professional 'gentry.'"

Lorna looks at Maggie, then says, carefully, "What else is it that makes you angry with Gib?"

"His influence on Jack."

"But he's Jack's father. Isn't he entitled to any influence?"

"See! That's what makes me go crazy about all this — my father, Gregor Glenn Scott the Third, is Jack's father, but he isn't — Hurley John Gibson, late of the Ozarks, is Jack's father, but he's not, either!

"Gib knows that Jack is his natural son, but can't acknowledge it. Jack has no idea that his biological father is the ranch foreman and, in a fit of adolescent anger, fires his own father from a brand that survived only because of the efforts of that same man.

"God! The lies and sick secrets that I have had to live with for the last twenty years have just about driven me over the edge! I hate secrets and lying more than I hate anything else on the face of this earth."

Maggie's voice had attenuated to a whisper. The last word comes out as a desperate croak. She puts her chin down and begins to cry, softly.

Lorna scoots over and takes the shaking shoulders in her arms. Maggie puts her face on Lorna's neck and begins to sob. Immersed in her own lies, she has stuffed these particular tears for a very, very long time.

From the north come the sounds of another flight of geese, calling through the pristine autumn air passing below their softly beating wings.

In the back of the sobbing woman's mind, a small girl's voice whispers: "That will be the nine and fifty, Mama. They have come, at last."

Chapter 10

Gib is sitting in front of Maggie's desk, working his big, rough hands in a nervous clump on his lap. He is clean shaven and has a fresh haircut. The nearly-forgotten smell of his favorite hair tonic and bay rum after shave fills Maggie with an ache for her childhood days on the ranch; when God was still in His heaven and all was right with the world.

"I didn't think that you were ever going to come and see me," she says, softly.

"I didn't think I was ever gonna get an invite," the big man says, defensively.

"Fair enough." Maggie looks at Gib for a moment and then turns her gaze away. "Jack knows that you are here. I had to tell him."

Gib's head comes up quickly. His lips draw thin in anger. "Zat so?" he says.

Maggie continues. "He's worried."

"Zat so?"

"I told him that you were doing fine. He wants to phone and say 'Hi'… But that will keep for a day or two. I know how much you hate phones."

Gib nods and his mouth loosens. "Does he know…?"

"Cody's a small town, I'm sure he knows you were court-ordered. I don't think he knows you are on the alcohol rehab ward. I implied that you were here, on my ward, with my people. Which isn't the exact truth, but…"

"Hell, I'd rather he thought I was with the drunks and the junkies than over here drooling on myself, with the rest of the 'old folks'." He looks at Maggie with a sly smile.

She takes it in stride, even smiling at the jibe, then uses the opening to say,

"Gib, I want you to move over here from your ward. The evaluation period is almost up and I've seen the report. You are not an alcoholic personality. You will be referred back to the court soon and I think it would do you good to accept a transfer over here and avoid going back to court. Why don't you stay?"

"I can take care of myself."

"I know you can, but it would be easier if you stayed here for a while. You are going to be on probation for some time, at the very least…"

Gib looks startled. "For what?!"

"For not taking care of yourself, that's what. I hate to rain on your parade, but you have one count of larceny and two counts of assault, and a charge of interference with a police officer hanging over your head; plus some others. If you leave here you are going to be looking at some jail time, no matter what. Interference with a police officer, alone, can get you a full year in jail."

Gib looks at her, skeptically.

Maggie continues. "I'm not telling you what to do, I'm only giving you an alternative to being run through the court system." She pauses. "Why not stay here until you get straightened out?"

"I think that I am straightened out."

"I can't agree."

"Well, Missy, I am. You don't know everything."

"I know enough to assure you that you need some more time to deal with some things — things that have been buried for a very long time — things that cause your feelings to need anesthetizing. You can't possibly have dealt with your issues in this short a time."

"Well, I think I have. It's been plenty of time."

Maggie looks at the ceiling in exasperation, then fixes Gib with a clinical, professional look. "I can't make you do anything, Gib. You always told me, 'Do what you have to do.' I'm telling you the same thing."

Gib stands up and goes to the door. "Thank you. I think I'll just do that." His face has set itself into a neutral mask. "I've got to get back to my ward."

"Very well."

"I need to thank you for the Wranglers…and the boots." He looks down at his feet. "And the belt. It's the nicest one I ever had."

"You are welcome," Maggie says, softly.

Gib goes to the door and opens it. But Maggie's voice stops him before he can step through.

"Gib."

"Huh?"

"I love you." She stands.

The tall man drops his head and puts his face in a large hand. "Oh, Lord…" he says, and his shoulders begin to shake. He closes the door so no one outside can see.

Maggie, whose face is now wet with tears, walks to him, puts her hand on one shaking shoulder. He turns to open his arms, Maggie steps into them and he puts his wet cheek on the top of her head.

"Oh, Missy, the last time I saw you, you were still my little girl," he says. "I can't get used to you bein' the boss, and knowin' more than me."

Maggie can't speak. Gib goes on. "I been lost for quite a while…I prob'ly could use some help."

❄ ❄ ❄

Security's office is small, with a desk, a filing cabinet and two chairs. An open vault, which holds the residents' valuables, seems larger than the room.

"Sign here," Security says, handing Gib a sheet of paper with a hand-written inventory on it.

"Wait a damn minute, here. Who opened this box of my stuff?"

"I did."

"How come?"

"Hospital policy. Can't have folks sneaking left-handed cigarette makings or anything else illegal into the place. Gotta have rules about that."

"Dammit, this is my plunder and nobody else's — private stuff. If a man was to get caught goin' through another man's stuff in a bunkhouse he'd likely spring a leak or two, and that's pure fact."

"Sorry, but I have my job to do. I didn't chop the lock off your duffle, though. And I darn sure coulda, if I'd been of a mind to do it."

"Well, goin' through my boxes was bad enough. Damn it. My stuff — and no one else has the right to put one finger on it unless I say it's all right." Gib signs the paper and pushes it across the desk.

Security stands. "Here, lemme give you a hand. It's a hike over to Seniors Chalet."

"Thanks, it'll save me a trip or two."

Security closes the heavy door, spins the wheel and stoops to pick up Gib's boxes. They walk in silence across the hospital grounds. Gib had talked to Security about Maggie's proposal and Security had assured him that being admitted to her ward would save him a lot of grief at the hands of the district judge in Cody. It was a good deal for everyone because, essentially, he would be serving his jail term in the hospital.

Hell, things were getting way too civilized. In the old days they'd have given him three days and maybe a hundred dollars fine, tops.

When they reach Seniors Chalet, Gib holds the door open and Security walks in. "Sorry, but I don't have anything for a tip," he says and grins. Gib's face is still red when they reach the Nurses Station.

"Here's good enough," Gib says.

"OK," Security says, and sets the boxes down. "Good luck, I'll be seeing you."

"That's another thing I like about you," Gib offers.

"How's that?"

"You don't run off at the head," Gib says, referring to their silent trip across the grounds.

"Thank you. I take that as a real compliment."

"Too much runnin' off at the head going on around here. Every damn body has to tell ya how they're feeling, what they were feeling forty years ago, how they plan on feelin' in the future — pure bullshit." His voice goes into falsetto. " 'My dad whipped my inner child's ass just 'cause the misunderstood little tyke burnt down the chicken house and the flames jumped to the barn and corrals — I haven't been able to hold a job ever since I growed up, because of that lickin Pap laid on me! Boo-hoo.' Buncha rank horse shit if you ask me."

Security laughs. "Give 'em heck, Gib," he says and turns to leave. He is still laughing as he walks back through the doors.

Gib turns and raps on the glass of the station and Dewey appears to open the door.

"Good morning," he says. "Let me give you a hand."

"Take them boxes, I'll handle this duffle. Where we goin'?"

"Follow me."

Gib falls in behind as they walk down a corridor to an open door. "Here you are, Mr. Gibson."

"Hmmm. This ain't half bad, y'know."

"This is the newest building on the grounds. Two years old. Is there anything I can do — help you unpack, maybe?"

"Nope, I'm all growed up. Which chest o' drawers is mine?"

"That one there. Well, I'll see you in a bit. One of the other residents is coming by to show you around."

"Wonderful," Gib says, sourly, then follows Dewey to the door and closes it behind the aide.

Gib pulls open the drawers to his dresser and begins to unpack. Socks, shirts, t-shirts and handkerchiefs are tossed, unsorted, into the top one. Wranglers are folded into the second and odds and ends thrown into a third.

He drags his duffle across the floor, sits down on the bed and opens the combination lock. He slides his long arm down the side of the canvas bag, to work something up. He removes a pistol wrapped in a lightly oiled cloth. It is a .45 Colt automatic with black military grips, worn and shiny. A warm smile crosses Gib's face as he studies the gun he'd had since his days fighting in Korea.

"Hello, Sissy," he says. "Welcome to the Old Farts' Home. The cops got my single-action but they missed you." He releases the clip, checks the load, then clicks it back into the gun.

He gets up and slides the pistol under the mattress of his bed. He still has his hand under the mattress when the door flies open and someone comes inside.

Gib jumps to his feet and turns toward the door, an angry look on his face.

"Whatcha hiding, a jug?" It is Dan Williams.

Gib's face changes into a radiant smile. He holds out his hand and walks to his friend. He grasps Dan's right hand and clasps their grip with his big left paw.

"Dan, I honestly have never been more happy to see anybody in my whole life. Siddown." He motions to a chair.

"Well?" Dan says, looking around. "Whatta ya think? Pretty nice huh?"

"This is it, huh?"

"This is it alright. Whatcha been workin' for all your life."

Gib smiles. "I knew I'd never wind up loungin' on satin and fartin' through silk, but this is close enough for an old SOB like me, I guess."

The two men laugh, loud and long.

Dan wipes his wet eyes. "I slipped outta the meeting when Dewey come in and gave me the nod. Let's go down to the kitchen and get a cup of coffee, there's a coupla fellas that're anxious to see ya again. We been waiting fer ya for weeks, Gib."

Gib runs his hands over his iron grey hair. "Who else is here, for Chrissake?"

"You can see for yourself."

Gib and Dan walk to the dining area. It is vacant at the moment so they go to the coffee machine and pour two cups. Dan cadges a can of evaporated milk from one of the kitchen people and they find a table. They are busy catching up when two men entered the room. Dan smiles, waiting for Gib's reaction, but he just sits, staring at the newcomers. Dan glances at Gib, then at the others. He dips his face in embarrassment.

"Hell, dontcha know Moon Mullins and Ole Olsen?"

Gib is mortified. "Oh my hell!" He stands, his face red, and puts his hand out as he steps around the table. "Moon! What happened to all that black hair of yours?"

"Oh, I got it wet and it fell out. Ole here kept warning me about that soap and water, but I just wouldn't listen."

"Py de gods! I bin a'listenin to dem vater chokes for t'irty year from dis Englishman an' it's bin t'irty years too long. I wisht I vas a swearin man sometimes, so I cud tell him vat I'm really a t'inking."

"How you vas, Gip? Py de gods, it's good to see you agin!" The Norwegian's eyes are leaking tears. Good old, soft hearted Ole.

"And I'm glad to see you too, Ole. I haven't seen you since…when?"

"Last time vas Labor Day veekend in Meeteetse, nineteen and seventy-five — ven you shlapped de poop outta dat drunk LU hand who vas peein' on de side uf de bar."

Gib grins. "During the parade and in front of all the kids. Heck, I'd forgotten about that — boy, that's been a while."

The four old cronies laugh and sit down, falling into warm and familiar conversation.

A Norwegian from western Minnesota, Ole always had the top button on his shirt buttoned, whether inside, outside, a hundred degrees above or a hundred below. He smoked a pipe, smiled a lot, and shared everything he had. But he could be a melancholy man. And only one person knew his history — the big man sitting across the table from him at the moment; the man who had saved him from his own self-destruction. Gib Gibson.

Now, as he looks at this much older version of the man, Ole's mind goes back many, many years. He remembers seeing the tall figure towering above him in the hot rail yard, the face blacked out by the blazing sun behind the cowboy hat. He feels again his agony and desperation, then the strong hands and gentle voice as he is lifted to his feet. Gib had helped him to stumble back into the world of the living. This man had brought him out of the alcohol-soaked horror that his life had been for the two years he had tried to blanch the memory of the dead child.

Ole wipes a cold sweat away from his forehead. He must have wiped a million cold sweats from that same place, since that day when he had felt the little bump beneath the old Ford truck he'd just backed out of the barn. He had gotten out of the vehicle to find the owners' child lying in the dirt, the tiny boy's eyes wide with shock, his entrails pooched out onto the dirt.

He marked the re-beginning of his life from the day that he had shared his secret with this man. "You're only as sick as your secrets," he remembered Gib telling him.

The four men talk and talk. Old memories and shared experiences on the vast range lands of Wyoming and Montana are taken out and burnished. Pain, and the passing of good men they had known, were given a quick, sympathetic swipe. Against great odds, they had survived the Great Depression, World War II, the Korean War, the withering away of their beloved occupation, and other of America's real tough times. The great joy of survival and reunion made the moment shine for them, just the same.

As they visit, taking turns at story telling, Gib keeps a tally of all the people who enter the room. One person in particular catches his attention. The man, built like a professional wrestler, has large, piercing black eyes set in a round head cased with slicked-back hair.

He had walked straight to a table next to the wall of the dining room, taken a seat, and been staring ever since. Gib had met the gaze a couple of times and found nothing threatening in it, only honest curiosity.

A minute later, Gib's attention is caught by the scurrying entrance of the disheveled and shaggy man Security had pointed out at the ball game.

The man stops at the hot water urn and pours a cup of hot water, surveying the room and the kitchen area the whole while. He plops a tea bag in the water, adjusts a folded newspaper tucked under his arm and joins the large man with the piercing black eyes.

Gib, half tuned to the conversation at his own table, covertly watches as the long haired little man quietly chatters and gesticulates, occasionally wiping spittle from his stubbled chin. The big man who is the object of his chatter smiles and stares in the direction of Gib's table the whole while.

Bang! The palm of Ole's hand slams onto the table top to punctuate the story he's telling.

"God damn it!" Gib's hand had jerked and spilled his coffee. He takes napkins from the dispenser and mops at the spill as he apologizes to Ole. "Sorry about the cussing...you surprised me."

Ole is an extremely pious man. Taking God's name in vain would draw a real protest from him. The cow camps that had included Ole were almost always a model of mild oaths. "Py de gods" was his only expletive, and it referred to his native country's pagan pantheon.

"Dot's hokay, Gib." Ole says, and takes a cube of sugar from the bowl. He places it against the front teeth of his bottom plate and begins to suck his coffee through it. In the old days his smiles had been marred by the black stumps of his bottom front teeth, victims of this Scandinavian habit.

Gib leans forward and says, "Say, Dan, don't look now, but who's that big guy over there against the wall with the slicked-back hair?"

Dan leans back in his chair, sneaks a peek, and says, "Joe Echeverria. He's a Basco sheep herder who's been here forever."

"And who's that hairball with him who's yakking ninety mile an hour?"

"That's Red. Real name's Herb Silver. He's real different."

"How so?"

"For one thing, he's Communist and ain't afraid to tell you, neither."

"A what?"

"He's a real live Communist, and proud of it."

Gib leans back heavily in his chair and turns a hard gaze on the little man across the room. Almost as if he felt Gib's eyes on him, the little man slowly swivels his head and meets the stare. The big Basco observes the exchange of looks and grins.

"He's a Communist? Then how come he isn't in jail?" Gib says, holding the stare.

"It ain't against the law." Moon says.

"Hell it ain't. Gotta be." Red has broken the stare so Gib turns his attention back to his friends.

Dan continues. "Yeah, he was a Wobbly. Worked all over the place — including Canada and Mexico. But they threw him away over in Utah, for throwing bombs. He claims that Utah Copper and the Mormons railroaded him. Who knows? Anyway, he served a good spell, and when he got out his whole family had disappeared. Couldn't find a trace of them, so he came back out west and finally ended up here. Pretty interesting guy when you get talking to him."

Moon chimed in with a chuckle. "Hell, I worked with him back in the 30s."

Everyone's face turns to Moon.

"Back then, I was dressing tools in the Teapot Dome oil field when he showed up and got hired to help me in the bit shop. Of course, he was trying to get us all to join his One Big Union. I didn't care much for his politics, or the fact that he had about as much mechanical aptitude as that sugar bowl. But he was interesting company, and he made the time go by. Like Dan said, he'd been just about everywhere trying to organize working stiffs. He'd followed the grain harvest up into Canada, worked in the orchards and fields of California trying to sign up the spics — he'd been down in the oil fields of Campeche and spoke the lingo real good. And he was always going on about working with some guy down there named Traven. Even showed me some letters and a book by the guy, as if it was supposed to mean something to me.

"Anyways, he took his commie act over to Lance Creek, then comes back to our camp, on the dodge. I put him up for a couple of weeks in my shack, he was beat up real bad. Then I came back one day from my tour and he was gone. After he disappeared, word got over to Teapot that he'd shot a couple of goons in a bunch who were working him over with a sack fulla tong dies."

Moon takes a sip of his coffee and stares at Gib. "He damn near died on me, they beat him so bad."

Gib glances up, meets Moon's look, then leans forward over the table and sips at his cup. He knows that implicit in Moon's look is the fact that he owed Moon his own life. "Hmmph. I hear he's a dope dealer."

"Yup. I've heard that, but I don't know it for a fact. Heck, the way I see it, he's just another old fart down on his luck, and with no place else to go." Moon sweeps his chin in an arc. "Like the rest of us here at this table."

Gib drops his face. "Mebbe so, but I don't want nothing he's passing out."

Moon stares at Gib as the conversation changes back to cow camp stories. He remembers the first time he ever saw the man, slumped in his saddle and looking like death warmed over.

Dan had brought Gib to a line shack on the Jordan place near Iron Mountain, where Moon was spending the summer. Shot in the gut and worked on by some horse doctor, the ride from Cheyenne had just about put an end to him.

Moon hid him while Dan went over to the Nickell place and picked up his plunder. Then he came back to nurse Gib until he was well enough for them to light out north. He and Dan had been on the dodge too, just like Red.

A few days before, Dan had left Iron Mountain with his brother, Dal, to go to Cheyenne, for the rodeo. He had come back with Gib instead of Dal, and the two of them had been the same as brothers ever since. After they lit a shuck for the Wind River country, he'd heard that Dal was killed by Union Pacific goons, then pitched into the Laramie River. He never did learn how Gib had come to get shot in the deal. Neither he nor Dan had ever brought it up again, except to say thanks, and he was too much of a gentleman to ask. Those had been tough times for most folks, but harder for some.

He turns his attention back to the conversation, about a Sunlight Basin roundup gone bad. Dan is talking.

"So there we were, still October and the weather as nice as it could be. The country was steep and broken up in places so we were taking it pretty slow, making sure that we combed the place careful. Them damn cows can get wild as deer when they haven't seen a man all summer, you know.

"Well, on the seventeenth, the wind started coming in from the north and she was spitting snow by noontime. If it had been blowing in from the west it woulda been all right, but we suspicioned that we were gonna get a norther. And we weren't ready for a lot of snow that high up, God knows …"

"God knows nothing."

The men at the table turn their eyes to the speaker. Red, smiling a green smile through his ragged mustache, adds, "There is no God, gentlemen, he's a fiction and nothing more."

The men turn back to the table, studiously ignoring the man.

As I was saying," Dan continues, here it was only mid October and it's blowing like hell, snow piling up and them cows heading for the timber with their calves… Man, it was hard work, and getting harder by the minute as we pushed for Dead Indian. We knew that…"

"You knew that you were putting your life on the line for a rich man who cared more for the cows, and the profit they represented, than he did for the men working them," Red interjects, completing the sentence for Dan.

Dan's face flushes. "Old Man Brown cared about his hands."

Red reveals his stained teeth again, "And how much were you getting for your labor?"

"I worked for a dollar a day, and every one of them looked as big around as a Ferris wheel."

Red sees his opening. "I'll bet they did. And how much was this Mr. Brown profiting from your labor?"

"Heck, I don't know. I was just a cowboy, not the damn bookkeeper."

"Well, you may rest assured that it was a good deal more than a dollar a day. That's how the blood suckers accumulate their capital…"

The sound of Gib's chair scraping on the floor breaks into Red's budding lecture. When he stands, he towers over the untidy little man.

"Mister," Gib growls, "you just made two mistakes. The first one was when you interrupted a private conversation that had nothing to do with you. The second mistake you made was when you called Old Man Brown a blood sucker, because he happens to of been a friend of mine."

Red looks up at Gib, then turns to the three men still sitting. "And who is this, Mr. Mullins?" Then, turning back to Gib, he offers his nicotine-stained fingers for a hand shake. "I don't believe we have been introduced. My name is…"

Gib cuts him off. "Your name don't mean nothin' to me, mister." He looks down at the proffered hand and adds, "And you can keep that to yourself."

Red steps back a pace and his manner becomes as hard as Gib's. "Ahhh, the champion. The man of the hard fist. The do-for-others-what-they-fear-to-do-for-themselves. I recognize you, Mister Gibson." Red's voice grows softer, venomous. "I have met you a hundred times — in the orchards, on the docks, in the oil patch, in 'the amber fields of grain.' You were everywhere in America the Beautiful that I went." He steps back two cautious steps, still staring up into Gib's pale eyes.

"My name is Silver, Mr. Gibson, and my game is guile rather than fists. But I fear no man — believe me when I say that." He smiles, coldly, then turns to leave the room.

Dan looks at Moon. "Judas priest, what was that all about?"

Gib, watching the man leave, says, "Just getting a coupla things straight. Getting them straight right away."

Moon Mullins pulls a toothpick from his mouth and says, "The man may be old and small and smelly but he's no one to screw with, believe me."

"He don't show me diddly-squat," Gib says.

"Fine. But watch him."

Chapter 11

It is night. A big full moon is looking over Carter Mountain, driving the night back into the trees. Inside the ranch house, Anisa pulls the stopper in the kitchen sink and, wiping her hands on her apron, watches the funnel begin to take shape in the dish water. She closes her eyes, puts her hands on the small of her back and massages. She is pregnant.

She takes the dishrag and wipes the counter, the stove top and cleans the grease spatter from the side of the refrigerator. She rinses the rag and drapes it over the faucet to dry.

The moon has pushed its big belly over Carter Mountain and is poking its light into nooks and crannies, throwing great luminous washes over the pastures. Glancing out the window over the sink, in the north field Anisa sees a brooding haystack standing stark in the brilliant moonlight.

She walks to the light switch and douses the electricity. She goes through the door and moves easily through the front room, around the big old-fashioned furniture squatting in the dark. The large, multi-paned front window frames the porch supports and the lilac bush on the lawn, silhouetted to black cutouts by the moonlight. Cool night air floods the house when she pulls the front door open to step onto the porch. She goes quietly to one of the supports and lays her cheek and shoulder against the weathered wood of the upright.

JC is asleep in his room, the only other person for miles. Jack, with the guides and horse wranglers, had left at first light with their long strings of horses. They were moving all the equipment needed in the hunting camp for the next two months. Anisa closes her eyes and asks God for a bit of luck to go with the hard work.

She moves down to the log column at the end of the porch, crosses her arms against the light chill and leans against the support. She can see the river and its bends clearly. The moon has sheathed it in silver serpent skin where it moves beneath the bluff, then curves out of sight down the valley. The canyon breeze rustles the cottonwoods and their leaves, whose silver undersides flash and plash against one another, as if the river's reflections were animating them. It is a magic night. And she has it all to herself.

Something catches her eye. The light bulb over the big barn doors is out. The bright pool of light that usually lights the barnyard, warming the corrals and the water trough, is gone. Instead, an indistinct jumble of vertical and horizontal linear shapes huddle together in front of the bulk of the barn. She scans the shapes and sees nothing really amiss. The place is deserted, all the animals gone to the mountains with the men. The thought reminds her she is alone with JC and she wishes the friendly circle of light would reappear and ensure her sweet dreams.

Anisa shakes off a small shiver and walks back down the creaking boards to the seldom used front door and enters the old house. The night sounds and smells are left behind, replaced by the spice of the apple pie she baked while she cleaned the kitchen. JC loves apple pie with his breakfast and she wants to thank him for his sweet company.

Oh, JC, she thinks, you are growing so big, so fast. A shard of pain enters her breast at the thought of her good, sensitive, boy so anxious to move into the world of men. And he is so much like his father — naive and trusting.

She walks down the hall toward the bedrooms, quietly opens the boy's door and steps inside. He is lying on his back, his upper half bathed in moonlight. His mouth is open and he is breathing noisily, his legs twined in the bedclothes.

His mother moves to his bedside, untwines his legs from the blankets and straightens them. He gives a contented sigh and rolls onto his side, his hair falling down over his eyes.

She bends and runs her finger gently through his hair, brushing it back onto his forehead. He moves at her touch, but remains deep in his slumber.

Anisa watches him for another moment and then, as contented as he, steps to the old rocker next to the window. She picks up the afghan from the seat and sits down, putting the knitted piece over her lap and legs. Through the glass she can see the lustrous rampart of The Citadel mountain rearing over the pastures and hills. The weathered face is thrown into relief and she notes that she has never seen it with as much character before.

She rocks slowly and looks again at her son. Her eyes move about the room. Each piece of furniture, each relic of yesterday's childhood, has deep meaning for her and she smiles sleepily at the memories they evoke. Her eyes move back to the luminous rectangles that are the window. Her eyelids flutter.

She raises the hem of her night gown, steps onto the wide window sill and moves through the glass. She feels the dewy grass under her bare feet for a couple of steps, then leans forward a bit to push off. She clears the fence and gains a hundred feet of altitude. She feels speed first, quickly replaced by the delightful sights and smells of the perfect Indian summer night.

She gains altitude, banks to the north and heads toward The Citadel. Fourteen head of cows had been missed in the roundup and she needs to find them.

Flying over the pines and broken rock of the giant rubble foothills, she soars into the high country, dodging hoodoos and other jutting formations reaching out as if to snag her from the air. She is nimble as a bat in her flight, dodging easily from side to side, swooping and soaring at will.

She searches carefully but sees no sign of the missing animals. Cresting a ridge, she turns and follows it until she is skimming the huge scree and talus fans at the foot of The Citadel's towering cliffs. She does a lazy roll onto her back and looks straight up the thousand foot rock face dimpled and shadowed, creased and gouged into fantastic grimaces which change as she flies.

The perspective makes her queasy after a minute so she rolls over and swings away from the high wall. She soars to the head of Hardpan Canyon.

The cool air in the canyon chills her stomach and legs. The smells rising from the tumbling waters and redolent pines fringing the silvery creek fill her head. She turns her eyes toward the ranch. It is easy to pick out, though distant under the beaming moon.

Her eyes zoom to the ranch house. All is in order, all serene beside the glinting river and glittering trees. Then something moves.

Something is walking sturdily from the big gully which opens onto the hay field behind the ranch. Covering ground fast, the creature is staying on the unlit side of the draw. The dark bulk moves through a patch of moonlight. Silver highlights wink and flash along the broad back before it dashes back into shadow. The route leads directly to the house. And her son.

Panic grips her and she banks sharply, falling swiftly toward the creek and canyon in a steep glide aimed for the runway beside the ranch. The side slip pushes her stomach into her throat as she loses altitude rapidly. Too rapidly. She is losing her power to control the diving flight.

Wobbling, no longer aerodynamic, she waves her arms to regain control. But there is no more lift. The canyon bottom rushes up. Her eyes tear with the violent rush of air that grips at her night dress and windmilling legs. Something snatches at her blurring vision as she plummets — something is flashing the moonlight back at her in frantic semaphore!

It is the glinting wreckage of a small airplane. It is…

Anisa throws her head back and draws in a long, panicky gasp of night air. Sweat is running into her eyebrows and down her sides. Tears course down her face and a knot of anxiety pounds under her breast bone. She puts her hand on her belly, to reassure the little being held there.

She holds the breath, lets it out as she wipes her face. She glances at JC. He is lying on his side, his face composed.

She moves her gaze. The room comes into sharp focus. All is normal. Nothing strange or out of the ordinary. Except for a very faint alarm in the air.

As she tunes her senses she becomes aware of an almost audible hum. A faint smell of ozone wafts by in the unlit parts of the room. Her jaws clench and her ears began to adjust to a faint buzz.

Anisa closes her eyes and throws her senses outside the house. She knows every rock, every yard of irrigation ditch, every splice in the fence wire. Her senses swiftly follow the boundary fence and begin a sweep of the north fields that she had seen in her dream. They range frantically over the fields, to the mouth of the draw and back again. Then she focuses on the haystack two hundred yards away. And he is there. Striding into the moonlight and bounding purposely for the house.

A moan escapes her. Jack had described this presence. Her heart falls from her. She grips the arms of the rocking chair and leans her head against the back. All energy drains from her as she realizes how defenseless she and her children are. Her newly acute senses pick up the beast as he bounds over the picket fence and quickly crosses the yard.

She feels him at the back of the house. His noiseless footpads are cautious as he moves down the wall to the kitchen window. He snuffles deeply there, and she knows his hunger as he drinks in the rich smell of the warm pie on the cupboard.

She senses his vigilance. He is in the heart of his ancient enemy's territory and she is paralyzed with fear — a narcosis — as he moves around the end of the house, directly toward the window that Anisa is sitting by!

The bear tentatively tests the long wooden porch that runs the length of the south side of the house. He sets his front paws gingerly on the porch, his rear feet still on the lawn — knowing the thin boards will not hold his great weight.

A faint squeal slips into the room. The next nail shrieks very, very near. She can now hear a careful snuffling sound, smell his reek. She closes her eyes for a second to blink away the drops of perspiration from her eye lids. When she opens them again, she can see only a bright rim of light visible at the top of the window open an inch at the bottom. Then she sees his eyes!

The bear's massive, scarred face is only five feet from hers. He is staring directly into her. A fan of flaring silver hair rings the luminous amber of each huge, ominously intelligent eye. The effect is hypnotic. Terrifying.

The blinkless gaze turns to JC's slim form. The animal places his nose to the opening at the bottom of the window and concentrates his senses. He draws in a long, yet delicate breath, bringing the organic essence of the house into his lungs, concentrating on the body on the bed. Then, with a grunt, he steps back and wheels away. He had not found what he was looking for.

Moonlight fills the room again. Anisa takes her hand away from her face. She looks again at JC, notices his open eyes and stricken face. His chin trembles and the pillow under the corner of his mouth is soaked with drool. Her heart returns to her chest. She throws away the afghan, goes to her terrified child's bed and takes him in her arms. She drags the covers over them, places her face next to his. They lie there, sleepless and speechless, until the morning sun finds them.

❆ ❆ ❆

Gib wakes with a start. A gamey odor fills his brightly lit room and for a moment he doesn't know where he is. His brain finally turns on and he recognizes the odor as his own. The nervous sweats of the summer past had come back. The bright light in the room comes from the full moon.

He sits up and swings his long, scarred legs over the side of the bed, gives a sigh of resignation: Another lonely moonlit night to wade through, a night ripe with ripples and shadows, night full of resurrected memory and feeling, a dead friends night.

It was hell to get old. He hated it.

He waits for the cobwebs to clear from his head, trying to remember the dream that he had wakened to escape. Something bad…something about Moon. Oh yeah, the fire at Moon and Arlee's place.

He stands to walk to the window, leans to look at the moon's scarred and luminous face. He had gazed at the visage many thousands of times, and it never looked the same to him. The moon changed like the face of a woman you have loved — fixed and static only when lost to memory.

Gib scratches at his stubbly cheek. The sound rasps in the quiet room. He drops his hand to his chest and takes a breath, the sigh joining the rasp in the emptiness of the small institutional space.

Once upon a time, when they had all been young together, Moon had been one of the toughest men in the country. Double tough.

He'd been raised in the sand, prickly pear and scablands of eastern Oregon. His dad was a rancher and a horse trader who left Moon and his kid brother alone with the horses and the marginal place for weeks at a time, while he traded in horse and female flesh. Occasionally he would come back with some angry, profane woman who would stick around until she could find some way into town and onto the bus. Then he would turn mean again, drink, swear, hit, then round up a few head of stock and leave again.

Those were the years when mechanical machinery was taking over the harvesting, making the old forty-horse-drawn equipment outdated. Moon's old man bought the draft horse stock from the dry farmers in the Palouse country, then sold them to the Jap truck farmers on the coast. Part of the boys' work had been to break the cross stock he got from breeding his grade horses with the draft horses whose colts he sold to rodeo producers. They were big, rank horses and he got real good money for the ones Moon and his other son rough-broke. Horses they topped off were worth even more, but the boys saw none of the money for themselves. Their lives were just hard work and then more hard work.

When another younger brother had been old enough to move to the ranch from town, where he lived with their mom, Moon saw his chance. He had ridden in small, local rodeos in Oregon, Washington, Idaho when he had managed to escape the ranch for short periods. There he had gotten a taste of the gypsy life. So, when he'd fled the ranch, the scablands, and his dad's heavy hand, he took to the life like a flea to a dog — hopped aboard and never had a second thought about what he'd left behind. The life of a circuit cowboy may have been spare for the rest of 'em, but for Moon the existence was more like a vacation. Not one minute of the circuit was half as tough as working for his old man, on that deeded waste in eastern Oregon.

Moon worked the shows from California to Florida, Florida to Montana and back again. When he wasn't rodeoing, he worked ranches all over the West, blown about by any breeze or whim which caught him. Then he met Arlee at the night rodeo in Cody. She was a trick rider from Red Lodge, Montana and they fell in love on a moonlight ride back over the ridge from a dance at Bear Creek.

They hooked up and, with both of them working the circuit together, saved enough to buy a place north of Cody, on the Montana line. The Clark's Fork is a long piece of water, and they were the happiest couple on the river. Until the winter of 1949.

Moon blamed the fuel he was burning for blowing up the stove, but no one knew for sure. The temperature was twenty below zero and he was in the barn harnessing horses, to feed cattle, when he heard the glass in the windows shatter, followed by a big whoosh. He had run to the house but it was no use. He couldn't even get near. The little house had gone up in what seemed like seconds.

Sadly, Arlee had saved all the birthday, holiday and greeting cards, their fan mail and posters. Then, on an impulse, she had papered the walls with them. Those walls had been a great comfort to her when she went through her bouts of chronic bronchitis.

The flimsy paper had turned the cabin into a holocaust in seconds. At first, Moon blamed the damn fuel and the greeting cards. Later he would blame himself for everything associated with the tragedy.

Gib was driving to Red Lodge that morning and found Moon wandering along the road, burned and in shock. He had taken him to the nearest ranch and then gone into Bear Creek for the doctor. The cabin had been little more than embers by that time.

When Moon got better, he went to the Hoodoo to thank Gib, who had put Moon to work around the ranch so he would have something to do while he was getting over things. Gib hadn't forgotten that in 1936, when he and Dan had been running from Union Pacific railroad thugs, Moon had taken them in. It was a small enough way to show Gib's thanks. Besides, what goes around comes around, and it was Gib's turn to pay.

Those events had conspired to bind the men to one another in a way that few could understand. And now here they were, again. All of them — Dan, Moon, Ole and Gib. The only one missing was Dan's brother, Dal, but he had been dead a very long time now. Somehow, his death had served to bind them all together, had given them their collective destiny — in a damn institution with people who knew nothing of them and their lives. People who cared nothing for the times they had lived and the things they'd seen, and done. For the men that they had been.

I wish I had a smoke, Gib thinks. Sometimes I wish to hell I'da never quit.

He puts down his reverie and looks again at the moon. She's a big 'un this time, he thinks, raking his ass with his fingernails. He turns and walks to the little sink. Reaching for his water glass, he hears a scurrying movement in the hall outside. He steps quickly to the door and noiselessly pulls it open an inch.

Across the hall, Echeverria's door is standing open. Gib hears a hissing of hurried instructions and then he sees Red hop out the door, pull it closed and scurry to his room. The door closes quietly behind him.

What the hell is that SOB up to? Gib asks himself.

He opens his door carefully and leans out enough to see Security and Andy walk up to the nurse's station, rap softly on the glass and beckon the aide to accompany them. He has a big black flashlight in his hand.

Gib pulls his nose in. He hears the two men walk by and stop down the hall, then a quiet but authoritative tapping. Gib pulls his door open a crack and hears some indistinct, questioning noises come from Red's room. Then Security's quiet, but firm voice.

"Open the door. Now."

After a few moments, Gib hears Red.

"What could you possibly want at this hour, Mr. Purce?"

"I want to do an inventory of your little apothecary, Mr. Silver."

"Clever. A little humor in the wee hour, but I'm afraid I shan't let you. I have a right to my privacy."

"Sorry, you gave up that right when you got your butt thrown in here by the judge."

"That was a very long time ago."

"And you have a very long time to go, as far as the law is concerned. Especially if I find any evidence of criminal activity. Get out of the way."

"Only under protest. If this is a criminal investigation you need a warrant."

"That's why this gentleman is here, to note your protest."

Gib smiles. "That little Commie's got his tit in the wringer, with a big black man cranking on the handle. Damn, but this makes me happy."

The search, however, does not live up to Gib's hopes. After a few minutes' muffled thumping and sliding noises, he hears a chortle from Red. Security's reply is not distinct enough to hear clearly. However, Red's reply is.

"Hope you enjoyed your little midnight drama."

"Just doing my job, Red." Security says. His voice is strained.

Suddenly the corridor is filled with Red's shrieking voice. "Mr. Silver to you, you shvartzer bastid! Now get out of my room and stay out!"

A monstrous slam of the door is followed by dead silence, then the sound of retreating foot steps as the two searchers walk down the hall.

Gib goes to his bed and sits down. He considers going to the nurses' station to tell them about the traffic preceding the search, but decides not to for a couple of reasons. One, he knows that Echeverria would end up in as much trouble as Red and, two, what goes around comes around, every damn time. And Red's turn in the barrel would come, sure as sunrise.

Chapter 12

"Just how old can them damn bears get, anyway?" Gib asks, aloud. Maggie frowns and says, "Old enough, I guess. Anisa said there was no doubt that it was your bear. Jack was convinced of it the morning after the bear tore up the hunting camp, and all the old timers on the river say the same. They say that one back paw turns in from a bad hip, and the tracks around the house were enormous."

"But, it's been over twenty-five years since that scut just about put me under — and he was no youngster then — biggest damn bear in the world, looked like to me. Hell, he flipped me in the air like I was a gopher. And that was twenty-give years ago. No, more than that."

Maggie nods. "He must be on his last legs, though it certainly doesn't sound like it."

Gib looks out the window and says, distractedly, "Getting older and meaner, sounds like to me." He pauses. "I know exactly how he feels."

"You should," Maggie thinks. "You and that bear are two of a kind." Aloud, she says, "Jack thinks that he has come down from the mountains looking for you. Why would an animal do something like that?"

Gib maintains his thousand yard stare. "Don't know. I could only guess."

"What's your guess?"

The old man shrugs his shoulders, untwines his big, rough fingers from his lap and puts them on the arms of the chair. "He wants to go out with a fight, maybe." He stands. "Too bad I ain't up there because, the way I feel lately, I think I could give him exactly what he's looking for."

Maggie frowns. "I thought that you were glad to be with your friends."

"Oh, I am. But I'd rather be sitting and shooting the you-know-what in the Irma Hotel coffee shop than…" He waves his hand at the institution. "This ain't no place to be. No offense, Maggie, but I can't get used to this place and I know I never will. Being cooped up like this is killing me."

Maggie stands and walks around the desk. She gives Gib a hug and says, "Well, make the best of it for now. It's a lot better than jail. I am working on a letter to the judge in Cody…and some other things. Hang in there. It's not forever."

Gib turns back to her. "Being forced to stay here damn sure makes each day seem like forever. I hate it." He leaves.

Maggie goes to the office door and closes it. You are just as wild as that animal, and always have been, she thinks. No past and no future — every day is the first because it could be the last. She knew that Gib had come to the ranch fresh from a war, and from a rumored life before that. There had been stories…

But, once at the ranch, this man had been a part of her life — after death had carried everyone else away. He had always seemed invulnerable and dependable as a rock. But he had never, really, been there for her. He'd only been a guardian, though she was thankful for what he had done.

Emotionally, she'd always had to do for herself, while at the same time longing for someone committed absolutely to her well being. She had needed a mother for a very long time. But, for most of her life, she'd only had herself.

❋ ❋ ❋

"Looka dere, Moon. Dat Florence is puttin de 'cute' on Gib again."

Moon pegs out his Cribbage hand, "Fifteen two, fifteen four, six, and a Jack for knobs." Then he follows Ole's bemused look across the room where a little peroxide blonde has Gib cornered.

"If you took the top of that gal's head off and looked inside it would be cram-full of peckers, like a bowl of cocktail sausages. But, I guess that's what happens when a woman discovers sex after sixty-odd years and eight kids." He gathers up the cards and hollers, "Hey Gib, whyncha come over and play a little Crib?"

Gib waves his hand and excuses himself from the woman. As he sits down, he says, "My lord! That woman does not have a lick of sense."

"Looked like she knew what she wanted."

"Well, she's gonna have to find someone else for the job. She's hornier than a nine-headed reindeer."

"Heh, heh. Say, what did Maggie want?"

"Oh, Anisa phoned her — she's got a problem that she wanted to talk about. Jack's up in the hills and she's been alone with the boy…and there's something going on up there they can't handle."

"Like what? Or is it none of my business?"

"Oh, gimme a while to do some thinking on it. Then I'll tell ya." He stands up.

"Whatcha got planned for tonight?" Moon asks.

"Oh, I gotta go to the dentist and get a coupla loose back teeth yanked, so I'll probably be doing some laying down. Why?"

"We got our Social Security checks today. We usually play a little poker to celebrate. Ya wanna set in?"

"I don't think so, I don't know if I'll be feeling up to it. Dang it, that doc's trying to get me to have 'em all yanked, and gimme store teeth."

"Might as well give up, Gib. You're putting off the inevitable. Heck, remember how glad you were when you got them glasses that you didn't want? Give it up."

"Yeah, maybe. But I don't believe in doing anything before it has to be done. I ain't dead yet. When I am, then they can do as they damn well please — take them all out and hang 'em around their necks, if that's what makes them happy."

Moon and Ole grin knowingly at each other. That's Gib all over.

Then Gib smiles, too. "Tell ya what — come by around eight o'clock. If I feel like playing we'll set down. Bring Dan along so we can play four-handed."

Ole offers, "Mebbeso ol' Florence wud be likin' to set in de game."

Gib grimaces and says, "That woman would drive a snow man crazy. Maybe you ought to go over there, Sportin' Life, and take her mind off me for a while."

Ole blushes and the others grin at his discomfiture. A life-long bachelor, sex is a mystery to the little Norwegian. Women make him wary as a long-tailed cat in a room full of rocking chairs.

As Gib walks away, he remembers the first time he'd seen the tidy little man. It had been in the Billings, Montana, rail yard where Gib had walked behind a stack of rail ties to take a leak. There he'd found Ole lying on a filthy blanket. Flies were walking all over him, drawn because the man had fouled his pants. Completely disgusted by the sight, Gib was turning to go when the man opened his dim eyes, looked up, and quietly said, "Help me."

As it turned out, Ole was another one of the good ones — the real good men. He had come out of Minnesota to the West, by way of a horror in North Dakota, and skidded to his fly blow lair in a freight yard. With Gib's help, he found a place in the Big Horn Basin as a cowboy.

Minnesota was famous for its great crop of Norwegian bachelors and Ole was one to the bone. He did the things for himself other men depended on women for — or did without. He would sew, iron, doctor, bake, trim a Christmas tree. And he knew how to pray and mean it.

He was also a favorite of the ranchers' wives because he could lay out a garden and make it grow, even in Wyoming. He knew what would grow, where it would grow, knew what insects ate what, what blighted, what stunted and what made the whole thing flourish.

Ole had been the one who had laid out Laura's garden, the garden for which she was famous all up and down both forks of the Shoshone River. The garden, studded with colorful vegetables and dense with flowers, flashed into Gib's mind.

Set beside the little apricot orchard, he could see the tall pink hollyhocks, smell the sweet peas, hear the bee hum. He could also see the slight woman — standing in the garden, her straw hat hanging from her hand by blue ribbons. She was fingering a damp strawberry blonde curl back from her forehead, a slight smile on her mouth, above that upturned chin, below those wide and wanton brown eyes.

"God forgive me," Gib says aloud. A wash of pain runs down his throat and he swallows it back. It was always like this when he allowed himself to think of the woman on that summer afternoon so very long ago in a distant world of passion and pain which had passed all too quickly.

❊ ❊ ❊

Maggie picks up her phone and dials the ceramics studio. "Hello, Lorna, would you do me a favor? There are a lot of things, donated from an estate, coming into the charity room and I'd appreciate it if you would go through it for me. I have a meeting with Doctor Hillyard and can't get away…wonderful, thanks."

Maggie puts down the phone and leans back in her chair for a moment to think. Doctor Hillyard had called it on their first meeting. She had been back in Wyoming for only a few months and already she was making plans that would mean her leaving the institution some time in the next year or so. The man was a good psychologist. She had to give him that. He had known her better than she'd known herself. She stands and sighs, not really ready, emotionally, for the meeting.

Lorna catches sight of Dewey on her way from the ceramics studio. His long legs are moving him swiftly along with the lanky grace of a cheetah. She calls out to him and he changes direction to join her.

"What's up?" he asks.

"Doctor Scott asked me to look at some trove in the charity room. It's from an estate, and she said it included some interesting things. Wanna go take a peek?"

"Sure. I was on my way to the cafeteria, but this sounds like much more fun."

The hallway outside the charity room is a jumble of boxes and packing crates. A standing wardrobe and a steamer trunk plastered with labels have been opened, and volunteers are doing an inventory.

"Look at this," one says, as she pulls a fox stole out of the wardrobe and holds it to her nose. "It's a little mothbally but it's clean."

Dewey leans down and opens the top box of a stack. He removes a record. "Fantastic! Look at all these 78s. There must be a couple of hundred — and they're all in their original sleeves."

Lorna opens a second wardrobe, full of evening clothes. Opening a drawer, she removes something and calls to Dewey. "Hey, get a load of this!" As he looks over, she pops up a top hat. His eyes light up.

"What have we here?" He puts down the record, strolls to Lorna to take the hat and places it on his head.

"That's not all, look at what else is in here." She hands him a silver-handled cane.

"Fantastic." Dewey tips the hat jauntily forward and poses with both hands on the head of the cane, his feet spread. He slides one shoe across the floor, producing a soft rasping sound.

"Me and my shaaadow, strolling down the avenue…" He goes into a Fred Astaire soft shoe routine, then changes to a short tap flourish. He bounces the cane on the floor, spins and snatches it from the air. He bows. The volunteers and Lorna applaud happily.

"Why, Dewey, that was a professional turn!" Lorna says.

"Ah, all those lessons Mom made me take were not for naught. This is fun, what else do we have?"

Lorna holds up a dress, sequined from hem to halter and trimmed with feathers. "There is a set of tails in here, too! Wheee!"

Dewey puts on a top coat trimmed with a fur collar. He then pantomimes removing a large cigar from his mouth. "Say there, Lady, do you have Prince Albert in a can?"

Lorna answered, "Yes, but we let him out for air on Sundays."

"Da-da-da-dum-ta-da! Say, Lorna, I have a great idea."

"What?

"Why don't we have a 1930s costume party this month, instead of the usual dance? There is enough stuff here to dress up most of the people. The women in the sewing circle could put together the rest. What do you think?"

Lorna brightens even more. "You know, I did some dancing in college and I'm pretty limber for an old broad. How would you like to work up a Fred Astaire and Ginger Rogers routine? Maybe there are some others who would like to be in a show."

"That would be fun. Let's."

"Doctor Scott will love it. We've been trying for a week to come up with something to break the monotony around here. Some of the people are getting real restless."

"It's that Gibson fellow. He paces and prowls like a lion — up at all hours, walking the halls and staring out the window at the moon. Ever since he showed up the other men have been galvanized by him." Dewey frowns. "He's a very charismatic man — and I'm not sure that's good for the rest of them."

Lorna says, "Maybe. But remember how it was before he came? We couldn't get some of them out of bed for breakfast, and weekends it was even worse. Maybe he's a bad influence only when seen through the eyes of an institution that expects regimentation and strict observation of the rules. I'll bet that he must have been something when he was younger."

She remembers the conversation she'd had with Maggie. This was the man who had fathered Maggie's brother — and with a woman everyone thought invulnerable to the rough charms of men like Gib. Yes, he must have been something when he was in his prime.

✳ ✳ ✳

In Doctor Hillyard's office, Maggie is sitting warily across the desk from the distraught man. The subject of the conference is Mr. Herbert Silver, Communist.

"This man is a bad influence, Doctor Scott. He flouts the rules religiously. He involves otherwise innocent people in his subversive enterprises, he actively sets up conflicts between the staff and the residents, to say nothing of the fact that he is wholly grandiose, a borderline personality, and pathological liar. And now he threatens to become some kind of martyr for the New York liberals…oh, how I loathe the ACLU."

Doctor Hillyard and the states of Wyoming and Utah had been served with papers, summoned to appear in federal court. The papers sit on Hillyard's desk, along with a new book on the history of The American Communist Party. "Doctor" Herbert C. Silver was included in the book, along with his version of the events leading to his incarceration, and subsequent remandment to a hospital for the insane. His comments on his history of treatment were, at the very least, bizarre. One result had been that the authors of the book had engaged the American Civil Liberties Union to investigate the whole affair.

Maggie can't help but be a bit amused at Doctor Hillyard's discomfiture. He is staring at the stack of papers as if it were a pile of dog dung. She picks up the book and turns to a bookmark. "Hmm, how did everyone miss the fact that Mr. Silver has a Ph.D.?"

Hillyard leans back in his chair and chokes out, "That is hardly the most salient fact in the matter. To me, it is of no importance whatsoever."

Maggie puts the book back on his desk. "And what is the most important fact of the matter? And what am I supposed to do in all this? I'm only the unit administrator, charged with the daily care and therapeutic regimen — I'm not a politician and this smells like politics to me."

"You are, de facto, a party to this lawsuit because of that role. You have been roped into this whether you like it or not. I called you here because I am bound to let you know what is going on. We will be meeting with the state's attorney general down in Cheyenne. They haven't set a date, but you and I will be driving over there together. I'll let you know when."

Maggie retrieves the book again. "May I borrow this?"

Doctor Hillyard waves his hand. "Get it out of here."

"Thank you, it should make some interesting reading."

"Interesting! Please, Doctor Sc…" A dry click comes from Hillyard's spastic throat. "That man and his history are anything but interesting. He is a pain in the ass, and nothing more!"

Maggie stands and looks down at the nearly apoplectic little man. The top of his shiny head is a hot and glistening red.

"Well, American Studies was one of my favorite subjects. I think I'll enjoy having a historical person around. Hmmm, 'Doctor Herbert C. Silver, Ph.D.'…how interesting." As she steps to the hall, she hears a sibilant hissing behind her.

"Doctor Sil-Si-S-S…"

She remembers Hillyard's doctorate is in education. Professionally speaking, Red outranks him by a mile. And now he is famous.

❄ ❄ ❄

It is dark at eight o'clock, when the poker game is being organized in Gib's room. Ole and Moon are placing Gib's extra blanket on a card table while Gib and Dan sit on the edge of the bed, talking quietly.

Gib is saying, "So I guess the big SOB come down to Eddy's place first. He peeled the side off that old trailer of his while Eddy and his dog was sleeping inside. That got everybody's attention — and scared that old hermit shitless in the meanwhile."

"Would me too," Dan says, riffling a deck of cards.

"Then he went on down river and pretty much did the same thing to Anisa and JC. All he did was stick his nose in the window of the boy's room. But she was sitting about five foot away from his ugly snout. JC seen 'im too — scared the kid so bad he's havin' nightmares every night."

"You two got your signals straight?" Moon asks as he puts the rack of poker chips on the table.

"Nah, we don't need no signals to trim you two," Dan says. "Gib's bear is back on the South Fork. He was telling me about it."

"What? That damn thing was old enough to vote the last time he came down, and that's gotta be twenty-five years ago. At least."

Ole is pulling on his old pipe, and jetting smoke into the room, the only way to tell he was excited.

"They sure that it's the same bear?" Moon asks.

"Same scar across his face, and his left rear foot is twisted from where I potted him in the ass that time."

"Who is Gip's bear?" Ole asks.

Dan smiles and says, dramatically, "Once upon a time there was this big old griz that came down out of the Absorkees and decided to kill his way clean across the basin to the Big Horn Mountains. He was so big you could water a cow for a week outta one paw print. But, before he could get really rolling, he made a side trip to the Hoodoo and met his match…"

"Oh for hell sakes, let's play some poker." Gib is now irritable.

"Ah c'mon Gip. Itsa purty goot story so far!"

"Well, it's an old one and I don't want to hear it again. Somebody deal while I get myself another pain pill. That Doc just about come up with my toenails when he pulled that big back one."

"Gonna get 'em all yanked?" Moon asks as he sits down.

"Dunno. Hate the thought of it. Who's dealin?"

"I'll start if no one minds," Dan says. "What'll it be — a little Blind Baseball with aces, kings, fours, whores, and one-eyed jacks wild? Or do you guys wanna play Stud and lose yer asses?"

"That's more like it," Gib says. "Let's play. How about a little Draw to warm up on?"

"Draw she be." Dan crashes the cards together smartly, then slams them down in front of Ole.

"Cut!" he cries, "And make it bleed."

The four old friends hunker down and slide into their card game. The feeling is good, real good, to be together like this again. Kinda like old times. When they were young, full of piss and vinegar, and bent on living forever.

❋ ❋ ❋

Maggie hears the anticipated rap on her door and says, "Come in, please."

Red enters the room and stands at the threshold.

"Please sit down, Mr. Silver. Or perhaps I should address you as Doctor Silver."

"Please don't. Those days have been dead for eons, it seems." He takes the chair.

"You know why I've asked you here?"

"I assume it's about the lawsuit. I must tell you now that I cannot talk to you or anyone else about it. My lawyers have been emphatic about that."

"Actually, I want to talk to you about your invitation to address the American Studies faculty and students at the University of Wyoming. The Chair, Doctor Yoder, phoned to ask if I would prevail upon you to accept the invitation. Apparently, you rejected it."

"Those days, that history, is dead for me. Living it was more than enough."

"Is that it? No other reason?"

"Yes. What else would it be?"

"Well, a little fear of the outside world would be understandable, considering how long you have been…"

"Institutionalized?" Red said, completing her sentence.

"Well, yes."

"I must admit that's part of it. But not all, certainly."

"Well, your experiences are valuable to other people, it seems. They want to hear about them."

"The intellectuals! Hah. They study, arrange symposia, write books, but they know nothing about the realities of life. They have never lived. As for myself, I have lived every moment that was given to me. Now I want to be left alone to live what I have been given to suffer."

"That smacks of martyrdom to me."

Red looks at Maggie slyly. "You might save that opinion for the court room, Doctor." He stands. "I think that I should leave. My lawyers would recommend it, I'm sure."

"I'm sorry if you think that we're here so I can entrap you. I'm not." Maggie looks at a photo of her stepchildren sitting in a frame on her desk. "I am simply trying to get a grip on some things, for my own understanding. You see, until recently I thought that I had studied all the relevant material and, so, had all the answers. I had been trained in some of the best schools in the country.

"Now, I find you here — a man with impeccable academic credentials who chose an activist life and even chose to cross the line into a place where your very life was at stake. And your freedom."

Red grins a death's head grin. "And I am paying the price for presuming to practice my beliefs. I am a political prisoner — in the United States of America!"

"The state of Utah found you guilty of conspiring to blow up private property. And killing a man as a result of that conspiracy."

"A man who wasn't even supposed to be in the building."

"He's dead. You are lucky that you are not still in prison."

"Same thing."

"Hardly. You wouldn't be getting away with the things you get away with in this institution."

Red smiles slyly, then looks at the black square that is Maggie's window. "Doctor?"

"Yes."

"I am going to assume that this conversation is covered by doctor-patient confidentiality."

"OK. Agreed."

"Do you have any idea what an anarchist's job is?"

"Yes. I think."

"No, you don't. Not unless you were in the Weather Underground or the Black Panthers, which I seriously doubt."

"You're quite right. There were no chapters of either at Smith or Georgetown. And I'm a little too young for even that generation of subversives."

"Bad organization on the part of the students. A lamentable lack of conviction on yours." Red pauses. "Well, I helped write the textbooks, the 'cookbooks', for that particular generation. That's what this guy Mishkind writes in his book." He gestures at the thick text on Maggie's desk.

"But I didn't write any screeds, songs, or broadsides. I was an illustrator! I made things perfectly clear for the bastards!" The last word comes out as a rasping expletive. Red lights a cigarette, steps to the black window. He stares out into the darkness for a moment, and then begins to speak, falling into the cadence of a practiced lecturer.

"The reason I am a prisoner here is that I worked for the One Big Union. Do you know what that was?"

He sees Maggie's reflection shake its head. "I thought not. Well, Miss Fancy Pants, I'll tell you what it was — it was the biggest dream The Little Man ever had." Red's voice catches, and he pauses. "When I was a child, my father and mother sewed for pennies a day, literally. For pennies! In those days the ugliest face that money ever put on was bare for all to see. 'Capitalism' they called it, but it was greed at its liveliest.

"Imagine men working underground in the mines, sixty hours, and more, each week — for pennies an hour. And children working there in the dark and dust for even less. Children eight, nine, ten years old. Children. And each child put ten dollars a day into the treasuries of the plutocrats who ran, make that 'run', this country. A million children, ten million dollars. A day." Sweat has formed on Red's forehead. Ash fallen from his cigarette litters his shirt front.

"Of course, the men and women contributed even more to those treasuries. More money, more shorn fingers, more lives…it was horrible.

"So, to answer that kind of power, we envisioned all working people in One Big Union. One big fist to shake in the baldest face that money ever wore!" Red gestures with his bony old fist. But the feeble caricature in the reflecting glass turns him around, making him ashamed of his old age, and his present helplessness.

He turns and walks to Maggie's desk. Her eyes are glued to the man's flushed, animated face and fiery eyes. She doesn't even blink when he drops his cigarette butt in her coffee cup, to die with an emphatic "phut!"

He steps back and continues. "So where do you go to start a union like that? Everywhere. And we were everywhere — in the mines, on the docks, in the orchards and fields, the factories and on the oil rig floors. We rode the rails, sang songs, held meetings, fought the cops and the goons, were murdered and mutilated." His voice trails down to nothing, for a moment.

"And it didn't work. We tried building up the men and tearing down the bosses, by organizing and sabotage. We pleaded. We threatened. We promised. We told God's own truth, and we lied until the taste of it was too much of it, even for us. But the lazy giant of American labor wouldn't be moved — too ignorant to be inspired, too brutish to know virtual slavery — even while experiencing it." Red goes back to the black square.

"We began to lose ground. Money rallied its troops. They beat us, maimed us, cut off our balls — literally cut off our balls — threw us into the jails and the prisons. Killed us. We tried to fight back but it was no use." Red turns his face toward Maggie. His face is wet with tears which he doesn't bother to wipe away.

"I went to prison in Utah and I didn't last very many years there. They broke me and I went crazy. I have been accused of having feigned it. But when I was taken to the hospital it was no fiction, believe me. There are almost ten years of my life that I cannot remember. Ten whole years for which I have absolutely no memory, not even a glimmer.

"Then, one night I woke up in a darkened ward full of beds and sleeping strangers. I saw a lighted door way and walked out through it. There was a startled man sitting at a table in the hall and I walked up to him and said," Red chortles and pats the window glass, "I said, 'Where am I?' What a cliche!

"But, you know, when you've been totally insane for ten years or so, it would be a perfectly reasonable thing to ask, wouldn't you say?" He looks at Maggie, arching his shaggy brow.

Maggie's intent eyes never leaving Red's enraged look, replies, "Yes. I would."

"Thank you." Red turns back to the blackness to wipe his face. "No, Miss Fancy Pants, I don't think that I will address the American Studies Department at Windswept Junction U. I don't think that they would have the heart, or even the capacity, to understand the times I lived through." Red turns from the window and walks to the office door to open it.

Maggie's voice stops him. "But what you have is valuable, there must be some who would care, could understand."

He turns to give her a crooked smile. "Only in theory. These are feeble times peopled by very small souls which are still gripped in the same moneyed, though now velvet, fists. Look at AT&T, look at the new and brutal Disney. Observe Microsoft." The crooked smile becomes a grimace.

"Imagine! Single corporations lay off 50,000 people or more at a whack — millions of people thrown out of work in any one fiscal quarter — designed to put those workers' well-being in the corporate pocket and throw their working lives away. And those people don't have the will, or the means, to raise the faintest cry from their feeble little hearts."

He steps to the hall, his hand on the knob. "I know about those feeble hearts — the feeble-minded brute of American labor broke mine," he says, tapping his chest as he turns away. Red gently shuts the door.

❄ ❄ ❄

"Aces and eights, the dead man's hand," Gib says, showing his cards.

"Not good enough. Spade flush." Moon fans his cards on the table and whoops. "Gimme that money. Gimme, gimme, gimme." He rakes the winnings to his side of the table.

"It's your money. And your deal," Dan says and pushes the cards in front of Moon.

"Now give me a minute here, Daniel. I want to sort out the dough with your fingerprints on it. You've been hanging on to it so tight, I'm going to have to have it ironed."

"Send it out and have it done, you can damn sure afford it. Room Service, please! How about some Lo-Ball, for a change?" Dan says.

"Fine with me," Moon answers. "You must have a death wish."

"You alvays call fer dot Lo-Ball."

"I like Lo-Ball, I win at Lo-Ball," Dan answers, shrugging his shoulders.

"Lo-Ball's the only game he's got figured," Moon heckles. "Simple minds, simple pleasures."

"Oh hell, if it's going to upset all you codgers, let's play something else." Dan is irked by the fact that it is true. He can keep a card count in his head only when the game is Lo-Ball. Sometimes he feels he has known these people way too long.

"Who iss Gip's bear?" Ole asks, out of the blue.

Dan glances at Gib, who seems unperturbed by the subject. "Well, I won't embroider it this time. Like I said before, this big griz hit the South Fork country twenty-some years ago and raised holy hell with the livestock — cows, sheep, horses, just about everything with blood in it. He was on a rampage of some kind 'cause he wasn't killing to eat. He was killing just to be killing.

"He finally worked his way around to the Hoodoo and Gib jumped him while he was feeding on one of their cows…"

"Anybody interested in playin' some cards?" Gib asks, mildly. "Moon's got 'em dealt."

Dan looks at his hand and says, "Betcha a buck."

"I'll see that," Moon answers. "Go on. I've heard it a couple of times, but it's a good story."

"Anyways, Gib jumps him on the cow and pops a bullet into him, just as he turns to jump into the timber. Off he goes, rolling rocks and roaring like all get out. Gib figures he's got 'im now and sticks the steel to his horse. Down the hill they go to catch the bear before he can get away." Dan stops.

"Ya, and den vat?"

Gib takes up the story. "The SOB was waiting for me behind a rock fall — rushed us head-on and I got piled up. Horse boogered and threw me. By the time I got him gathered up again, the bear was gone."

"Dat's all?"

"Nope," Dan says. "Show him your scars."

"For hell sake, this ain't California. I ain't haulin' my britches down at a card game."

"So, vat happened?"

"About three months later he jumped me — ambushed me cleaner'n hell. He had the wind in his face, so the horse couldn't smell him. He'd dug behind a log next to the stock trail that I rode just about every day. It was a flat, damned ambush. He put a lot of thought in it."

"Vy come he didn't kill you?"

"Oh he planned on it, I'm sure. But he messed up — threw me up into a tree and I hung on like a limpet."

"That's the part I don't get," Moon observes. "What was he doing, throwing you up into a tree?"

Gib's eyes take on a hard stare. "He was playing with me. Celebrating, I suppose."

"You mean like a coyote tossing a mouse?" Moon asks.

Dan interjects. "Bit Gib clean through, too. Can you imagine how big that bear has to be? Gib ain't no small man and he bit him clean through!"

Gib's mood had soured. "Dammit, let's play some cards. That's enough story tellin' for one night."

Dan answers, "Well then, give me something to play with. All I been getting all night is bobtailed straights and gutshot flushes." He tosses his cards in the middle of the table disgustedly and then stares at the partially open door. All eyes follow his stare. Red is standing on the threshold. He gently pushes the door open, and steps inside.

"Mind if I sit in?" he asks quietly. "It looks like a real long night, over in my room."

"No room. Not enough chairs," Gib says, an edge on his voice.

"I could bring one over from my place." Red's voice is conciliatory. Hopeful.

Moon takes his cue from Gib and says, "These is twenny dollar chips, Red. The game might be a little rich for your blood — don't want you getting gouty over a little card game."

Red walks to the table and pulls a wad of bills with a rubber band around them from his pocket. He removes the band, snaps five one-hundred dollar bills from the wad and lays them on the table. The four men stared at the money in shock.

"I'll take my chances," Red says. "I may be old, diabetic, and have a bag instead of a bladder, but gout is one thing I don't have." He pauses. "I'd be more than happy to buy a seat."

Gib looks up from Red's money to the man himself. He glares at the untidy little man and says, "We're trying to tell you that there's no room here. Your money's dirty, far as I'm concerned."

He tosses in his cards. "I lost track of the game, let's keep the pot where she is and play something else."

"You call it, Gib," Dan says.

"Let's play some Spit."

"Suits me. Suit you guys?" The others nod nervously. Red hasn't moved and Gib's shoulders are hunched, as if he were set to spring from his chair. It is a bad sign that all, except Red, have seen before. The room is thick with tension. They are hoping that Red will leave. Pronto.

"Spit?" Red asks, real condescension resonating in his voice. The atmosphere in the room becomes electric.

Dan cuts in, trying to mitigate the tension. "Spit. You deal the cards and someone says 'Spit" and the dealer turns over the next card and that's wild. Then…"

"That's simple enough," Red says, staring at Gib. Gib stares back, his blue eyes darkening to gray.

Moon says, with a wary edge to his voice, "Let's you two be friends, now." The two men's stares remain locked.

"Trust a cowboy to come up with a game vulgar enough to be called Spit," Red says, mildly.

It is meant as a personal insult, and Gib takes it exactly the way it is intended. He stands quickly, his long legs toppling the table and scattering chips and cards. "You little asshole! This is my room, and if you aren't out of it in two seconds I'm gonna make you wish you'd never been born!"

Red's eyes narrow and he plants his feet. "Do it, you redneck son-of-a-bitch."

Gib skirts the sitting men, who were righting the table, and is on Red in one stride. As he reaches the much smaller man, he grabs him by both shoulders. And freezes.

Red's eyes glitter. A hard-edged crack defines his mouth. He has a small pocket pistol in his hand and it is poked into Gib's belly.

Gib's face loses color as he looks down at the cocked pistol. His chin drops. He looks at the crazed little man in front of him, then the color rushes back into his face.

"Why you little bastard, never pull a gun unless you shoot. I've got one of those too."

Gib sweeps Red's gun hand up, knocking him off balance. He then dives across the room, jamming his hand under the mattress. It comes out holding his .45 automatic.

Red glimpses the action and puts a bullet through the light fixture. The crack of the pistol in the small room is ear-splitting. In the dark, Dan, Ole, and Moon can be heard humping for cover, over the sound of Gib's cursing.

Red flees the room and turns down the hall toward the rec room. Gib jumps to the door and snaps a shot after the fleeing man. The roar of the .45, and the ricochet of the big slug off the tile walls, is awesome.

Red peels into the last room before the recreation area, but his head pops back into view almost immediately. Gib pulls his head back into the room just in time to hear a bullet buzz by, followed by the smart pop of the pistol. The little bastard could shoot!

Gib kneels and looks quickly into the rec room. Dewey, wheeling an old lady in a wheelchair, is staring down the hall at him. He is paralyzed.

"Get the hell out of the way!" Gib screams.

Dewey awakes in terror, propels the wheelchair and its occupant across the room then jumps back from the action. The surprised old lady squeals happily as her wheelchair shoots across the room, does a dido, then comes to rest with its handles against the wall.

Dewey covers the distance to the nurses' station in two long strides. He grabs the PA system microphone and shouts, "Code 99, Code NINETY-NINE at Seniors' Chalet! My God, I've got a gunfight going on over here!"

Red scurries from his hiding place to the center of the rec room. He thrusts a couch onto its back and dives behind it. At the same time, Gib barrels out into the hall, his gun held low for a quick shot. Red pops his head up from behind the couch and hurries a shot down the hall, toward the lumbering man.

Almost too late, Gib throws himself through an open door as the *Crack!* of Red's pistol whips past him. He lunges part-way back through the door. With no time to aim, he blindly throws a wad of lead, and its roar, in Red's direction.

The little old lady in the wheelchair hears that one! She jumps in surprise and then smiles with interest when the big TV set explodes. She reaches up with both hands, turns down her hearing aids and scrunches down to watch.

Dewey peers over the dutch door and sees Red. He is on his knees and elbows behind the overturned couch. A painting jumps from the wall in a rain of glass splinters and, almost before the roar from Gib's pistol is heard, Red strikes like a snake. He fires a suppressing round to ricochet, whiz, and sing down the hallway.

Gib is sweating. He sets his mouth grimly and steels himself to expose his head for another shot. Moon jumps into the room.

"Damn! Don't do that, I almost shit myself!"

Moon grins and says, "Here."

"What?!" He sees that Moon has brought him his new glasses. Gib puts them on. "Now I'll chill his shit for 'im," he mutters.

Behind the couch, Red is now sweating, too. The break in the gunplay has given him a moment to think. He realizes that no matter how this falls out, he is in very grave trouble.

Gib chances a peek. This time the whole scene has tightened to sharp focus. He pulls the pistol up and sights on the manufacturer's label on the bottom of the couch.

"God damn these rednecks!" Red whispers and looks quickly over the couch, to see a nightmare come true. His enemy's face is stuck out the door, and in front of it is the muzzle of a gun, spewing fire.

At the moment Gib squeezes the trigger he sees Red's horrified face appear. The recoil from the big gun obliterates the picture. He is secondarily aware, however, of one of Red's arms disappearing from view. It is flopping like a hooked trout in fast water.

Inside the nurses' station, Dewey sees the result as the slug center punches the couch label. The first thing is a cloud of dust, lint, and balled-up gum wrappers boiling out into the room. The second thing he sees is Red hinge in the middle and do a loose flop onto his back. Dewey closes his eyes at the sight, then screams, "Stop! STOP! Red's hit!"

Silence melds with the gun smoke. Dewey stands and edges warily out of the nurses' station. Red is moving slowly now, drawing up first one leg and then the other. Dewey starts toward the old man on the floor — and he seems, to himself, to be moving in slow motion. An avowed non-combatant, he is numb from shock. Horrified, Dewey sees a dark stain spreading over Red's side. "Oh my God! he whispers as he kneels beside the man, who is pressing his fingers into the stain.

Red slowly slides his thumb across his fingertips, then he puts them under his nose. "Phew," he says. "Shot my piss bag."

Dewey slumps beside the fallen old man and says tiredly, "I simply do not believe this shit."

Dan and Ole moved tentatively into the rec room. The front door flies open and the clattering footsteps of Security and his men are heard. They stop out of sight and Security shouts, "Dewey? DEWEY!"

"Yeah?"

"You all right?"

Dewey looks up at the now-appalled old men and asks, "Is the party over?" Then he turns to shout down the corridor, "Yeah. Everyone's okay — c'mon in. The party's over."

An hour later, Gib is standing in front of the old Jolly Roger restaurant. He can see a half-dozen cop cars, with flashing overheads, across the Bear River at the hospital. The red and orange strobes are softened by the mist of a light autumn rain. He turns up his collar and pulls his cowboy hat down to obscure his face.

Good, he thinks to himself. If everyone's up there, they won't be down here looking for me. He sees a set of head lights come out from under the railroad underpass. The pickup's orange blinker signals a turn that will take it in front of the Jolly Roger. Gib steps from the shadows and puts out his thumb for a ride. He looks like an ordinary Wyoming hitchhiker, a cowboy needing a ride out to one of the many ranches north of Evanston. But, inside, he is almost screaming for the vehicle to stop. It slows down for a moment, then passes by.

Gib puts his head down, trying to keep the knot in his gut from projecting itself out of his mouth. He was so upset that he was afraid that he might throw up. Oh God, I am so sorry. Please, please...I am so sorry.

He is desperate with remorse. He has shot a man, and for no good reason. Out of plain damn meanness, as much as anything, although the little shit had challenged him outright. Now Gib is in it up to his eyes. After the last episode, in Cody, this one would see him to the state pen for sure. A second, and this time armed, assault charge is very serious business, no matter how you cut it.

After Gib had seen Red hit, he'd panicked and run back to his room. Moon had sent Ole and Dan into the rec room to check how badly Red was hurt. Then he had grabbed Gib's duffel and the money from the poker game and chased Gib out the back door of the building. They decided that Gib should try to make it to some friends' ranch south of Cokeville. After that — who knew?

"Hey Buddy, you want a ride or not?"

Gib spins around. A pickup had stopped and almost backed into Gib.

"You bet," Gib says. He tosses his duffel into the back and hurries to the cab.

Thank you, Lord, he thinks as he gets in. Thank you. I promise that this is the last time I'll ever ask you for anything. Promise.

Chapter 13

Late on the night of Gib's escape, an exhausted Maggie enters her house and flicks the hall light switch. Nothing happens.

"Oh, what next?"

She walks to the picture window, looks out and sees that the neighborhood is dark, no street lights, nothing but darkness.

A moon only now is working its way to the horizon, still hidden behind the range of hills to the east of Evanston. Light shines from behind the clouds and hills, pushing a shaft of light through a scant opening to illuminate the bottoms of thickening storm clouds. They look like pewter rubbed to a dull lambence. Even as she watches, the light disappears. Almost audibly, night falls back onto the country.

She had wanted to make herself a pot of tea, but her stove is electric, she remembers. The house is too dark to negotiate a search for the hand lantern in the kitchen. So, she decides to go for a walk.

Outside, the first breath of air moves her briefly out of her despondence, takes her away from the horrors of this day. "Winter," she murmurs to herself and reaches up to button her coat's top button. She drops her eyes to the sidewalk and begins a slow, thoughtful stroll up the hill.

Love. All day long she had been thinking about love and what she understood of the whole deal. "Damn little," she comments, aloud, then glances about to see if she'd been overheard talking to herself. She walks alone.

Alone. God, what a ghastly word. But here she was, again, her parents were long dead now. Her ex and his kids were as good as dead, it seemed. None of them would communicate, ignored letters, didn't return messages left

118

on answering machines. Her mentor, Doctor Brewton, had died while she was in the middle of the divorce, making everything harder to take. Before him, Chamberlain, the only man she'd known intimately except her husband, had finally gotten his wish and exited this world on a motorcycle at a hundred miles an hour — sliding, spinning, tumbling, and finally free of himself on a rain-slick expressway in New York. Then Annick, her roommate from college and best friend for 20-odd years, had died in a car wreck in Italy. No more phone calls came at four in the morning, to simply talk or, almost as often, to report in detail on her latest marriage or liaison.

For most of her childhood and on through adolescence to her first years in college, Gib had been her de facto father. He had been the guardian of the ground under her feet. The more she knew, the more complicated her feelings. But, she had never felt anything but love and respect for the man. Also, she knew that he loved her. Simple.

And now Gib had run away and was gone from her care, perhaps forever. He was avoiding the consequences of another folly, but this one had very real consequences. The sheriff had explained Gib was now looking at a minimum of two-and-a-half years in the state penitentiary at Rawlins. Even under her care, he had not been able endure his stay in Evanston for the four-month evaluation period ordered by the judge in Cody. As wild as the elk in the hills, a prison stay would kill him.

Maggie stops and looks around. She hasn't the slightest idea where she has wandered, but somehow it seems unimportant at the moment. She glances at the sky and sees the faint glow of the moon behind the clouds. Mist dampens her upturned face as the breath from the clouds' invisible passing overhead drifts gently down. She drops her head and walks on through the neighborhood, making random rights and lefts.

As she meanders, she begins an inventory of her loved ones. She starts by including all the people she presently feels any real fondness for. Some colleagues were winnowed out, along with her erstwhile in-laws. Faces come and go as she edits her way down to the people who were in her life to stay. Jack, Anisa, JC. They were family, they stayed. Gib was trying mightily to cut himself off from her but he stayed, too. Then the three other old men who had worked for the ranch. Moon, yes. Dan, yes. Ole, yes. Lorna and Security? They were keepers...

Glancing up, she recognizes her car parked in the middle of the block and feels suddenly oriented. She has wandered back to her own house.

At that instant, she knows what she is going to do. What has been missing is the sense of family and belonging familiar to her as a child. She would begin a gathering of the ones she loved. And she knew where she would go to begin it.

❋ ❋ ❋

Sheriff Burns has held his office for over twenty years. Before that, he'd been a deputy sheriff since the age of twenty. Altogether, he had thirty-five years in the business, so there was little in life he hadn't seen. Humans were as inventive about their mischief as they were about all else they did. The Butterfly Farm, as he called the hospital, had exposed him to some of life's weirder manifestations, certainly. But a shootout at the old folks' home had stretched his experience to a new latitude.

This thing wasn't as simple as it looked at first glance. The combatants were 69 and 74 years old, and when perpetrators were in that age range he had a different sort of deal. Ordinarily, you punished miscreants so they would find the straight and narrow and not go on to ruin their lives. But these two old farts had already lived most of their lives — and were still acting like a couple of randy adolescents trying to prove themselves to the world. Hell, they'd already ruined their lives!

Sheriff Burns takes a pull on his pipe and looks out his office window. It is drizzling rain. Gray clouds hang low on the mountains and mist clings to the river, its fingers laced into the bare willows. Winter wouldn't be long in coming now.

He blows the smoke into the room, continues his train of thought: The matters of the previous charges against both men. Gibson was already looking at a felony assault charge, plus some miscellaneous misdemeanors that qualified him for a minimum year in country jail or more in state prison. This little affair would most likely mean real prison time because it came so hard on the heels of the first screw-up. The judge would have little choice but to add it to the other scrape.

The other man, Silver, was already under life sentence for murder, conspiracy against the state, conspiracy to commit murder, and as many other offenses as a long-dead Utah Attorney General could conjure up. Silver had the convenience of being classified insane, even though he was as normal as most on the outside. Maybe more so, based on the sheriff's interrogation.

Nah. No sense in bringing charges against someone with a built-in and iron-clad defense — "I've been certified nuts under several jurisdictions — how can you claim I knew what I was doing?" And just as well, too. Hell, the guy would be damn near eighty by the time he was readied for any sentencing.

As for Gibson, it wasn't so easy. He'd escaped the legal grasp of the state while under arrest. And he was considered sane. The escape, alone, was good for three full years in Rawlins — the standard sentence for indulging one's self in perfectly rational behavior.

Unlike the one against Silver, this case wasn't going away.

Sheriff Burns leans forward and pushes the intercom button on his phone. "Tricia?"

"Yes, Bob?"

"Forward the report on Mr. Gibson to the prosecutor's office as soon as you're done. Also, put a note on Silver's paperwork that the guy is officially nuts and the county might as well save its money. Recommend no prosecution. Sign my name."

"Yes Sir. It's all typed up and ready to go."

He smiles ruefully. He hates it when she knows what he is going to do before he does. "OK. Thank you."

The Sheriff of Uinta County stands and looks back out the window. The mist and light rain fit his mood — a perfect day for a last round of solo golf. Before the imminent snow makes it impossible to play.

❄ ❄ ❄

Moon and Ole are sitting in Gib's empty room, dressed for the 1930s theme dance in the gym. Their dejection is a gross contrast to their gay outfits.

"Hey, did he make it up to Julian's ranch?" Dan asks, as he comes through the door and joins the other two.

"Yeah," Moon answers. "I phoned Truman and asked if our package had made it and he said that it had — UPS was there way before breakfast time."

"Now what's he gonna do?" Dan asks. "The sheriff didn't seem likely to cut him any slack. My God, three years for just leaving the grounds without permission?"

Moon shrugs. "If he'd shot Red — and he was trying, sure enough — it would mean a lot more time than that. Hell, we didn't know that Gib had only punctured his piss bag. We thought he was killed for sure. I'da left for the high country my own self…and damn near did."

"It wudda bin a real lonesome place here wit bot' of ye gone," Ole observes, then puffs on his pipe. "Oh, yer goot comp'ny, Daniel, but it…"

Dan waves his hand. "I know exactly what you mean. I was a basket case when Gib got here. He sure did liven the place up, just like old times." His voice pinches off. "I hope he clears the country, but it's probably the last any of us will hear from him. He ain't much of a writer."

Moon snorted. "He ain't any kind of a writer and neither are any of us. Can you write good?"

"Nope."

"Ole?"

"Nope."

"See?"

Ole's soft sucking on his little black pipe is the only sound in the room.

Moon asks Dan, "Do you remember when you brought him up to my shack on Iron Mountain?"

"Yup. We put him in a bunk, then waited for him to die. But he was riding less than three weeks later, and we lit out for the Wind River Rez. I guess he's seen worse than this."

"That's exactly my point. Nobody's going to put him in prison. Nobody's going to kill him. He's probably going to live just as long as he wants to live — not a day more and, damn sure, not one day less."

Dan stands up. "This conversation is getting me down. Let's go to the dance."

"Suits me," Moon says.

The three old men walk out of the room and Moon closes the door.

"Hell," he says, "This was no place for a man like him, anyway. He'd be better off dead."

When they reach the building, a mirror ball showers scintillating light about the gym, which has been transformed into a nightclub. Cutouts of palm trees, pastel lighting, and other touches create a facsimile of a 1930s Art Deco interior. White tablecloths cover the tables and a horseshoe bar has been set up. A distinguished looking old gentleman is making a champagne punch in a large cut-glass bowl as he gossips with a silver-haired woman in a short skirt and a pill box hat. Her tray of candy cigarettes sits on a table close by.

When the three cronies enter the faux nightclub, Florence, her cleavage on the verge of cascading from her costume, breathes, "Your coats, gentlemen?"

They give Flo their overcoats and start toward the bar.

Ole says, "Dere is s'posed to be champagne, I hear. I haf neffer tasted de stuff, und I'm purty darn sure dis is goin to be my last chance."

When they reach the bar, Moon crooks his finger at the distinguished gentleman. "Señor Bodegero, I'd like water and fresh horses for my men here — then a quart of tequila and two women for me."

The man smiles. "I'm afraid those days are gone forever, my friend. How does champagne punch sound, instead?"

"Sounds fine as frog hair. Drive on."

The three friends wait for their glasses, then raise them in a toast.

"Gib," says Dan.

"Yah."

"And better days," says Moon.

They drink their glasses empty, then put them back on the bar. Moon draws a circle over the empties with his finger. The bartender refills them.

Dan turns to look around the room. "This place reminds me of New York, when Gib won his buckle at Madison Square Garden. Boy, he was the toast of the town. We got drunk with the governor, some senators, congressmen, a half dozen working girls…" He shook his head. "It was a good time to be alive."

Moon smiles a crooked smile. "Y'know, when I really think about it, just about every memorable time I ever had was when I was hanging onto that man's coattails."

Dan drinks down his punch. "Let's not get off on that again. Change the subject."

"Glad to — look what just come through the door." He points.

Red is strutting through the crowd, heading toward the bar.

"If that little prick starts anything, I'll…" Dan growls, through gritted teeth.

Red slows his pace a bit when he sees the three men at the bar. But he continues his way, to stand at the other end of the counter. "Excuse me, Sir. I would appreciate a little service down here." He is twirling an empty glass.

"You ought to be feeling pretty good after four glasses. Are you sure another one won't be too much?"

"Ah my dear man, my capacities are the stuff of myth. Pour, Mr. Bartender, pour."

"Well, it's your funeral."

"Don't be insensitive, I'm a very sick old man." Red raises his glass to the men at the other side of the bar. "Gentlemen! *Salud, amor, dinero, y el tiempo para gustarlos.*"

Dan raises his glass. "And so's yer mother."

Moon pinches Dan's sleeve and says, "Looks like the show is about to begin. Let's go get some chairs."

Dewey, dressed in top hat and tails, is standing on the stage, speaking into the microphone.

"Ladies and Gentlemen, welcome to the Club Lido!" The audience, warmed by the champagne and the party atmosphere, give him a loud round of applause.

He doffs his hat and says, "No show would be complete without girls would it?"

"Noooooo!"

"Well then…" Can-Can music swells on the PA system. "Here they are… Girls!… Girls!… Girls!"

The curtains open and a dozen women, dressed in net stockings and red sequined outfits, enter while doing a kick-and-shimmy routine. Their exaggerated makeup and synchronized steps show the hard work and hours of preparation which has gone into their routine. The response from the audience inspires them, and their confidence transports them back many years. Their kicks go even higher. The crowd goes wild.

"Who are they?" Moon shouts over the whistling and clapping.

"Beats me!" Dan hollers back.

A man at the next table shouts, "That's the gals from the square dance group!"

"You got to be kidding!" Moon exclaims. "Hell, they're good!" He stands up to join the rest of the room, clapping his hands. "C'mon, Dan, Ole, get with it — yer only old once!"

The other two stand and crane their necks to get a look at the chorus line over the lively crowd.

Crack! The flats and props are exposed as the lights in the gym come on. The music stops with a squeal and a scratch. The chorus, caught in a high kick, clatters their taps to the floor like an impulse of metal hail. Then, from the back of the room, comes a shriek.

"STOP!" The whole room turns to the rear, where Red stands next to the switch bank. He is reeling. "Stop this…undignified…this masquerade! Are you going to let them take your pride, your…are you going to let them have that, too? My God, look at yourselves! Fools, one and all."

Suddenly he clutches at a rope, his face turned a horrible gray. He leans against the wall, then slides down to dump limply onto his side. "I feel very, very bad," he croaks.

As the staff rushes to Red's side, and residents crowd around the care givers, Moon dips from the abandoned punch bowl and offers it to Dan.

Dan, leaning on the bar with one elbow, gestures with his glass at the crowd, saying, "Trust that walking horse blanket to screw things up for everyone else."

Ole waves away the dipper. "I vunder iss he gonna die, you t'ink?"

Moons dips himself a glass. "Nah. One thing about Red, though — he does love a crowd."

Chapter 14

Jack and his head guide, Buck, ride down the Ishawooa Trail in the rain. Comfortable with one another's silence, they haven't spoken for hours. Horseshoes click and pop on the rocky trail as the two riders, and their three horses, work their way down the valley, over which hangs the bottom of a misting, grey cloud bank. Up higher, it was snowing and Jack's mind agonized about the damage that the heavy snow would do to an unattended camp. The tents would be crushed if too much fell. But they'd be a real mess to clean up, no matter what. The snow-laden camp, however, did not rank as the biggest mess in his life at the moment.

When they brought the first party of hunters out, he had been confident his money troubles were over. The first week of the hunt was a great success and his hunters had complimented the whole operation, from the beauty of the country to the abundance of game. A group of rich California farmers who hunted the Rockies every year, they were looking for an outfitter to take their business to. And they had picked Jack. It was the mountain West's equivalent of having a Medici crook his finger, selecting you for his patronage.

Gib's bear managed to change all that luck. Buck had come into camp one morning and told Jack he'd found enormous griz tracks when he'd gone out to bring the horses in from the meadow. He described the one slewed foot, and added that he'd followed the trail to the edge of the camp. Jack had felt bound to tell his hunters the truth, just to make sure that they would be more vigilant than usual. They canceled the hunt, and insisted on going to town. They hadn't asked for their money back but the second hunting party, which were more rich California farmers from the same area, had also canceled, then demanded the return of their deposits. The cancellations threaten to swamp his new business altogether. If something isn't done, the ranch will be ruined. Also, not being able to repay his sister the promised money on time added humiliation to his mix of feelings. Failing again.

Jack lifts his eyes and scans the canyon side to side, ignoring the drizzle of rain water falling from the brim of his hat and splashing on his yellow slicker. Fall had shown up in full force here at the lower elevations. In contrast to the naked trees and bushes in the high country, all the vegetation down here was bright with vibrant reds, oranges and yellows. The color lightened his mood a bit as he reconsidered his situation. How was he going to salvage his hunting season? What were the options?

His hunters were from a place where only the worst about grizzlies ever made the news. Getting them into the mountains had been an impossibility. Now, his and Buck's hunt for the bear had ended in nothing and they were heading back for the ranch in defeat. Jack had hoped to run the bear down for the Game and Fish people. But, what had been ample sign at the ranch had turned into nothing once the bear hit the rock of the mountain sides and game trails. He and Buck had combed the country around the ranch for five days, but the bear had turned to smoke.

Jack had to come up with something before his third party arrived and got wind of the situation. The local newspaper had picked up the story and was keeping the bear on page one, fanning local talk. The incoming group was a bunch of first time hunters, so rumor of a rogue bear would surely flush them like grouse too.

He is also worried sick at the possibility of the bear returning to the ranch while he was gone. Anisa's father and brother are taking turns staying at the house, but he was still worried about JC. The boy's two encounters with the bear have changed him. He's too quiet, and he isn't sleeping well. One morning Anisa had found him curled up on the floor next to their bed in a sleeping bag.

Jack recognizes JC's passage — the new awareness of the abyss yawning at a man's feet all his livelong days. Jack would have liked to spare his son that awful revelation, but he also knows the knowledge is important for everyone. It helps to keep you honest. And strong. The hard, razor edge of reality comes with the understanding that, finally, your parents are helpless to protect you from the world, and your mortality.

"Jack!" Buck's voice jerks him from his thoughts and back into the drizzly canyon. He twists in his saddle and looks back at the guide, who has stopped his horses. Buck's gloved hand is pointing. Jack looks at the wet trail and sees what he should have seen for himself — dishpan-sized bear tracks, inches deep, going in a beeline down the trail — the spoor headed in the same direction as they are. Toward the ranch, now visible in the distance.

❄ ❄ ❄

Gib points down the highway. "I need to get out at that ranch road, right there."

The young cowboy who is driving nods and begins to brake the pickup. When he had pulled onto the gravel turn-off, he holds out his hand and Gib shakes.

"Thanks for the ride, I appreciate it."

"No problem. I was glad for the company, it's been good visiting with you."

Gib gets out and takes his warbag from the back. Then he waves, steps back and watches the pickup shift down the highway and out of sight. A nearby sign reads: Cody 45 miles.

He crosses the highway and starts down the narrow road leading away to the west. He knows Carl Seifert takes his family to Meeteetse every Sunday for church, then cafe food at Lucille's. He needs to hurry before Carl returns, and Gib has to explain why he needs horses, equipment, and food. He is not in an explaining mood. Besides, Carl is one of the few people left in the country Gib feels he can borrow from, and this is as good a place as any to start from. It does mean a damn long, rough ride from here, over Carter Mountain and down to the South Fork, and the Hoodoo.

When Gib nears the ranch he whistles to Carl's dogs and they come running. Blue, the Aussie cowdog, runs the bunch and Gib knows he will keep the rest of the dogs in line. When Blue accepts Gib's presence, the other dogs trot suspiciously alongside, growling. They are not really convinced that all is kosher, but they don't want to risk an ass kicking by Blue.

When Gib reaches the place, he goes to the barn and saddles a big lineback buckskin. The stripe is a genetic artifact from the prototype horses of the ice ages, and it usually indicates stamina and common sense. Gib rubs the big horse's face and the horse responds to the touch by rubbing his jaw on Gib's shoulder. "I'll bet yer Carl's ride," the man says. "Good, 'cause I'm gonna need one hell of a horse, where we're going."

Twenty minutes later he has packed what he will need on a second horse, a little bay mare. Then he leaves a note for Carl, and is soon slapping the buckskin across his ample bum with the lead rope, the mare scampering along behind.

They jump the little creek running by the corrals and fade into the dimming landscape, the waning sound of their progress the only thing left in the ranch yard except tracks and Gib's note.

He pushes the horses hard, trying to gobble up as much ground as possible before full dark. Because of the gray weather there will be no stars or moonlight, and the ground between Carl's place and top of Carter Mountain is not familiar to him. But the saddle horse knows the country and can see well enough to keep them away from major obstacles. They will go until Gib is comfortable that no one could follow and overtake them. Then he'll make camp and start again at first light. He sits back in the saddle and begins to think, as the horses swing along into the gray hills.

It's a fairly easy climb up the southeast side of Carter, if a man has a good horse, Gib thinks. The ones he picked out are strong and work well together — the buckskin isn't goosey and doesn't kick, while the mare doesn't bite or try to pass.

Tomorrow will get us to the north side of the mountain if we push it. Then we'll drop down of Aldrich Basin and cross the highway at the TE ranch road. I can scout the place the next morning, and see what I can pick up for sign. It's been a week since the bear was at the ranch and, what with this rain, it's gonna be slim pickins unless I ride right up to the house and ask what's been going on, which ain't exactly likely. There's probably been sheriffs all over the place by now, but they'll play hell getting a glimpse of me.

A vision of the ranch as seen from the high pastures on the flank of Carter Mountain flickers on the screen of Gib's mind. In the total blackness of the misting night, the white buildings are like a hologram in front of his blind eyes. The reality of the picture makes Gib actually reach out with his gloved hand, to scatter the vision. Other illustrations, of memories from the long ago coalesce from the scattered fragments. He settles resignedly in the saddle, powerless against the visions bobbing on the night.

An airplane appears, a Callair, taking off from the strip in the pasture. It disappears into the sun. He sees an irrigation ditch with wildflowers and grasses growing thick along its banks. It runs by a little orchard of apricot trees. A pulse of expensive perfume fills his head — a cry loops out of his throat, shattering the next scene: Laura looking up at him with a seductive smile as she sits in the grass and flowers, her arms clasping drawn-up knees. The top of her dress open to the sun, her mouth an irresistible invitation.

He suddenly drives his spurs into the buckskin and both horses snort with fear as he lashes them into an insane sprint, into the damp, black gut of the chilling night.

❄ ❄ ❄

Maggie holds the phone with her right hand. Her left cups an aching forehead. "That's all the note said? Nothing about where he was going? Or why?"

She chews her bottom lip as she listens to her brother's answer, then says, "He can't just be heading off into the mountains for no good reason. He never does anything on a whim." She pauses, "I think it has something to do with that bear. As a matter of fact, I'm positive that's it."

Jack speaks for a few moments before Maggie answers, "If he makes up his mind to do it, a fifty mile ride over a mountain is no real obstacle for him. You know that."

Maggie's door opens after a couple of taps on the wood. Doctor Hillyard's secretary sticks her head in and gestures at her watch. Maggie nods and the woman closes the door.

"Jack, I have to go see the hospital administrator again. This business with Gib and the other resident has turned into a major deal. I am in serious trouble with the hospital board, and the good folks down in Cheyenne.

"Which reminds me, I need to sit down with you. I have an idea. Tell you what, I'm going to drive up there this weekend and run it by you and Anisa." She pauses. "No, I want to present the idea to you both in person. I'm afraid that you are going to need some convincing. Talk to you later. Bye, and love to Anisa and JC."

She puts the receiver in the cradle and stands. Glancing at her watch, she picks up a notebook and Red's file. Then, taking a deep breath, she exits. The meeting with Hillyard is going to be no fun at all.

When she enters the administrator's office he motions her to sit down. He continues reading from a report on his desk. A few minutes pass and he signs two documents, sighs and closes the folder.

"Hello, Maggie. Let's see what we can salvage out of this mess."

"I've done as much as I know how. The investigation has been made. The reports are written and ready for review…"

"Well, there is a fair amount of political damage that has fallen out over this. This is a state institution, after all, and it is overseen by politicians — sorry to say."

"And they want a scapegoat."

"Frankly, yes. But I'm not inclined to give them one. They can have a few strips off my butt — but you are going to have to make nice. Real nice."

"Keep a low profile."

"Yes, of course. The row that Mr. Silver caused at the dance would have been of little or no consequence if it hadn't been for the champagne…"

"Which I talked you into."

"…which you talked me into. Plus the fact that the attorney general's grandmother is a hard-shell Baptist and a resident on your little corner of the campus. She is not one of your fans."

"What she is, is a controlling old bag. Besides, that woman should be either under private care or in another, more therapeutic, situation at this institution. She's nuts."

Doctor Hillyard raises his hands, palms up, and points them at Maggie. "'Nuts', the good doctor says — all psychiatric jargon pared down to the nub; reduced to one incisive, inclusive, descriptive, naked, clinical term: 'nuts.'"

He turns to gesture theatrically at his library of clinical texts and studies. "What a waste of time all this is — I think I'll have it carted away and have my grey-headed Momma make me a petit point sampler that reads: THEY'RE NUTS. It's a lean concept. I like it."

Maggie smiles. "What can I do to keep a state's attorney general at bay? I would guess that my head would be an appropriate blood price — is that what you are disinclined to discuss?"

"No. Thank God that this is Wyoming — a gunfight in the old folks' home has more than a little appeal in a place where the old code still gets a nod, even from the state's own lawyer. But there are some very real legal considerations. Both these men are under indictment for, or have been convicted of, felonies. This is no trivial deal."

Maggie snaps, "I have never pretended that this was in any way trivial."

Hillyard's face reddens. "Doctor Scott, I am trying to be as congenial as I can be about all this. In point of fact, my butt has been scorched by half a dozen people, one of them the governor. Also, there have been at least a hundred inquiries from national, even international, media reps. I have had joshing calls from professional colleagues, even one from our jester ex-senator in Washington. I am not a happy man, Maggie. Professionally speaking, this has made me look very bad in a very large way."

Maggie leans forward. "I'm sorry, Bud. What can I do to help?"

"Well, as you said, you have done all that you can do — except to police that bunch of post-erectile adolescents over there! As for our incorrigible Doctor Silver, I am going to give him back to Utah."

Maggie draws in her breath. "So he becomes the scapegoat. You can't sacrifice him that way!"

"Oh yes I can! We took him only because their old institution was overcrowded. They now have a larger facility and they are going to get him back." He gestures at the paperwork on the desk in front of him. "He is their pain in the ass now."

"But he's sick. That diabetic shock incident has really drained him. Besides, the man is almost eighty years old, and all his friends are here. It would be criminal to send him away from this place."

"Criminal!" Doctor Hillyard puts his hand over his heart, leans back in his chair and turns his face to the ceiling. "Lord, forgive me for what I am about to say."

He rocks forward, puts his hands on the desk and looks Maggie straight in the eye. "Mr. Herbert Silver has been convicted in courts of law of so many felonies that you would break both ankles if you jumped off the paperwork. He has committed federal, state, local, neighborhood, foreign, domestic and state hospital crimes that beggar my ability to catalog them — including conspiracy to commit murder. Dr. Scott, I am not the criminal." His eyes are hard as turquoise in his hot little face. "And now I am royally pissed off at your charge. He goes back to Utah. Period."

❄ ❄ ❄

In the late morning, Gib reins his horse up on the first patch of grass they have seen for more than a mile of pure rock. The high world of the Absarokas is mostly rock. A patch of good green feed this late in the fall is something he must take advantage of, he has been driving the horses very hard all night. They will have to drop down off the face of Carter Mountain to get to the valley of the South Fork, a steep, treacherous trip.

He rustles around in his saddlebag and comes out with an apple. He sits on the brow of the grassy slope, takes his pocket knife out, cuts a piece from the fruit and puts it in his mouth. Then he puts the binoculars to his eyes and looks down into the shadowy valley. He fiddles with the focusing knurl until Villel's little subdivision comes into focus, drawing a snort from the man.

"There's getting to be too damn many people in the world," he mutters with disgust. "Where in the hell do they all come from, and how did they find us clear out here?"

The answer comes to him above the cliffs, looking out over the beautiful valley and mountains. They probably came out to heal up from what had happened to them in other places. Just as he had done in 1951, home from the Korean War.

"Yeah," he mutters, "I guess ever'body's got to be someplace."

The only thing doing at the Hoodoo are chickens scratching in the drive. He sweeps the binoculars west to examine the foothills below the mountains. The Willwood badland formation behind the ranch stands out with its distinctive colors, riven by Bobcat, Houlihan, and Hardpan creeks. The pink, yellow, and purple sediments run in bands below the dark reddish-purple volcanic rock piled on top, for a thousand vertical feet. Ancient volcanoes off to the east had buried the country, first with pumice and ash, then molten ejecta had buried that in turn. The last debris had cooled into a vast plateau of rock that sat on top of the badland clays and sandstones. Water, snows, creeks, and eventually rivers had etched their way down through the great plateau and finally created the valley below. He looks out into more than a thousand feet of verticality. The sight gripped one in the gut, as a tap root of beauty, fixed long ago in the mind of primitive man. At the moment, however, Gib thinks of it as a helluvva good place to hide, if you are a mean old bear— or a mean old man.

"Well, Horse, there's the little blind canyon where that one old cow always had her calves," Gib says, leaning out to see around the buckskin, which has grazed into his line of sight. He pegs a small stone at the horse's ribs and the animal jumps out of the way.

The man returns the glasses to his eyes and continues his examination of the hills. They are now picking up more light as the sun rises over his right shoulder. The reddish volcanic rock takes on a pink glow and, as always, gives Gib peace. This valley had been the home of his heart of hearts for more than half his life. "God, help me," he says aloud to the heavens, " I am homesick, and can't go home."

He puts the binocs down on the grass and leans against the rock. He remembers the first day he came up the South Fork, to the Hoodoo. He knew of the Big Horn Basin when he'd been cowboying in the Wind River country to the south. And so, while he was trying to stay alive in the mud and snow of Korea, he'd promised himself that he'd move to a place where warm winds blew and snow didn't rule the country all winter. After his discharge he took the Burlington Northern to the end of the line, which was at Cody. The trains ran right up to the foot of the mountains, then had to back out of the place. That suited him just right.

Judge Scott had hired him over the phone. Gib was standing in the station-master's office, still in his uniform, a piece of paper in his hand with a number: 252-R. A rancher friend had given it to him, knowing the Judge needed a cow man. The Old Man had come across the river in his big Buick, picked Gib up and they'd driven out to the Hoodoo. It was noon, and hot, but the house was set under big river cottonwoods, so it was a pleasure to drive into the cool and welcome shade. A sober-faced blonde girl of five was standing on the lawn. Her father had introduced her as Margaret Glenn. He remembered that the little girl had called the Judge, "Father." Not Dad or Daddy. Father.

They had gone inside and Gib had been introduced to one of the most beautiful woman he had ever seen. Laura. "Hello," she'd said, looking at his military decorations, then directly into Gib's eyes as she spoke to her husband. "I heard you drive up. I didn't know you'd brought company."

"Mr. Gibson is our new cow manager," the Judge had replied.

"A hero for a cow manager — you do aim high, Judge, as always." She had stuck out her hand and said to Gib, "I'd like to hear about that Silver Star ribbon sometime."

But the subject never came up again. And when those people were gone from this life, Gib was just about the only one left who knew he'd been decorated. The uniform had finally fallen to rot and he'd burned it, along with the ribbons and almost all else from his generation's war.

The glow of the moment winked out. The weight of the years and their other losses came back. He looked down again into that broad, fair valley. It seemed impossible that it was no longer part of his life. But then, as the Judge himself and his people before him must have finally realized, the ranch was larger than their own lives and the name would long outlast their own. Of course, the Judge hadn't lived to see the next chapter of their generation's story, the one including the end of Laura's life.

She had sent for Gib on the afternoon of her last day. He had entered the front room, where they'd set up a bed for her next to the south windows with their view of the river and the trees. She looked terrible, wasted, but her eyes were as clear as her mind.

She'd held up her hands and said, "I see my life ebbing by the state of my hands — I haven't the courage any more to look in the mirror." Over the last few months, indeed, her beauty had melted like cotton candy in the rain. Watching her as she wound down and down, her life being etched away, had been all that Gib could bear. She had held up her hands for a long moment as she examined them, and he'd known that they were surrogates for the beautiful breasts that she had lost to the cancer, and the doctor's knife.

Then she told him to sit and hold her hand, and he obeyed her. Even though they had shared the same life after Judge Scott's death, this occasion was only the second time in their lives she'd allowed him any intimacy, and he was profoundly thankful. She was the only woman he had ever loved.

She talked of their betrayal of the judge, commenting briefly, as if to put her sins behind her. Then she'd said, "I'm giving you my children — and the ranch — until they reach their majority. If it were any other way, and Jack were not your son, I might have sent them back east to my relatives. But, in that event, they might not return. And that would be another crime against the Scott name…and one against you. Also, I am giving you a lease on real life by handing you this responsibility. Otherwise, you would wander the world feeling sorry for yourself, and losing that self in the process. This will keep you here on the Hoodoo, and the ranch will be as much as yours — until you find yourself where I am at this moment."

He had sat with her the rest of the afternoon, until the sunlight had melted away to the west. The doctor had showed up just before dark. She'd sent Gib out of the room and half an hour later the doctor came into the kitchen to say she was gone. Gib was no stranger to morphine overdose, it was a common practice during the war. So, he went in and sat with what remained of her until the coroner came to take it away. Then he'd gone back and sat next to the bed, to be near the faint impression left by her body. He'd left sometime later in the night — when the moon came up and her words had begun to haunt him: "The ranch will be yours until you find yourself where I am at this moment."

When he was younger, Gib never imagined the world without him in it. But here it was. And now, standing on the brow of Carter Mountain, he could feel his feet on the threshold of a room enormous beyond his imagining. The little space of his own life was almost through. His time was done and the ranch could no longer be any sort of refuge. His generation had had their run. He felt unneeded, unwanted, unloved, and finally alone. He choked on the fact for a long moment. But then he thought of that enormous room and he wanted to step into its new strangeness, to put this familiar life, pain and people behind him. Oddly, the willing acceptance of that realization gave him a new and larger sense of peace than he had ever felt before.

Gib raises the glasses again and returns to his study of the mountains and hills beyond the ranch. As he moves the field of view, his gaze picks up luminous dots above Bobcat Creek. He steadies the binocs and verifies a string of elk making their way back from water. He knew well the ridge where they are heading, to lie down and bask in the morning sun. Over the years he had killed a number of their brethren on those rocky narrows.

The glasses move his view further west and he looks up the length of the Ishawooa drainage. The big creek is a corridor to the Yellowstone country and the home of the bear. Somewhere among those mountains, hills, rocks, quakies and willows is what he has come looking for down all the miles and years.

Suddenly, a blink of light focuses Gib's attention. He studies carefully until he sees an antlike figure going down to the creek. He knows it to be the hermit Old Eddy, going to the creek for water. "What'd ya do, get yerself another ratty old trailer house to replace the one that bear tore up? When they said you'd moved to town I knew it was a lie — yer too damn mean to be scared for long. Heh, heh, but I bet you had to clean out your drawers after looking that hellhound in the face, smelt that rotten breath of his."

Gib wraps the neck strap around the binoculars and walks to the packhorse, picks up the halter rope and leads her to the saddle horse. He then swings into the saddle. As he is about to put the binocs into their case tied to the saddle horn, another wink of light catches his eye. He puts the glasses to his eyes and sees a car pulling up in front the ranch house. "Looks like the kids've got company, Horse." Then, casing the binocs, he makes a half-dally around the saddle horn and says, "Hup!"

The two horses step out in unison and start down the mountainside toward the trees, and the river far below. On the other side of the valley, the mountains stand waiting for them.

❊ ❊ ❊

"Sounds like we've got company," Anisa says, wiping her hands on her apron. JC follows his mother to the window and peers around her at the woman getting out of the car.

"Who's she?"

"That's your Aunt Maggie. Jack! Your sister's here."

Jack's voice comes down the hall from the bathroom, "What?"

"Maggie's here!" Anisa pushes the door open and steps onto the porch. She raises her arm and waves. "JC, go help her with her suitcase. Maggie, you look wonderful!" They meet on the walk, throw their arms around one another and hold on, tight, for a long time. JC watches them carefully. Something about their embrace tells him, for the first time, about a private corner of the world, reserved only for themselves.

"Hi, Maggie."

"Hello, Jack. How are you?"

"Good as can be expected. How about you?"

"I'll be better when I get my hug."

At that, Jack walks down the steps and takes his sister in his arms.

Behind the Senior Citizens' Chalet, a 1952 Studebaker Landcruiser is parked by the back door, its motor running. Dan sits behind the wheel. Ole is sitting in the front seat beside him.

"Ho boy, dis is vun bad idea, I'm t'inking."

"Well, yer welcome to stay here if you like."

"No, I mean shtealing Doc Hillyard's car is vun bad idea."

"We're only borrowing it for the trip north. There's a big difference."

"To you, maybe. I'm t'inking dat ve should ask de Doc first, if we are yust borrowing."

"OK, have it your way — we're stealing the damn thing."

"I vas afraid of dat." Ole wipes his brow with a big bandanna.

Dan hits the steering wheel with the heel of his hand. "Why'n hell did Moon have to invite Red along? He's piss-poor company, talks all the time. And he smokes like a chimney."

"Moon sez he's known him vun long time an' he don't vant him dyin in Utah — said no good man should be caught dead in dat shtate. I t'ink it vas a choke."

"Well, it'll be no joke if we get caught idling our butts here behind the building. It won't take Security very damn long to figure out we're doing more than washing Hillyard's cars. What kind of a man collects Studebakers, for hell's sake?"

"Here dey come," Ole says and hops out to open the rear door as Moon and Red scurry out the back door, cardboard suitcases in hand. They jump inside as Ole pushes the door shut and jumps in front. Dan pops the clutch. The tires chirp and the ponderous old car wallows down the gravel drive, around the end of the building, and accelerates smoothly across the grounds. For better or for worse, the three are on their way back home, dragging along a dirty little commie.

❄ ❄ ❄

Jack has been listening to Maggie for half an hour and hasn't said anything. Now he looks at her carefully as she waits for him to speak. Anisa watches them both.

"You want to turn the ranch into an old folks' home." His voice is neutral.

Maggie puts her tired face in her hands and looks at him with all the passion she can muster.

"We can run it parallel with the bull operation, and your outfitting. There is plenty of room for the buildings. We can begin with modular structures, and then replace them with permanent structures as we go along. We can get federal financing and the state will help, too. There's also private money out there, but it's mostly in the form of matching funds and we'd have to come up with half. I've checked it all out."

"I don't like that federal part," Jack says. "Once you take a penny from the feds they figure they own you, and can dictate whatever they please. They end up running you. It's a bad idea."

"Well, we would need a quarter of a million dollars for seed money, and that would take years to round up. But, I hope you can see your way clear to agreeing with me in principle. Just think of it — a community of people who built this part of the country, a place where they will be treated with respect, and in the surroundings that they love. It will be like the old days. I've even thought of calling it 'The Home Ranch.' We'll have an oral historian who will write down the residents' stories. We'll publish memoirs. We'll…"

"Maggie."

"What?"

"This all sounds pretty grandiose, to me."

"Not at all. I know that it will work. Besides, it would make the place pay for itself. And I would be doing what I love to do while you would be doing what you love to do — ranching and hunting. The whole family could pitch in. But, best of all, the people will have a place that honestly cares about them. They'll be home, not in a home."

Anisa puts her hand on Jack's arm. "I like the idea. I like it all."

Jack's voice has an edge. "Well, it sounds good all right. Especially liked the part when you said that it would make the place pay for itself."

"Jack." Anisa's voice holds a warning. But, he has his chin down and his shoulders up, ready to play the ass. They all know this attitude, including Jack, but he can't help himself. He's just like his father.

"I have worked my butt off, trying to make this place pay. I have done everything humanly possible to make things go. But, there has been a conspiracy by everyone, from every U.S. president for the last thirty years, down to the local federal bureaucrats, to kill ranching. And that doesn't count all the assholes from California and New York who come out here full of prescriptions and proscriptions, wanting to run us off the land after more than a hundred years, just so they can raise their yuppie larvae where the water is still drinkable and the air is still breathable.

"I am sitting on top of millions of dollars' worth of real estate, and still have to work seven days a week, fifty weeks a year. I go to town only when I absolutely have to. Hell, I've got holes in almost all my underwear and Anisa darns our socks — how long has it been since you saw a darned sock, Maggie? She had to learn it from her grandmother, for God's sake!" Tears of shame start from his eyes.

"Jack, please. I didn't mean to…"

"I know you didn't mean to, but you did. You have no idea what it's been like the last few years."

Since Gib has been gone, Maggie thinks. Perhaps the issue is abandonment, rather than the grim economics of ranching. Does Jack know who Gib really is?

Jack had puts his face in his hands. His shoulders shake. Anisa, whose own eyes are wet, is gently tugging at the long, ragged hair over his collar. He hasn't had a town haircut in months.

After a minute he puts his hands down, takes out his handkerchief to wipe his eyes. He leans back in his chair and looks up at the ceiling. "I've wanted to do that for years. Lord, it is so hard for me anymore. I guess I just don't know what I'm doing. I have to admit it."

Maggie says, "Jack, almost everyone else in the business is going through what you're going through. It's the times as much as anything. That's why I know that we can make a go of things if we get some money coming in from something that isn't tied to the ranching economy — or to the new people with no history in this place — or anywhere else, for that matter.

"Listen. People get old and have to be taken care of. That doesn't change just because people start eating chicken instead of beef, or the rich move in and take everything over, or the banks make whores out of everyone with their cheap money, then end up with title to the land.

"And besides, Jack, it's the right thing to do. We could make this place have some moral importance by giving those good people a place to be genuinely comfortable in their last days."

Jack looks at his sister, embarrassed at his breaking down in front of her and his wife. "It's a lot to think about, and I just don't have the time to spare right now. I have ten hunters in town that have to be moved thirty miles into the wilderness. Plus, Gib is on the run and out there in the mountains by himself, and that damn bear is trying to put me out of business altogether. My plate is more than full."

He stands and steps toward Maggie. "Talk it over with Anisa. I'll set down with you when I get back from the hills." He stands and steps toward Maggie. "I never got around to saying 'welcome home,'" and he stoops to give her a hug.

The smell of hay, denim, leather, human and horse sweat brings a flood of fond memory.

Chapter 15

Old Eddy watches as Gib and the two horses start up the hill in back of his trailer. They disappear quickly out of the light from the Coleman lantern the hermit holds in his hand. As they wink out into the frosty dark, the only evidence of their passage is the occasional clack of horseshoe iron on the ledgy sandstone. The old man holds the hissing light until he can hear nothing more over the sound of the creek. He then climbs the steps of his trailer and pulls the door shut.

He sits down amid the stale heat, the grease smell and the lantern light. He pulls Gib's graniteware plate across the table to put on the floor with his own. He reaches over to the stove and grabs the fry pan which contains the remnants of eggs and potatoes, fried together in lard. With a heel of bread he wipes the grease pooling in one side of the pan and shoves the mash into his toothless mouth. He then places it on the floor next to the plates, wiping his hands on the greasy thermal underwear he wears year round. "Clean 'em up," he says.

From the dark rear of the trailer, a blind dog creeps from under the bed and goes to the pan and plates. He licks cautiously because the hermit is a man of great mood swings. The isolation and his daily disputes with God have made him more than a little mad.

The man picks up his black pipe, pulls the pound tin of Prince Albert toward him and packs the pipe to the charred rim. Lighting it with a wood match, he turns off the hissing lantern. The licking sound from the dog and the sucking sound from the pipe fill the darkness, relieved only when the pipe's ember pulses, dimly lighting the hermit's leathery face.

Gib had shown up sometime after dark. He had halloed the house while he was still a quarter mile away because he knew Old Eddy could be lying up somewhere in the black with the wire-wound barrel of his rifle pointed in any trespasser's direction.

Despite his constant disputations with the Almighty, he was no anchorite. Rather, he was a trapper and a poacher who had passed his life outside the traffic of the world since returning from his military service in the South Pacific. The world did not care. This he knew. He also knew the world gained meaning only through other people, and that being estranged from human companionship meant estrangement from the universe itself. But when he had come back to Wyoming from Kwajalein he no longer cared.

"Gib," the old man says aloud. The dog freezes at the injection of the name into the dark. He waits for the moment to pass, then goes back to his licking.

When he rode up to the trailer, Eddy had known what the man had come for and a small rejoicing had risen in the old man's breast. The bear had brought fear back into his life. But this man, Gibson, had arrived to bring fear into the life of the bear. And death.

Dawn fingers the curtains always drawn against the world. Slivers of light fall on the table and the hermit puts down his cold pipe. He picks up the cleaned plates and frypan, and sets them on the small counter. He pulls on the felt liners of his winter boots, then rises to take the water bucket out of the sink. He opens the door and a couple of his resident flies buzz out into the cold air, only to quickly circle back into the hot interior of the trailer.

When he reaches the rocky trail that leads to the creek, the old man puts his bucket down and probes inside his mostly buttonless fly and longjohn bottoms, until he finds his withered penis. He then raises his grey, stubbled face to the bluing morning and dampens some dry stalks of thistle. Finished, he pulls the front of his trousers out, to put himself in order. Sighing, he wipes his hand on his underwear top, picks up his bucket and makes his careful way down the path toward the rushing creek below.

※ ※ ※

The morning has turned to bedlam at the Hoodoo. Fourteen horses have been saddled for riding. Fifteen pack horses and mules are being loaded down with two weeks' supplies for the hunting camp. The guides and wranglers are finishing the packing while the dude hunters stand around, trying to look Western.

Inside the house, Maggie, Anisa and JC survey the mess in the kitchen.

"I'd forgotten how exciting a big hunting trip can be for these people," Maggie says, "what with everyone crowding into the kitchen at 3:30 in the morning, with their stories and questions."

"Dumb questions," JC observes. "Did you hear that one guy ask Dad if they were going to be staying in cabins?"

"Oh JC, they're new out here and don't know what to expect. Be generous."

"Yes, ma'am. But they still ask some awful dorky questions."

"Anisa," Jack hollers from the front room.

"Yes?"

"Which one of these boxes has those hunting vests? We need to get these guys in hunter orange before we leave the place."

"They're in the Clorox box. The one with the meat sacks on top."

"OK, got 'em. Jeanie, come get this box and give it to Monte so he can get those guys outfitted."

Anisa turns to JC. "It sounds like they need another pair of hands. Give me that dish towel and go help the wranglers."

"Yes ma'am!" He throws the towel on the table and dashes to the coat rack for his down vest and hat. He is gone in a flash.

"He's so big now," Maggie says, as she scrapes a plate into the garbage.

"He grows inches at a time, it seems. His voice is changing."

"I noticed."

"It embarrasses him so much when it cracks on him." Anisa pauses. "I'm going to have a baby."

Maggie looks at her sister-in-law and her face is beaming. "Really? That's wonderful."

Anisa looks at Maggie. "I'm not really sure, to tell you the truth. Babies are expensive. Plus, we need all the hands we can muster around here. Jack counts on me a lot in the spring, but I can't be feeding cows, or helping to calve if I'm big as a dead bull."

"Oh, I'm sure it will be fine."

"Things have been so hard for us since…" Anisa's voice trails off.

"Since Gib left," Maggie adds.

"Yes. Oh, Maggie, you'll never know how hard we have tried, but it was only your money that has kept us afloat."

"Well, I'm not worried about the money, it went to good use. We still have most of the original ranch. Besides, I am confident that we can put this ranch/retirement/outfitting package together. God will find us a way. He supports all honest enterprises."

"I hope you are right. But life has a way of sneaking up on you sometimes."

Maggie, stacking dishes in the dishwasher, glances out the kitchen window. "Well, speaking of life sneaking up on you…"

"What is it?" Anisa joins her at the window. "Who are those people?"

"Four of my people from Evanston. They're AWOL from the hospital, especially the one in the baggy pants and dirty jacket." She puts her hand on her forehead. "I haven't been sneaked up on, Anisa, I've been ambushed. The attorney general's grandmother is going to have my butt."

Anisa looks puzzled. "Maggie, sometimes you have the strangest life."

❄ ❄ ❄

Gib finds the bear's trail almost immediately after the sun comes up. The bear's many sets of tracks join at the edge of Houlihan Creek, below a little bowl of pines above and visible only from the set of cliffs above it. Apparently, the bear has been laying up in the hideout for at least ten days. He'd been wading the creek for most of a mile before clambering out on the upstream side of some slab rock fallen into the water. Then he had walked the ledgerock to the pine glen below the cliffs.

"Jack shoulda known enough to check here, Horse. It's the closest place to the ranch to hide, and one of the easiest to get out of in a hurry." Gib gets stiffly down from the saddle and ties the two animals to a tree. He then removes the rifle from the scabbard and quietly levers a cartridge into the barrel. At that moment the wind changes and the two horses jerk back on their halter ropes, their ears prick and nostrils flare. The big buckskin's eyes roll, and he snorts.

"Whatsamatter, you don't like them stinky ol' bears?" he whispers. "Well, neither do I — if they're the kind I'm thinking of." He checks the knots again, making sure they are secure, but still capable of being slipped with a minimum of effort. It wouldn't be good floundering around, trying to loosen a horse, with a wounded grizzly bear hot on your ass.

He slips the safety off on the rifle and walks cautiously down into the little glen at the foot of the cliffs. In a few minutes, he finds the bear's bed beneath a big Douglas fir.

"That's a right nice bed you made for yerself, Bear — must be two foot deep in the middle. All the stub ends are tucked down so they don't poke, and the branches are flexed so they spring up. Couldn't of done better myself. Nice layout." Gib turns his face to the wind and takes a deep breath through his nose. "And you ain't been gone so very long, neither." He raises the rifle to his chest, then puts every bit of his concentration into a careful look around the bower. His eyes search the rocks, the trees, a hollow which might reveal a patch of fur, or a big amber eye. His wrung nerves make his right knee shake as he spins carefully around, but nothing is left of the bear, except tracks and reek.

The man examines the area carefully, noting where the bear has entered and exited, where he has lain in the morning sun, where he has made himself a shallow hide near the game trail the ranch riders used. He finds scat filled with Hereford hair, and wonders if Jack knows how many cows are missing to the big animal. Probably not.

He returns to the horses and leads them to the edge of the bowl. Below him lies the ranch. He had been as faithful as a hound to the brand. Damn near forty years, and what had it got him? A lot of memories, nothing more. He'd raised those kids, built the ranch, kept faithful account. He'd worked his soul as hard as he'd worked his body, seven days a week, a lot of the time. For what? He had not coveted one square inch of the place...

And then his bullshit alarm goes off. For the first time in his life he is given a true picture of the reality of his life down there. In truth, he had coveted the whole place. He had fallen into a hell of a deal. Gib Gibson had become synonymous with the Hoodoo and, with time, people had mostly forgotten about Judge Scott.

And when Jack had come of age he had been less than honest. He had left out things that the boy needed to know, if he was going to master the wild fluctuations of ranching economics. He'd consciously excluded Jack from decisions that would have given him an even hand in the managing — historical clues telling a smart man when to sell and when to buy, when to dump the calves, or keep them to feed through the winter. Gib had hoarded access to friends with pasture elsewhere, who would give a man a fair price for his cattle because they had good winter grass.

"Jesus," he whispers. "I am truly sorry, Son. Your failure is really mine."

The moment of clarity made Gib's conscience burn. For the first time in his life, he sees himself for what he is. A fallible human, just like everyone else. For more than three years he had been feeling sorry for himself, looking foolish with his self-indulgent drinking. He had been looking for sympathy, something he hated in other people.

"Horse, it's like Moon says, 'If yer looking for Sympathy, go to the dictionary — it's in there with Shit and Suicide."

He neck reins the buckskin onto the game trail running around the lip of the hidden basin. They move from the trees and into the mid-morning sun. The day had broken clear and still and it promised to be warm. Good. He'd almost suffocated while sleeping in Old Eddy's hot trailer. But his bones had needed the warm bed — something he would not see again for some time.

He picks out a faint trail in the sagebrush and they ride north into the Ishawooa. They travel less than a mile when they cross another, larger, trail. The buckskin snorts and jumps to the side, his ears pricked. In the middle of the junction is a large pile of bear scat. The man swings down from his horse, kneels to poke at the excrement with a twig. The dung clings, showing that it is very fresh. He tosses the stick, remounts and stares down at the scat. Then raises his eyes to the drainage leading into the Yellowstone country.

Gib grins. "You leave that pile there for me, Bear? Good...I like a challenge."

They ride to a game ford in the creek, where the rider stops to water the horses. He takes out his binocs and scans the terrain up ahead. Nothing obvious. He is putting the glasses in their case when, far above and a quarter mile away, he hears the sound of a loose rock rolling against a boulder, then the swishhh of running scree.

He stares at the rimrock above. After a moment he remounts and says, "Prob'ly nothing, Horse, just rotten rock. The rock is always running in this country."

He moves his eyes over the high terrain again, and the wrinkles around his weathered blue eyes deepen as his jaw sets. A sharp hiss comes from between his teeth and he knees the horses forward. "Let's go, we ain't getting nothing accomplished down here. Time to go back to work."

Chapter 16

Hunters, wranglers, guides, and other people are coming and going through the front room, getting ready to leave for the hunting camp. They have been joined by Maggie's deserters from the hospital.

"What are you people doing here?" Maggie asks the four old men.

"Maggie," Moon says, "the place just wasn't the same with Gib gone…" He looks sheepish.

"You know that's no excuse for leaving without notice and," she nods her head at Red, " for bringing Mister Silver with you. You know that he is court committed."

"Well, that's something else, too. They're fixing to send him down to Utah and that just ain't right."

"I don't think it's fair either, but it's out of my hands, and yours too, I might add. Bringing him up here has only made things worse."

Dan offers, "We know that Gib's up here someplace, and we come to help."

"And how do you know that?"

Dan looks at Moon, who says, "He spent a couple of days at the Julian place, near Nugget. He told Truman before he left he was coming up here. Said that he was going to pick up some things at the LU, then drift over Carter to the South Fork."

"And did he say what he was going to be doing up here? We haven't seen anything of him, so far."

The men look at one another again. This time Dan explains. "He come for the bear. I doubt you'll get wind of him here at the ranch."

"He knows the law is going to be after him," Moon adds. Then, with a shrug of his shoulders he says, "He'll die before he goes back to any jail — or hospital. That's plumb certain."

Jack joins the conversation. "I know that hurts, Sis. But it doesn't have anything to do with you or what you do. You know how Gib is." His voice is pained. "He loves you, but he's going to have it his own way, and the rest of the world be damned."

"That's him, alright," Moon agrees.

"But this bear vendetta solves nothing," Maggie says. "It's illegal, and a federal offense in the bargain. He's doing nothing but piling more woe on his own head. At this rate, he'll never be able to come back to civilization…but, I guess, that's the point."

The men look at one another. Then Dan asks Jack, "What do you think? Can we find him? And if we do, what do we do?"

"I'm turning the camp over to Buck and Jeanie. They're going to take the hunters to the mountains while we take a look around here, to see if we can pick up any sign of Gib. If we find him, we'll talk. What happens after that is up to him. We sure as hell can't hogtie him and drag him back"

Ole says, "Dat vud be some real vork, sartin sure." He puts his little black pipe back in his mouth and smiles around the stem.

"About like packing butter up a bobcat's ass with a hot poker," Dan agrees. "A man could come away with some serious scratches."

❄ ❄ ❄

Buck leads the long string of horses, mules, and men out of the ranch yard. A few minutes pass while the caravan gets the kinks out of it, the wranglers riding along the column with whoops and hollers, pushing animals back into line. Jack rides drag, having decided to tag along for a few miles. He wants to take a look around the west part of the ranch for any sign of Gib.

Maggie stands on the porch with Anisa, to watch them go.

"It's one of the things that never changes," Maggie observes. "People have been going through that gate, on their way to the hunting ground, for more than a hundred years. I love this place, but this is the time I love it best — moments just like this."

"It's a hard life, but it's honest," Anisa said. "We could never live any other way. I don't know how other people do it."

"Do what?"

148

Anisa shrugs her shoulders, her arms crossed against the chill of the morning shade. "How they could possibly live any other way? It's all I've ever known, though, so I guess I shouldn't be making any judgments."

Maggie puts her arm around her sister-in-law's shoulder. "I've done a lot of other things, 'nisa, and let me assure you that you are one hundred percent right. Given a choice, this is the only way to live. And now that we've got some time to ourselves, let's talk about what we can do to keep this way of life." They leave the porch for the kitchen, and a cup of coffee.

An hour later, Jack cuts the sign of a single horseman leading a pack horse. The rider had ridden onto the main horse trail from the north, from the country above the junction of Bobcat and Houlihan creeks. Jack turns his horse onto the backtrail of the two horses and follows the sign uphill. At a junction with a game trail, he finds a large pile of bear scat. Beside the pile is a twig and some boot prints. The tracks were big and the heels of the boots which left them were run over. Gib.

Jack turns and looks to the west. The sun is still low, and he can see the last of his horse string switching out of sight above the Ishawooa. The snowy mountains rear up behind the dun hills and blue sage, above the faint yellow dust his people and animals have raised. Somewhere in that vast country, the man he loves more than any other in the world is moving away from him. Moving, again, away from the ranch, from Jack and his family. This time, perhaps, it is forever.

He watches the dust rise on the morning light. The ephemeral billows twist up, then thin to nothing. Gone. Just like that.

Jack raises his hand to the mountains. Then he squares his shoulders, reins his horse around, toward home, and kicks the strong animal to a trot.

Back at the ranch, he begins by saying, "Anisa, I found sign of the young bull that's missing."

"Oh, really? Where?"

"Between Ishawooa and Bobcat — in a massive pile of bear scat. With Gib's boot prints by it."

Moon slides to the edge of his chair. "Which way is he headed?"

"Upcountry. In the same direction as the bear."

"Yellowstone way."

"Yup. And that ain't good. If he chases that bear to anywheres near the park, he will have more problems than Job. Those Park Service cops think that the east boundary of the park runs next to the Mississippi River. And it will take a major law firm and a million dollars to get his ass out of the federal crack they'll put it in, if they catch him."

"Ya, but furst dey gotta ketch 'im," Ole says, his blue eyes twinkling.

"Well, during hunting season they are thicker than lice in Egypt."

"So, what can we do to help?" Moon asks. "We need to catch up with him, at least. Then we'll do whatever it is that needs to be done — including letting him go ahead on his high lonesome."

Maggie's voice is emphatic when she says, "You can't let him do that!"

Jack looks at his sister, puzzled. "What do you mean can't?"

"Can't is can't. Jack, that man is seventy years old. He has a heart condition, impaired circulation, and other disabilities that come from treating his body like a machine for sixty years. It is cold up there in those mountains and that, mixed with the altitude, makes him a prime candidate for frostbite, pulmonary edema, and a whole host of other things." She stands up. "What we need to do is phone the sheriff's department and notify Search and Rescue."

"Gib doesn't need any rescuing. If you phone the Sheriff, he is going to be up here with a search on his mind, alright. But it won't be the kind we need." Jack is losing patience.

His wife joins his sister, saying, "Jack, this needs to be dealt with. And Maggie's right. He's in no shape to be roaming those mountains alone, even tough as he is."

"Fine. We'll deal with it." He turns to Moon. "High lonesome or not, we're going after him. We'll get up there first thing in the morning and look for his trail. Then we'll do whatever has to be done when we catch up to him."

Moon shakes his head in mild disagreement. "Yes, we have to find him. I agree. But what happens after that, I would say, will be entirely up to Gib."

❄ ❄ ❄

The season is clamping its cold hand tighter on the country. During the night, the stars have shivered in a gunmetal sky barely burnished by a wan moon. Ice has crept from the banks of the stock tanks, and the morning light gives them the appearance of cankers. The ground is littered with a new layer of browning yellow leaves which gave up their grip on frosty twigs.

Maggie sits alone at the kitchen table, blowing on a cup of coffee. She is surrounded by the wreck of another breakfast eaten in shifts.

Jack enters the kitchen and leans back against the counter, picking at his teeth with a toothpick. "I'm sorry you got voted down like that. You're not the doctor up here, and those old guys can do as they see fit."

"I can accept the fact that they can do as they please. But I won't agree to it. I can't."

"Why not?"

"Because I am liable for their well-being, even though they may not be on the hospital grounds. I am still charged with their protection, as an employee of the state and as a sensible, conscientious, human being."

Jack dismisses the implication with a wave of the toothpick. "These men are from a generation which takes their responsibilities seriously, and helping a friend is a serious responsibility. It may not be in a written contract anywhere, but it is as binding as anything you or I have put our hands to. They weren't raised to suck the sugar tit and whine about their rights while ignoring their responsibilities. And I won't stand in the way of that."

Maggie doesn't say anything for a moment. Then she says, "Jack, I am talking about my whole professional future, never mind the potential civil liabilities involved. This is not an abstraction for me. This is very, very real."

She waits for him to comment, then continues. "And as for Herb Silver, it is my duty as the officer of a state institution to report his whereabouts to the authorities. He is an escaped felon, and we are harboring him. That, you may want to know, is a felony in and of itself and you and I could both go to jail for it."

Jack smiles a crooked smile. "And that's the difference between law and justice. Besides, no one is going to put either one of us in jail."

Maggie is sober. "We may not go to jail. But I promise you that we will be selling this ranch to pay the lawyers' bills when it is all over. Think about that."

He drops the toothpick in the paper bag-lined garbage can brimming with egg shells and pancake rinds. "I hate to think about that — but you do whatever you have to do about Red.

"However, as far as the rest of 'em go, we come as close to being family as they've got in the world. They know you're concerned, and they understand why, but all you're doing is making it tough on them. They've made up their minds to go and they need your support. Come out and say goodbye."

Maggie stands to take her coat from the back of the chair and put it on. She and Jack go to the porch. She waits there as he walks out into the yard, where the band of old men are waiting with the horses.

Jack goes to the packhorses and checks the lashing on each one, pulling hard against the ropes binding them to the pack saddles.

"Heh, heh," Ole crows, "you kin yank on dem lashings all dat you vant, Yackson. You von't find anyting wrong mit ours! Vill he, Partner?"

"Nope," Dan agrees. "It come back like it was just yesterday when I last threw a diamond."

Moon comes around the animals, sees Maggie on the porch and grins hugely. "I checked the punkin. There's frost on 'er that thick!" He spreads his gloved fingers four inches. They all laugh at the exaggeration.

Maggie is impressed with the transformation in the men. She remembers Dan, only a few months ago, having to be dragged from his bed. Moon has real color in his face, not the hospital pallor she has grown accustomed to seeing. But Ole is a real concern. She steps down to the yard and walks to him. "Ole, are you going to be alright?"

"Yes, Ma'am. I feel real goot."

"Do you have your medicine?"

"Ya, plenty. I vill be yust fine. Don't you vorry 'bout me, please."

"If your feet or fingers start getting numb, you tell Jack. And if you have any trouble at all breathing, or start to get dizzy, you all come right back down here. OK?"

"I vill, sartin sure."

Maggie gives him a big hug. In nervous reflex, his hand flaps weakly on her back. "I got to git."

"OK, you git."

Moon mounts and Jack hands him the lead rope of a pack horse. Ole and Dan pull themselves up on their horses, but with real effort. Maggie hopes their bulky clothing accounts for the clumsiness.

God, please watch after them, she prays.

Anisa gives her husband a long embrace and then Jack swings easily onto his horse.

"Maggie?"

"Yes?"

"I love you, too."

She raises her hand and her brother taps his mount with his spurs. Men and horses begin to undulate away, beside the frost-furred willows bordering the river road. Horses' hooves ring on the iron hard ground. Cold leather squeaks and creaks and the horses break wind explosively as their bodies adjust to the men's weight. The two women raise their hands in goodbye, but the men are intent on their business and don't look back. The blue light of dawn blurs them at the edges and, in a matter of moments, they look like some big caterpillar moving stiffly into the dark distance.

"This is little more than a Peter Pan expedition. I do believe that they never outgrow their boyhood," Maggie observes as she watches them go.

"This is men's business," Anisa observes calmly.

"That is male chauvinist poppycock, Anisa. I'm surprised that you can't see what's going on here. There's absolutely no good reason for all this! Gib runs off on a macho fool's errand and soon every other man in the country is lined out behind him. It's so…male."

"Maggie, this is Wyoming and things are still done the old way. Time will take care of it, I'm sure, but this is the only way they know to go."

"Jack knows better."

"Yes. Jack does know better. But his respect for those men, and their idea of what is right, is what he is going by. Jack has rules for himself, but he would never dream of pressing his ideas on anyone else. They are a generation which will be gone shortly, taking their customs with them."

"And not soon enough."

Anisa put her hand on her nose, to warm it. "Jack would say that it will be all too soon. He's a little old fashioned — he loves them, and what they stood for."

She raises her hand in goodbye, just in case anyone is looking back. "When, and if, women come to take an equal place in the world, I hope we try as hard as those good and honest men have done."

Chapter 17

Gib kneels down on one knee and presses a gloved finger into the bear's paw print. The soft mud takes the impression of his finger. He then presses outside the print. The mud feels granular from the night's frost.

"These are fresh as hot bread, Horse," he says softly. His breath billows from his mouth to rise and frost his eye lashes. The horse jerks his head, making the bridle's chin chain rattle metallically. Gib slowly stands and runs his hand up and down the buckskin's wide, intelligent face.

"Relax, if he was near we'd be well on our way to being pointed on both ends, and laying in the trail in a pile." The man lifts the left stirrup, hooks it on the saddle horn and adjusts a couple of inches out of the warmed cinch and saddle. Then he goes back to check the pack on the mare, and gives her a fond pat. "Yer a good little horse, Sis."

He takes the reins of the buckskin in hand and begins to walk stiffly up the trail beside a little creek whose course is marked by dwarf willows and fragile lenses of ice. He feels like his sleep on the frosty ground has driven spicules of ice into his knees. The sun has not yet reached down into this nameless little valley and he needs a stretch.

"He's staying in open country and makin' real good time. If this keeps up, Horse, that big bastard will be in Yellowstone by noon tomorrow." He reaches into his coat pocket and takes out a piece of jerked meat. Putting the leathery stick in his mouth, he begins to suck, hoping to soften it enough to gnaw some loose. The jerky is going to start a fire in his belly, he knows, but jerky is the best he can do for the moment. He wants to stay on the trail while it is fresh.

When he reaches the top of the little ridge above the creek, he gets into the saddle. Now warm, he rides easily, beginning to enjoy the morning. Only a half dozen puffs of cloud mar the deep blue autumn sky. High above, on the sunny rock, he hears the whistles of pikas remarking his passage up the valley. His eyes sweep along the sunline to the head of the valley, and then on around to the rimrock that still lies in shadow. His sweep of the terrain picks out the likely places in the talus for the small rodents' colonies. He then focuses on the hay mounds marking the nests they are building for the long winter.

He glances down to reconfirm the bear's passage up the valley. His eyes dart back and forth across the frosted grass and rock, but the bear's sign is gone!

Gib begins to course back and forth across the narrow valley, but he can not pick out anything. He spins the horses, to begin a brisk zigzag down the back trail. A hundred yards later, he finds what he is looking for.

The bear had doubled back. From where Gib sits on his horse, he can pick out a faint game trail that cuts up through the grass, then the scree, and on up to the talus. He can pick out a definite impression of the big animal's passage on the slide rock. The trail then disappears into a notch of rock in the skyline.

Gib surveys the scant trail. It is open, with no apparent hiding places, until it reaches the notch in the cliff's top. The notch is, perhaps, ten feet wide and a man would have to ride through it, at a steep angle, for fifty yards or more. No good.

Moving his eyes along the mountain's rim and upvalley, Gib sees what could be another game trail a quarter mile away, running at an opposite angle. That trail should bring him out on the mountain top, but a half mile to the west of the notch. Better.

"Hup," he says to the horses. They step out smartly, as he pops the reins across his chaps.

A hundred yards below the notch, in a shallow slump invisible from below, the bear lies flattened out like a badger. Waiting.

After a moment, he cautiously raises his enormous head until he can see out of the shallow depression he dug next to the steep, rocky trail. He sees the man and the two horses riding away to the west. He snorts. The spray from his nose is lit by the sunlight creeping down to the hiding place. The light reflected off the great yellow eyes turns the irises to black dots. A scar begins under the bear's right eye and meanders over his nose to his left cheek. The shiny black glitters like a vein of obsidian in the silver-tipped cinnamon hair. The bear puts his chin on the rim of the slump to watch the man, and begins to think.

Maggie puts the last of the silverware in the drawer and sighs. She runs her finger over the worn partitions separating the knives from the forks, from the spoons. More than seventy years' daily traffic in the drawer has left depressions in the wood.

While washing the silverware, she had found a table knife with one side of the handle caved in. She could remember very plainly the sunny morning on the porch when she had used the knife to pound a nail into a pull toy, bashing in the knife handle in the process. Maggie remembers the mild scolding, and then the fond pat on her head, from her mother.

She pushes the drawer shut, takes off her apron to hang the tattered, bleached fabric next to the fridge. The geraniums on the kitchen window sill are still blooming. Chinese red in color, her mother's favorite, they and their ancestors were sitting on that same sill before Maggie was born. Perhaps before her mother's own birth. With a start, she realizes that she is now older than her mother had ever lived. By almost ten years.

God, she thinks, how fragile and fleeting You have made this life.

She reaches out to a pot and breaks off a cluster of dried bloom. She then fingers the soft petals of one that still lives. "And, oh, how rich," she says, aloud.

"Who's rich?" The voice from the kitchen door makes Maggie start. She turns to to see Red, his face grey and drawn. She glances at the clock, now clicking past 7:30 A.M.

"Good afternoon," she says. "Everyone else has been up and gone for hours."

"Is there any coffee left?"

"Sit down, I'll pour you some."

"Thank you," he says, and takes a chair.

Maggie looks at him askance. The man had actually been polite. What could the matter be?

"I'll make you some toast and an egg."

"I'm not hungry." He reaches into his jacket pocket for a cigarette.

"No smoking in the house, Mr. Silver. Sorry."

"How uncivilized. Cigarettes and coffee were meant for one another."

"One poison at a time should be enough," Maggie says, raising her own cup to him and looking at him over the rim as she takes a sip.

"What's the matter?"

"Did you know that they are going to send me back to Utah?"

"Yes."

"I can't go. It would be more than I could take, truly."

"Yes, I know. I have retained a lawyer to see what can be done. To my mind, you have paid your debt and then some. He is a man who has a great deal of influence in Utah. An ex-attorney general."

The old man's face registers genuine appreciation. "I am obliged to you."

"And I am obliged to you. I am familiar with the great risks that people like you took during the Depression, trying to make things livable for the working people in this country. Not everyone has forgotten."

Red's face suffuses with cheer. "That makes me happier than anything else you have said. Including the prospect of being rescued from the institutions of Utah. They are some of the most infamous in the country. Thank you."

"I'll get your egg and toast. And you are welcome."

She opens the refrigerator and takes out an egg, then puts the poacher on the stove. As she slices home made bread for the toast, she says, "I am thinking about starting a retirement home here on the ranch. It would take some real money to get it going, a couple of hundred thousand dollars, at least. But there is foundation and federal money out there somewhere, I'm sure. It would take some time to get things going, but I would like to have a place where people like yourself could come. I would want a place where everyone was welcome, and appreciated for what they have done with their lives — try to have a genuine community, rather than an institution. What do you think?"

"I think it sounds a bit Utopian. But, given my history, something like that would appeal to me. Is that why you brought it up — knowing that I would approve?"

Maggie smiles. "Probably. I'm having a bit of hard time trying to get the rest of the family to see things my way."

Red takes a sip of his coffee and reaches for his pocket. He grimaces, and put his hand back to the cup. "Two hundred thousand dollars is a lot of money, even these days."

"I'm hoping that I can find matching money, so we would only have to raise one hundred thousand or so. Not counting your lawyer's fees." She shakes her head and puts the bread in the toaster. "Make that half a million."

Red taps the table with his finger. "You know, miracle of miracles, I just might have access to a half million or so."

"Well, get out your checkbook, Dr. Silver. If ever people needed a money miracle, we need one now. Every one of us is in the doo-doo up to our eyebrows."

❄ ❄ ❄

Sheriff Burns of Uinta County is driving to the Hoodoo, with Sheriff Nagel of Park County. They meet the school bus as they near the Hoodoo ranch road. The Scott ranch truck is turning around at the bus stop.

"That's Jack's wife there," Sheriff Nagel says, pointing.

"What do you think? Are we gonna get the runaround up here?"

"Oh, the Scotts are good, honest people. The folks up here can be real clannish and prickly, but they aren't the kind to break the law. I expect we'll get what we need."

"This Gibson character sure did have a runaway lately, didn't he?"

Sheriff Nagel frowns. "Y'know, I just can't figure it all out. Once upon a time he was one of the most well-thought-of men in this part of the basin. Then one day he ups and quits a place he's spent most of his life on. Then he takes off on a tear a mile wide and a thousand miles long. I just don't get it." He turns onto the Hoodoo road.

The Uinta County sheriff shrugs. "Who knows what goes on in men's minds. I've had lifelong friends, ones I thought were happy as any man could be, put an ought-six under their chin and ruin the wallpaper in three rooms — with the whole family sitting there, watching."

"There's an old story that Gib came over here on the run, a long time ago. But there's others swear they saw him get off the train, right after the war, in a sergeant's uniform with a chestful of medals. It couldn't be both ways. All I know is that things have sure changed for him, one way or another."

"And then there's this Silver character. He's got a record that would patch hell a mile, and if the two of them are up here together it's going to be a royal mess, no matter which way we have to sort it."

Sheriff Nagel grimaces. "The part I dread is if we have to charge the Scotts with harboring, or aiding and abetting. That would be the sad part, they are damn fine people." He shrugs. "But I guess that all depends on what they have to say right now. If they are straight with us then it's going to be OK. If they lie, it's their funeral. Here's the ranch."

"Nice old place," Sheriff Burns says. Then he adds, "Do you see what I see?"

"Where?"

"Over there, behind that shed. Looks like the ass-end of a Studebaker to me, and it's got county 19 plates on it. Hillyard's, it's gotta be."

Nagel turns off the engine and says, "Let's go get the story, and I hope it's good. Man, I tell you, when these old farts finally kick over the traces, they sure do make flinders. You gotta give 'em that."

Inside the house, Red looks out the window and shouts, "Let's run! The gestapo is here!"

Chapter 18

Jack pulls his face into the collar of his fleece coat. Leading his little band of searchers up a rocky, wind-lashed trail, blasts of driven snow sound like rice being thrown against their bodies and equipment. Though the path is becoming steeper and narrower as they go, Jack is mostly oblivious to his surroundings. He must trust his horse to lead the way safely to the top of the ridge.

When they finally gain the summit, he will bring his attention back to finding traces of Gib. But, in the meantime, he has a few minutes to think.

This quest for the man who had been the only father-figure he had ever known has been bringing old emotions to the surface, emotions long-buried. Traces and relics of the man were turning up everywhere. Only a few weeks earlier he had pulled a bale from a haystack and found a leather glove of Gib's, lost years ago. The glove looked as new as the hot summer day when they had been building the stack, and Gib had cussed the loss.

Another time, during the recent fall roundup, Jack was riding down from his grazing lease on the forest. The day had been long, and hot, and steep. He had stopped at Yellow Creek to water his horse. It was after dark and a big full moon was rising. On an impulse, he had ridden into a nearby grove of quaking aspen, to a clearing at the base of a big boulder. The fire ring from so long ago was still there, though only a circle of rocks in the moon-drenched grass.

He had been twelve when Gib took him on an overnight camping trip and they had stayed there. Gib Dutch-ovened grouse, corn on the cob in aluminum foil, sheepherder potatoes and hot rolls. Jack had eaten until he was round as a tick. He remembered it had been during a blue moon.

Gib had pointed at the bright disk and said, "That's a blue moon." Jack stared at the luminous globe until Gib chuckled. Then he'd told Jack a blue moon was the second full moon in the same month. He'd said that it came around only once in a lot of years. Since that time, Jack associated blue moons with the rare occasions when he'd had Gib all to himself, to learn from. Once in a blue moon; and then some.

Jack looks up. Instantly, his eyes water from the blast of wind slicing along the ridge line. Once on top, he reins in his saddle horse and gets down to the ground. The wind blowing across the warm seat of his pants chills him instantly. He walks a few steps, to stretch his legs, and looks back down the mountain side, where the other three searchers on horseback are filing up. Above them, flat-bottomed grey cumulus clouds were leaving skid marks on the sky as they coasted over the mountains in the distance.

As Jack watches the riders, he notices that Ole is lagging behind the others. He watches carefully for a few seconds, but there seems to be nothing wrong with the man. Tired horse, most likely.

He takes out his binoculars and, with the wind to his back, begins to survey the surrounding country. He can see a great deal of the rock-strewn, treeless terrain typical of the summit country in the Absarokas. The immense volcanic plateau is decaying into huge cirques at the heads of the major streams. The great rock bowls join one to another with bald ridges and undulating expanses of rock, furred with short, hardy grasses stunted by incessant wind. A man can see a great deal of the country with a pair of binoculars, but Jack's careful survey reveals nothing but rock, snow and sky. He puts the glasses down as the other men join him.

"Nothing, huh?" Moon says, wiping his runny red nose, then watching the wet streak on the back of his glove dry instantly in the sharp wind.

Jack shakes his head and places the glasses back to his eyes.

Moon pushes his ear down into his collar, to keep the cold wind out. "I don't need no ear ache," he mutters into his coat. It reminds him of a time when he and Gib had been hunting bighorn sheep near the Montana line. They had waited in a low pile of rock for some rams to work their way by. The wind glancing off the rock had given Moon an agonizing ear ache. Down in the hunting camp, later that evening, Ole blew his pipe smoke into Moon's ear. It was an old Norwegian home remedy, and damned if the remedy hadn't worked. When they went hunting, they always took Ole along as campjack.

"Whooeee! That wind's got an edge on 'er, don't she?" Dan shouts as he rides up.

"Yup. Some real weather must be moving in," Moon agrees. He turns and asks, "How you doing, Ole? You warm enough?"

The little man doesn't answer. He sits with his back to the wind, his gloved hands stacked one atop the other on the saddle horn. He coughs thickly.

"Ole!" Moon nudges his horse forward until he is beside the man, and gives him a nudge. Ole opens his eyes. They are unfocused and glassy. His windburned cheeks are the only color in a face now appearing sculpted from suet.

"Jack!" Moon shouts.

Dan and Jack turn their attention to the other two. Jack takes one look and shouts against the wind, "We've got to get him down off this ridge, and out of the cold."

"What's the matter?" Dan shouts.

"I don't know for sure. It's serious, though." But the wind carries Jack's words away.

"What'd you say?"

Jack pushes his mouth to Moon's ear and says, "We'll go back to that grove where Gib camped last night. It's out of the wind, and we can get a fire going there. You take off now and I'll bring Ole and Dan. Go!"

Moon leaves, hitting his horse across the bum with the reins.

"Dan!"

"Huh?!"

"You ride behind. Let me know if he starts falling!"

"Right!"

"C'mon, let's get out of here! This is no place for anything human, let alone a sick man!"

❄ ❄ ❄

Almost five miles away, to the west, Gib reins up on the lee side of a sheltering rock formation. He pulls off a glove and puts his hand up to warm his cheeks and nose. "Mares' tails and mackerel scales make big ships wear little sails!" he shouts to his horse, as he looks up at the attenuated clouds and scalloped sky. A rock the size of a golf ball rolls by, driven by the wind. "Damn!" he exclaims.

He climbs stiffly down, then hangs onto the saddle for a few moments while the blood flows back into his legs. He drops the reins and walks from behind the rocky shelter. The howling wind jerks at his clothes and tries to sail his hat off the mountain as he walks to the edge of a rocky cirque. The steep, north-facing crags at his feet are thick with pine trees the color of tar in the flat, blue light. Gib lost the bear's trail a mile back, but a sixth sense has led him to the edge of the alpine bowl below.

He stands, braced against the blast, for a couple of minutes, taking time to examine the small cornices of wind-drifted snow at the lip of the basin. He sees, two hundred yards away, the wide track left by the animal as it dropped off the howling rock plateau and down into the sheltering trees. Then the man retreats to the shelter, where his horses wait. "Horse, he's layin' down in the that bowl, out of the wind. You wanna go down there and snuggle up to 'im, to stay warm? Well, me neither."

He takes the panniers from the pack mare and stashes them in a crevice, along with the crossbuck. Then he unsaddles the buckskin and stores the saddle with the other items. He makes a wind break with the canvas manta covers. After he'd made his cold camp, he feeds the animals Omolene and pickets them in the lee.

After seeing to the animals, he spreads his sleeping bag amid the panniers and saddles, out of the meatslicer wind, and crawls into the bag. Swirls of cold curl in as the storm front gains strength. Gib fumbles in the pocket of his coat, which he has converted to a pillow. He takes out a piece of peanut brittle and puts it in his mouth. The candy is covered with pocket lint, but he patiently works it off the candy and balls it on his tongue. He spits it out. Then, as he sucks on the sweet, he begins to consider the situation.

It seems that if the storm were going to be wet, with snow, it would have happened by now. With no snow, it just might blow itself out. If that happens, the morning would dawn cold and still. One plus is the bear's biology would be prompting him to den up for the winter. That means that his blood would be slowing down his brain, preparing it for the long sleep.

"If it's calm at first light," he says aloud, "I'm gonna be on him like ugly on an ape before he knows what the hell is going on."

In his mind, Gib covers the distance to the cirque. Half a mile at most, maybe less. The walk would warm him up, and by the time he hit the timber it would be light enough to shoot. If he got lucky, he would catch the animal in his bed. Then, adios muchacho.

He rolls over on his side. A rock digs into his hip and he adjusts his position. He sighs at the rebellion he feels way down in his bones, because his body just doesn't want to do what it has to do, anymore. He hates being old, and everything else that goes with it.

But, I ain't done yet. The judge, the cops, and all the Hillyards in the world, can kiss my ass. I got one last run at doing things my way, and it s going to be on my terms, he thinks. He has made up his mind, and his body will follow, just as it always has.

As he begins to wander on the edge of sleep, faces begin to float up to the level of his consciousness. Old George, Ross Meeks, Moon. Good old Moon. Jack, Nisa, Maggie, the Judge. Young JC. Laura. Oh, God…Laura.

With a small start, he realizes that he's had a very good life — good friends, great enemies, and a love with a gravity given to few. He smiles as it comes to him that, in spite of the fact that he felt old, stove up, and is freezing his ass off on top of a mountain in the middle of a winter storm, he is probably as happy as he has ever been.

The little mare shifts her weight and crowds closer to the big buckskin, jockeying for more warmth. The sound of her iron shoes on the rock makes Gib surface from his reverie. Then he feels himself sliding back down into the well of memory. This begins his long, long, night.

Chapter 19

Gib didn't remember opening his eyes. It felt like he hadn't slept at all, simply closed his eyes and listened to the sound of the wind tearing at the mountains all night long. But, suddenly, the sky is open, grey, cold, and as still as the wreck of an ancient stone church.

He rolls out of his sleeping bag, pulls on his boots, and goes to feed the horses. He looses them from the picket rope, drops hay cubes on the ground for each of them, saying, "If I don't come back, you can find your way back to the South Fork. You're smart enough for that."

His rifle's steel stings, icy to the touch when he picks it up. He cradles the metal in his arm as he walks toward the lip of the cirque. Dense fog fills the valleys below. The ridge rocks are graced with delicate spikes of frost.

The man strikes out, his internal compass dead on. He makes his way down the center of the wide ridge, to the trough in the snow cornice, where the bear had dropped into the protection of the bowl. He follows the sign, walking down into the top of the fog and mist. He waits there a few minutes, to get the feel of the place, and to wait for the light to get a bit stronger. He will need light.

When he can see the mist take on a little color, he begins to drop down, moving quicker as his lean body warms with exercise. He licks his dry, cracked lips.

Gib stays in the wide furrow the bear left in the drifted snow, until he gets to the trees, where the spindrift disappeared and traces of the bear's passage waned. He cruises the edge of the trees, looking for a likely entrance into the dark grove. He will need soft footing to make his search silent as possible. He soon finds the entrance he is looking for, and moves into the black timber.

He cuts faint sign of the bear's passage as he descends into the fog-shrouded pines. His eyes pick up the impression left by the slip of the bear's heel in the stiff grass. Then he finds a broad impression, near a little seep of water. Deep marks disturb the frosty duff, where the animal has bounded over a deadfall log. The trail becomes more obvious by the moment, and the man moves with new confidence.

He carefully avoids the steeper places, with their slick grass and rocks, and skirts the brittle asterisks of dead branches at the margins of treefall. As he steps over another log, his boot descends on a brittle twig, and he barely catches himself before his weight causes an almost inaudible snap. He changes the placement of his foot, and drops, silently, deeper into the dark.

The way grows steeper, slowing his stalk. Then the terrain benches and, immediately ahead, he sees where a large windfall is piled up.

The jumble of downed pines looks like a hasty barricade thrown up to block his pursuit. Logs rear from the mass, like spars of a ship rotting in a dismal backbay. Tendrils of fog drape the broken branches, tentacles of mist rise from seeps that leak out of the ground under the wreck. He has found the place he is looking for.

The man moves quietly to the left for a few yards. No entrance. He moves in the opposite direction and sees nothing, until he glances over his shoulder and notices an oblique corridor into the dead pile. Cautiously, he glides into the dark entrance, his eyes picking out a way over and through the tangle, as his peripheral vision scans for a hidden bulk, a patch of hair.

He puts his hand on the slimy bark of a fallen tree, then places his leg over it. His foot dangles, probes, and finally touches the ground. Then he puts his other foot down and, once steady, stares into the obscure heart of the stack. There are two apparent ways into the refuge, so he pauses to consider his choice. But something tells him to look back!

Gib swivels his head slowly, to look over his shoulder. Above him, twenty yards away and outlined against the background of fog, a form is carefully rising. The outline of a bear's sloping shoulders and round ears rises cautiously above a black foreground. Instinctively, Gib throws the rifle to his shoulder and fires.

His brain registers the bear's muzzle dropping dramatically as its throat is caved in. Pink mist and rags of flesh make a brief aureole behind the animal. But, even as the man takes in the sight of the collapsing bear, he knows the destroyed animal is not his quarry. Too small for a griz, it is an innocent cinnamon bear, roused from a winter nap.

But, at that same moment, a howl of rage and fear explodes behind Gib's back, amid the windfallen trees. He spins in reflex, jacking another round into his rifle as he hears the sound of a dislodged log rolling from the drift of rotten logs. He pulls the weapon to his shoulder, sighting into the mass. But, his senses only record the bawling passage of the griz as he moves swiftly away in vocal, raging flight.

❄ ❄ ❄

Red stares at young JC. The boy has stood from the table and cocked his ear, as if listening to something. Then he says, "Dad!" and bolts for the door. He returns to retrieve his hat and coat, his mother joining him at the coat tree.

When Maggie and Red reach the porch, they see two horsemen under the light in the barnyard. JC is taking the reins of his father's horse while Jack goes to the other horseman.

"Maggie!" Anisa shouts, "Come here. It's Ole!"

"Red, go to my room and get my doctor's bag. It's on the chair next to the bureau."

"Right. I can help, I was trained as a medic." He leaves as Maggie runs to the people at the corrals. Snow is spitting, the flakes swirling and dancing into the cone of bright light.

Jack pulls Ole's foot from a stirrup and takes the reins from his grip. "OK, oldtimer, you're gonna be fine now. Maggie's right here."

"What's the matter?" Maggie asks as Jack helps Ole dismount. The two of them almost fall as Ole staggers on his numbed legs and frozen feet.

"I don't know," Jack said. "You're the doctor. All I know is that he has a hell of a time breathing."

"Ah, I'm yust fine. Don't you be vorryin 'bout me."

Jack takes the little man under his arm, waving Maggie away. "Let's see if you can get to the house."

"I kin get to de house. Don't you vorry. I'm feelin pretty goot, now dat I kin see a varm house. Boy, I neffer bin so cold in alla mine born days. Whooeee!"

"How you making it?" Jack asked.

"I got 'er on de downhill pull now. T'ank you."

Jack smiles. "Ole, I think it's time for you to get a milk cow, some carrot seed, and a set of bib overalls. I see retirement from the fast lane waiting for you."

"How 'bout yust de carrot seed and de bibbers? Milkin' cows is darn hard vork."

Red is waiting on the porch. He holds the door as Jack and Maggie help Ole up the steps.

When they set Ole on the front room sofa, Maggie peels off the old man's outer clothes, and examines him. "Jack, get his boots off. JC, you go get me a couple of pillows and a warm blanket. Red, get out my stethoscope, the sphygmometer and a thermometer."

"Anything else?"

"Yes. Anisa?"

"I'm right here."

"Phone 911. Tell them to get an ambulance headed this way. Now!"

❅ ❅ ❅

Joe Echeverria did not bother to remove his coat or muffler when he entered the bank. Now he is sitting across from a bank officer, a pretty woman with wavy chestnut hair, green eyes and a frozen smile. The two of them are waiting for the president of the bank.

That is OK with Joe, he doesn't mind waiting. Besides, it gives him a little time to look around. After all, it is the first time he has been off the hospital grounds in many, many years. The town has changed, the bank building is new. Much bigger, much nicer. The new bank pleases him.

Joe's cannonball head, with its large brown eyes and neatly raked hair, swivels on his invisible neck as he watches the progress of daily commerce. His hands, with their thick fingers laced, are set on the front of his heavy coat. All the bustle is quite interesting, relaxing even.

However, the bank officer is less relaxed. First, Joe had been brought to her desk by a mental hospital attendant. Then the huge man had demanded, with his thick accent and mangled syntax, three hundred thousand dollars of his money, in cash and immediately. For all intents and purposes, her day had ended in those few moments.

She sits across from the Basco, smiling her frozen smile, her fingers laced on the desk in unconscious mimicry, as she watches Joe's massive head swivel. Each time his large brown eyes sweep over her, they seem to dilate in brief recognition and then dismiss her. The hypnotic affect of each rotation causes her to be conscious of the beads of sweat on her upper lip, but also causes a lack of will to wipe them away — no wonder she shrieks when the bank's president puts his hand on her shoulder.

Everyone likes Al, the bank president. He is fair, and as accommodating as the law will allow, which makes him a popular man. He has a knack with people, and knows when to say "Yes" and when to say "No." He has heard what Joe expects and knows this is one of those times to say "No." But, of course, in a very nice way.

"So, Mr. Echeverria, you want to take some money out of one of your accounts."

"Yes."

"And how much did you have in mind?"

"T'ree hunret t'ousan' dollar."

"Well, may I ask the reason for a withdrawal of that size?"

"No."

"Uh, Sir…you must realize that you are not liquid enough to withdraw anything more than, say, four thousand dollars from any one account. Perhaps five."

Joe leans forward in a very deliberate manner and stares into Al's eyes. "Money is not here? You no got him?"

"No, no. I mean yes, yes! Yes, your money is here in a manner of speaking. It's just that it's not here in cash, and we can't get it for you right now. Today, that is."

Al's confidence is slipping as his gaze is drawn to Joe's brown eyes, flashing now with sparkling coppery highlights. He breaks the gaze and glances through the glass wall of his cubicle, looking for the hospital attendant. The man is intent on a Reader's Digest article.

He turns back to Joe, to say "Why don't you give me a few d…"

"I'ma come here to gets some my moneys — I'm not ask for all, jus' some of him. Now you tella me somnabeech money no can you give me." Joe's simple way of stating the facts as he understands them intimates a need for resolution in the simplest way possible. The now-pulsing red highlights in his eyes support that impression.

"It's just that coming in without notice and asking for that much money for no good reason is not…"

"Is notta what?! You gots my money for long time an' I'ma no say shitting t'ing to you. Forty year you papa write me some letter, and now you write me letter maybe two time a year an' tella me dis, tella me dat, send me paper to sign an' I sign him. I stay my moneys here an' I say not'ing. Now I say gimme some my moneys an' you gimme magpie talk. Gimme moneys — *now!*"

"Coming right up." Al springs to his feet. He has not lived this long, and a become bank president, by hanging onto an issue past its zenith. And this situation, he has no trouble recognizing, is heading downhill fast.

Half an hour later, Al watches from the front window and shivers as Joe mounts the step of the hospital van, sagging the springs. The attendant slides the door closed, walks around and gets into the driver's seat. When they are gone, he goes back to his office and sits down with Joe's portfolio, then exhales a big breath. He will be all afternoon figuring out how to rectify the three hundred thousand dollars he had placed in an open account for Joe.

On the way back to the hospital, Joe reflects briefly on Red's phone call of the day before. He had started off with a wonderful line of bullshit about the big cowboy and a grizzly bear, about it being on television and in the newspapers. Joe had tears as big as horse turds rolling down his face, from silent laughter, before Red was halfway through his story. Joe missed the grungy little man, and he missed him a lot.

When Red had finally gotten around to his pitch, Joe had seen no problem with the deal. What the hell, money didn't mean a whole lot to him, really. Red's proposition, on the other hand, was another thing altogether. The donation would mean he could be back with his little friend, the only one he'd had in more than forty years.

The van turns the corner and starts up the hill. At that moment, Joe remembers that he'd forgotten to ask the attendant where a man might find some chocolate-covered almonds, but too late. Besides, he didn't have any money.

❄ ❄ ❄

Sheriff Nagel has beaten the ambulance to the ranch. A deputy patrolling in the area when the 911 call went out had raised the sheriff at home. As he watches the medics slide the sick man into the back of the van, where Maggie waits with a stethoscope around her neck, Nagel turns to Jack and says, "Let's go inside and I'll take me some notes, alright?"

"Sure. There's coffee and cinnamon rolls. The family was going to have them after supper, but supper never got around to happening."

"Why don't you folks go ahead and have your meal. I'll have some coffee and one of those rolls while we talk."

"Just right. How about your deputy?"

"Rose has got to finish his patrol up to the end of the road. Lots of vehicles are parked at the trailheads and the local thieves like that. The Billings, Montana pawn shops get a lot of local hunting equipment at this time of year, and we try to discourage as much of that as we can."

Once they were at the table, Sheriff Nagel nods at Red and says, "I know that Doctor Hillyard has given all these men, except Gibson, leave to be here while under Doctor Scott's immediate supervision. That's fine with Sheriff Burns, and if it's fine with him, it's just dandy with me. But, even if it's none of my business, I want to register my concern that the other two men are in the mountains. That's stretching 'immediate supervision' more than a little, isn't it?"

Jack says, "I tried to get them to come, but they dug in their heels. They wanted to go on to my hunting camp, to see if Gib showed up there. Then they were going to try to talk him into coming back down with them. They've known him for more than forty years, and if anyone could get him to do it, it would be them." He takes a drink of milk. "I didn't feel like arguing with them. I had a real sick man on my hands."

The sheriff cuts a piece of cinnamon roll with his fork, spears it and puts it in his mouth. He chews, thinks, swallows. Then he picks up his cup of coffee. "What do you think the chances are of Gib coming down on his own — with his friends?"

Jack looks at Anisa. She looks back, waiting for his answer.

"Zip," he says.

"I appreciate your honesty."

"But that doesn't mean that I couldn't be wrong. Gib does as he damn well pleases."

Sheriff Nagel smiles. "I've been getting that impression."

Anisa asks, "What are you going to do, Sheriff?"

"After what I've heard, I'm afraid I'm going to have to send some folks up there after Mr. Gibson. You see, there's not just the fact that he's got some warrants out for his arrest. He's after a park grizzly and that's against another two bodies of law — state and federal.

"Gib has a genius for spreading his act all over every possible jurisdiction. He's wanted for assault in Nevada, Cody, and Evanston. Also, Park County and the state of Wyoming want him for escape, and now he's dancing on the toes of Wyoming Game and Fish, U.S. Fish and Wildlife, the U.S. Forest Service, and the National Park Service — to say nothing of the Greater

Yellowstone Coalition and the 'Save the Gerbil' crowd in Hollywood. So, you see, if I don't, at the least, go through the motions of looking for him, the other agencies and the newspapers are going to run me over."

Sheriff Nagel takes another bite of cinnamon roll, chews. He shakes his head and smiles as he raises his coffee cup. "You gotta give him credit — the man sure does know how to raise hell."

❋ ❋ ❋

The next morning, the sun is up over Carter Mountain when Jack comes into the house and says, "The deputies are coming across the bridge with their horse trailer. JC, go out and show them how to get their gear organized for packing." The boy grins and grabs his jacket, to fly out the door and down the steps to the yard.

Anisa answers, "He's really been looking forward to helping the deputies. I'm glad you gave him that responsibility." She steps to put her arms around Jack's neck. "You are a very good and sensitive man, Jack Scott. And a good father."

He kisses her on the mouth. "And you are a helluvva wife. Thank you for last night."

She leans back and smiles seductively. "I figured I had nothing to lose. I might as well let you have your way with me. The damage has been done, so to speak."

He reaches down and rubs her stomach. "Knocked up, huh?"

"Everyone on the river figured you'd get me in a family way, hanging around the way you do."

"Guess I'll have to make an honest woman out of you."

She raises her hand and flicks at her wedding band with her thumbnail. "Too late."

"Durn." He kisses her and she opens her mouth, inviting him in. He breaks off the kiss. "There are entirely too many people around to be doing that."

"Chicken," she whispers.

"And you are a tease. Just you wait until I get back."

"Promises, promises."

Jack reaches down and cups her bottom with his hand. "Lady, that is a promise."

"And I know that you'll keep it. You are, if anything, an honorable man." She breaks his hug. "Now go talk to your sister."

"Where is she?"

"Down at the cemetery, with your mom and dad."

Jack walks the hundred yards to the family cemetery, set on a little hill behind the house, overlooking the river. Maggie is gazing across the river at Carter Mountain, her hands in the pockets of her red down coat. The wind blows her hair across her face and she pushes the errant strands back with her fingers. The squeak of the gate makes her turn.

"Hello, Jack. Come give me a hug, I need one." Her eyes have circles under them.

"You got 'er," he says, and puts his arm over her shoulder.

"You know that I'm mad enough to spit."

"Yep."

"I warned you he was too frail for the trip."

"Yes. You told me, but he wanted to go."

"He is my responsibility."

"Maybe according to some state statue or hospital policy, but he is his own responsibility."

Jack takes his arm away from her shoulders, gently turns her to face him. "He wanted to go and he went. Now he is paying the bill for the trip. Besides, he isn't dead, he's just sick."

"Jack!"

"Sshhh. Listen to me. On the way down to the ranch we had to stop a half dozen times, so he could rest for a while. Once, we were on a point next to the trail where we could see down the valley for miles and miles. He was sick as hell, but he got a great big grin on his face and said, 'I prayed a thousand times that I would get up into these mountains one last time, and I did — thanks to God and you.' " Jack's voice croaks on the last word.

He clears his throat, pinches his thumb and finger together and says, "He was this far from dying on me, and he said 'Thanks.' Do you know what kind of a person it takes to do something like that? He wasn't afraid of dying, not one whit. He was happy that he might just get to die right where he sat."

Jack puts his hand on his sister's cheek. "I think that it would make Ole's God real happy if we make a place here for people like him."

Maggie pushes her face into Jack's jacket front. Her shoulders shake and he put his arms around them until she gains control. Then they walked back to the house to tell Anisa she is going to be having a lot more company.

Chapter 20

The search party reaches the hunting camp at dark, after a long, snowy ride. Breaking through the snow at the higher elevations has slowed them down. The lighted tents, glowing in the dark like jack o' lanterns, and the smell of the smoke from the camp make the men ache for a warm meal and bed. The exhausted horses pick up their pace, knowing that food and shelter wait for them, too.

"Hallo-o-o!" Jack hollers.

The sound of wood being chopped stops, and a man's voice answers, "Hallo-o-o!"

"Boy, I hope they got some supper waiting," Deputy Rose says.

"It's coffee I want, first, then something to sit on besides a saddle." The other deputy sounds beat. "My asshole is pooched out far enough to cut washers off it."

Buck and the wranglers are waiting when they reached camp. Jack gets down and, waving at a meat rack where two elk carcasses hang, says, "Looks like you had some luck."

"Two six-pointers. A couple of your hunters are happy as larks — and drunk as lords. One of 'em gave Jeanie a hundred dollar bill for getting him his bull. She's drunk, too."

"Good work, Buck. Maybe things have turned the corner for us." Jack adds, "I'm supposing that Moon and Dan made it alright."

"Oh yeah. They made it yesterday, late. But both of 'em are fine."

"Thank you, God," Jack says quietly. "What's for supper?"

Buck grins. "Steaks!"

Jack turns and points to Deputy Rose. "See that red-headed guy, there?"

"Yeah."

"Don't get in between him and the table — you could get run over. Coming up here, he ate enough gorp to carry a horse through the hunting season. Better hide the Omolene."

Rose grins hugely. "I'm still growing, I guess."

Buck gestures. "Well, go on up to the cook tent. The steaks are already frying. We'll take care of your gear."

The other deputy says, wearily, "Man, that is the most welcome news I've had since they handed me my discharge from the Army."

❄ ❄ ❄

It is the last sigh of day, and the snow is coming straight down, in flakes the size and delicacy of baby hands. There is not a breath of wind, and the snow piles up uniformly on everything. The dark pines are being redefined, then accented, and finally burdened until overflows sift down in slight cascades. All that evidences runnels of water are their muffled xylophone voices, ringing up through the white shroud.

Gib sits by his fire, looking out from his stout lean-to to watch the snowfall turn to steam on his sleepy horses. The fire throws a perimeter of pink light into the darkness, lighting the stout legs of the pines. During lulls, the firelight glances up the trees' fir undergarments. Then the huge flakes sift down again, returning them to modesty.

He leans over, picks up the coffee pot steaming on the edge of the fire and pours himself another cup. This snowfall is allowing him his first real rest in five days of constant travel.

"With this kind of weather, Ol' Ephraim is taking himself a nap, sure," he says aloud to himself. The buckskin looks over the little mare's back, and blinks in response. Gib puts the pot near the flames.

"What do you think, Horse? Is Eph on the run for his den, or is he just settin' us up — taking us into his neck of the woods, where he's picked the place for us to get down to business?" The horse snorts and shakes his head.

"I don't know, either." He slurps at the hot coffee. "But I do know one thing — this is the first good snow of winter, and this is the one that sends bears on a beeline for their hibernation bunks. The ones who are still out foraging, or raising hell like Eph, have to start taking care of winter business. They don't have much choice." Gib knows that animals' biological imperatives, like breeding and hibernation, aren't optional.

He takes another sip from his cup and, seeing the buckskin returning to sleep, adds a piece of wood to the fire. With a long stick, he pushes the log deep into the glowing coals, then tucks unburnt log ends into the flames with it. Little sparks fly from the new log, then flip into the air, where they are met by falling snow, and die with little spits of sound.

A small eddy of wind, pulsing from the approaching cold air cell, twines with the smoke from the fire and the coffee's steam, then hurries out into the dark and, as the impulse of air gains strength, makes its way through the pines, finally reaching, and rousing, the bear.

Small alarms go off in his great brain. He rolls over onto his stomach and stretches out his paws, but he cannot drive off the lethargy sapping his will. He knows whose fire he smells. He can even gauge the distance and direction, but he just cannot move. The breeze swerves, dances in another direction, taking the alarming smells with it. The bear rolls to his side, pulls up his paws, puts his nose under his arm.

Gib wakes with a start when a cold sprinkle of snow blows onto his face. He glances around. The fire is dying. Thin blue fingers of flame wave as the breeze fans them, then they fold back into the embers, flickering faintly as they are clasped from sight.

He pulls off his boots and puts them in the back of the lean-to, then unzips his bag and crawls in. Before he fastens the bag, he banks the fire with green logs, then lies down to watch the fire light dance on the shelter above. The wind calls, the cliffs echo the treetops' hushed voices. His eyes blink, blink again, then close.

Chapter 21

The camp cook fills Jack's cup with black coffee. "Thanks, that was a helluvva breakfast, Dutch,"Jack says.

The old man smiles his stained smile and says, "Backstrap, eggs an' potatas allus makes a prime breakfast. No reason to have anyone runnin' around hungry while there's meat in camp." He goes to his bunk in the corner, sits down and crosses his legs, then picks up his pipe and tobacco.

The tent is hot and smoky, but if the cook likes it that way God help the man who tries to usher fresh air inside by leaving a flap open. Dutch has the rheumatiz, and bellying up to the red hot stove while breathing meat smoke makes the old man feel better.

Jack smiles as he looks across the tent at a pie tin hanging on the side of the food cupboard. Dutch has found a marker and written on it, "You'll eat liver if I cook liver! This is my kichen — ferget the bitchen!"

The tent flap opens and the two deputies enter. Rose goes to the warmer and peeks inside. "How about a coupla those biscuits, Cookie?"

"Help yerself. They'll go to the camprobbers iffen you don't. Butter and jam's on the table."

The other deputy, Thompson, sits down after pouring a cup of coffee. "When we heading out?"

Jack pushes the sugar bowl to him and says, "Just as soon as everyone's ready. The hunters and guides are out of the way, so we can get organized any time. I just want to have a word with my two men first. I want to make sure they're fit to go — don't want another man getting sick."

"What's the plan?" asks Rose, around a mouthful of biscuit and jam.

"That bear is heading back for Yellowstone through Deer Creek Pass, near as I can figure. And wherever that bear goes, that's where we'll find Gib. It's just a matter of cutting their trail in this new snow and staying on it til we catch up to them."

Thompson shrugs. "You're the man. Just point us in the right direction and we'll follow along. This is your back yard, not ours."

"We'll set up your radio repeater when we get to the divide. Then we'll have communication with Sheriff Nagel. How long will it take?"

"Not too long — half hour, forty-five minutes."

Moon and Dan enter the tent and head for the coffee pot, Dan exclaiming, "She's a pretty one this morning. Musta got a foot and a half of new stuff last night."

Moon adds, "It's going to make for some slow traveling when we get a little higher. It musta really dumped up on the divide." He sits down next to Jack. "What's happening?"

Jack looks closely at Moon and says, "Guess we'll head for the Deer Creek country and see if we can find some sign in this fresh stuff. I'm sure that the bear is hot footing it for his denning ground, what with this change in the weather. Most of this country connects to Yellowstone through that pass. If we cut sign, we'll whip it up until we catch Gib. Then it'll be up to you...and the deputies." He pauses. "How you two doing? Feel alright?"

Dan shrugs, "Fine as frog hair. Why?"

"Just checking. How about you, Moon?"

"Don't worry 'bout me, just a little saddle sore. It's been a while."

Jack drains his coffee cup. "Well then, let's saddle up. It's gonna be light real soon — when we get the repeater set up, we'll check in with the sheriff's department and find out how Ole's doing."

❄ ❄ ❄

Gib wakes with a start. As he sits up and looks out over the snow laden grove, he feels something is very wrong. He unzips his sleeping bag, pulls on his boots. Then he reaches for his rifle, steps out of the lean-to and looks around. The horses are gone.

It is still as death among the snow-laden pines. The cliffs above have dragged the cold air to a standstill and wrung its clouds of most of their moisture. Everything is piled to overflowing with the fluffy ice. Trees are burdened to their limits. Downed logs have become indistinct lumps.

Gib's eyes sweep quickly over the surrounding scene. He sets one foot behind the other and raises the rifle to port arms as he concentrates his whole being into a careful inventory of the grove. His eyes move slowly from right to left, then back again across the scene.

Twenty five yards away, green deer brush and other small evergreens break the plane of white. The sides of tall stumps show patches of brown, and Gib assesses each dark object carefully, looking for something hairy brown with silver highlights trying to pass for a dusting of snow. There is a faint smell of ozone in the still air, as if an electric field had been set up around the man.

He begins to swivel around slowly, to survey the half of the scene that lies at his back. As he turns, the large burl on a log quivers, then changes to a grizzly's hump bearing an inch of new snow. The crest of the bear's head, ears flattened, eases up and the eyes, gorged with blood, rise into view. The bear sees the man's back turned. His moment has come.

A great howl erupts from the bear's throat as he rises on his forelegs, gathers his huge buttock muscles to drive himself across the short distance to his enemy. He vaults over the log, in full stride in less than a moment, roaring as he charges.

Gib's speeded up reflexes throw the scene into slow motion. He spins around to see the bear's neon eyes, his arched tongue, his great bristling hump, the arcing clods of ice flying from his enormous paws. He sees a string of spittle fly from the bear's gaping mouth, to drape itself on a pulsing muscular shoulder.

In an almost staggered motion, he steps into the charge, ignoring the avalanche of sound rolling over him. The rifle muzzle comes up as he gauges the distance. His finger takes up the slack in the trigger. The rubber recoil pad snags in the armpit of Gib's bulky coat. That millisecond is enough.

An electric flash of panic grips him. The old memory of this animal's power, the wounding grip of his enormous teeth, blows his composure away. He is lost. His finger grips the trigger in reflex. The big gun goes off, nearly in the bear's face.

The roar makes the animal close his eyes, flinch away, and break his charge. His rushing bulk pushes the man to one knee, but the bear spins back. The man is down, working the bolt on the rifle, struggling to rise.

The bear leaps again, his mouth open to finally rend his enemy's bones. The second roar from the misdirected rifle does not break his concentration. This time his heart sings as he gathers himself to charge again.

The bullet from the rifle buries itself in a large pine. The powerful thud of the heavy bullet shakes the tree, and the shudder dislodges a ton of snow. The bear, poised to throw himself over the last five yards, is buried by the heavy cascade. He inhales thick spindrift, feels the thudding bulk on his back and head. He swerves, mistaking the falling snow for a weapon used in the man's defense.

Gib, also in the blinding cascade, grimly works the rifle's action, taking advantage of this moment's grace. He feels the bear go blindly by him, the wake of snow from the bear's body pressing him back. The rancid smell of the hot animal fills his head. He feels the bullet lock in the chamber. He turns, he blindly points the gun and fires again. Now at the very edge of control, and hope, he jacks the smoking, redolent casing out and throws the long bolt forward again, but the finely oiled mechanism cracks hollowly on the bullet chamber, empty.

Chapter 22

Jack and the searchers are riding through deep snow in a patch of timber when he hears something up ahead and raises his arm as a signal to halt. The hollow "thump" of a hoof against a log comes through the trees.

"Elk," Moon says, quietly.

"I don't think so. Listen," Jack says, his head lowered as he concentrates on the sounds ahead. After a few moments, they hear heavily breathing animals moving toward them.

Moon smiles and whispers, "Betcha it's elk — and when them critters see us, they're going to tear this patch of timber up, getting outta here."

The men sit quietly, until Jack's horse stretches her neck and gives a great, shuddering whinny. It is answered instantly by another whinny, and the sound of horses laboring in their direction.

"I thought so," Jack says, and smiles. They wait until the big lineback buckskin, followed by the pack mare, come within a few yards, then stop to eye them.

Jack swings down and wades through the snow, talking in a low voice to the buckskin. He has stopped, his big intelligent eyes wide, his ears perked as he nervously shuffles his hooves. Jack reaches out carefully and grasps the lead rope, now frayed through.

"He's got an LU brand. It's gotta be Gib's horse."

"How fresh are they?" Dan asks. "Got any idea how far they've come?"

"They don't look like they've come real far, but it's hard to tell with the snow deep as it is."

"What are we gonna do with 'em?"

Jack answers, "We'll take them with us. Gib's gonna need them. Moon, you lead the mare and Dan can take the buckskin. You officers come up and ride behind me."

He grabs the mare's lead rope, then waits for the men to ride up and take their places. Then he remounts and rides to the head of the group. "We won't have any trouble finding him now," Jack says, spurring his horse into the fresh trail.

❄ ❄ ❄

Maggie puts down her pen, folds the letter she just finished and puts the paper in an envelope. She stands from the kitchen table, walks to the window and looks out to see Anisa returning from her ride. She puts on her coat and goes outside. The early morning is cold, but the sun is gaining strength and the air is warming. She takes a deep breath of air, sharp with the acidy smell of fallen cottonwood leaves. All over the Mountain West, things are readying for a long winter's sleep.

A skift of snow from the night's little storm still lies on the north sides of the ranch buildings, hiding from the sun. But winter will fall onto the country any day now. This day could be one of the last fine days before fall slips from their grasps. The place has returned to the quiet familiar to the women when the men's work takes them elsewhere. It is the quiet Maggie knew and loved as a child.

Beginning a game from her childhood, head down, she follows the patches and strips of sunlight on the ground, letting them take her where they will.

The sun leads her around the ranch's outbuildings, down the ranch road, then west along the river road. Before she reaches the bridge, she hears the hooves of Anisa's horse coming up behind her. She stops and waits while her sister-in-law dismounts. Then they continue in silence, the horse bobbing its head as it follows peacefully behind the two women.

They walk and listen to the river, each glancing up occasionally at the sun-drenched mountains with small clouds hanging from their summits. Magpies squawk in the trees and a raven croaks as it flies overhead, its wings swooshing like grain being scythed by hand. Each woman knows the other's thoughts, but neither wants to mar the beautiful morning with worried discussion of the happenings up in the mountains. However, when they give a big sigh simultaneously, they break into nervous laughter which turns into the real thing. Anisa bends over at the waist, with her hands between her knees.

"Stop, stop!" she says, "or I'll pee my pants!"

Which is exactly the wrong thing to say, as the picture sends Maggie into a laughing fit.

"Hold my horse!" Anisa cries and bounds off the road into the frosty willows on the river's edge. Maggie picks up the dropped reins, tears running down her face. By the time Anisa returns, Maggie is no longer shaking, but she has the hiccups from laughing so hard.

"*Boy*, it was cold in there," Anisa says, innocently. Maggie sets off again, and they laugh until they are helpless. Finally exhausted, they calm themselves.

Maggie wipes her eyes and says, "Oh Lord, I needed that."

"Me too." Anisa dries her face with the arms of her down coat. "All this morning I didn't know whether I needed to laugh or cry — I guess it was both. This waiting and not knowing what's going on up there — plus the fact that Red drives me nuts, sitting in front of that television all day and all night."

"He's lost without his friend, Echeverria, and he's more than a little bit institutionalized. It's another worry — and that laugh was a relief for me, too." A hawk cries high overhead and she stops to shade her eyes.

Anisa shades her eyes and looks up also. Then she says, "It's good to have you here, Maggie. Jack needs some family to fall back on, besides me and JC. I know how capable and honest a man he is, but I also know what a little boy he can be, especially when it comes to people, like Gib, that he loves — worships is more like it."

Maggie nods, "He is an innocent, alright."

"For the first few years we were married, I sometimes felt like I had two children to take care of. At first I ate it up, like when we were in high school, then when I was over in Powell, at college."

Anisa stops and looks down at the ground for a few seconds, gathering her thoughts. Spicules of frost are melting, creating a slick on top of the frozen dirt. Then she looks up at Maggie. "At first I thought that it was so romantic, being worshipped. I was one kid in a big family who got lost in the shuffle, pretty much. So, it was wonderful having Jack follow me around." She giggles. "He was such a jerk — chewing snoose and strutting in his boots when the other boys were around. But when we were alone he was gentle, kind. He made me feel like there was no one else in the world."

"For him, there really wasn't," Maggie comments. "Just me and Gib, and neither of us could give him what he needed, God knows."

"When we started…you know…in high school, it made him so happy. I didn't like it very much at first, but it made him…ecstatic. Or something like it."

Maggie nods. "For someone as starved for love as Jack was, I can see where real intimacy would inspire something like ecstasy in him."

"Well, anyway, we ended up having to get married and I guess everyone in the whole country knew."

"Probably not everybody."

"It sure seemed like it at the time, but we just drove to Thermopolis, got married and spent one night at the Holiday Inn. Then we went swimming the next day and came home to the ranch that evening. Gib moved out to the bunk house and that was that. He, Gib, had told Jack that it was the only thing to be done — to go get me at the college, and do what was right. Live with it." Anisa smiled. "And he was right. We've been mostly happy with one another."

"And you're a matched pair. Everyone sees it."

"If there's a problem, it's that our marriage is too perfect." Anisa bites her lip. "I know that sounds dumb."

"How can it be too perfect?"

"Jack decided that he was going to be the perfect husband, the perfect father, the perfect…everything. It gets to be too much. Do you know what it's like to live with someone who is trying to be perfect?" She slaps her leg with the reins. "Sometimes it makes me want to scream — Jack's need to please. His love can be a burden, I swear."

Maggie puts her hand on Anisa's arm when she sees tears in her eyes. "I know that it seems like betrayal to you but, you see, people raised in families where there is a lot of insecurity, like Jack and I were, can become perfectionists. It's based on a fundamental need to supply the emotional security they never had."

"You mean that it's…normal?" Anisa quickly adds, "I mean, that it's OK for me to feel the way I do?"

"Absolutely. Living with someone who needs to be perfect in an imperfect world is a very trying thing. Saints are saints and men are men. Have you ever heard anything of saints' wives?"

Anisa puts back her head and laughs out loud. "No, come to think of it!"

"You see," Maggie goes on, "Jack loves you and JC more than he loves himself, and that's the burden you are trying to bear. It's a burden that will eventually wear you out. They have no idea how selfish and insensitive it is, trying to please everyone all the time. They don't understand that knowing when and how to be selfish can be a gift — for both others and for themselves."

"It makes sense, when you explain it like that. All this time I've thought that it was my fault."

"And that's another part of it — making everyone else feel responsible for your own actions. It's a psychological spin that people from broken or dysfunctional homes put on the ball. He gets it from Gib."

Anisa takes a short breath. "Maggie…"

"Yes?"

"Is Jack Gib's son?"

Maggie puts her head down, then raises it to look at Anisa's face. "Yes."

Anisa glances back at the sky. "I knew it. You can't really see it in Jack, except for the eyes, but you can't miss it in JC, unless you try to. Does Jack have any idea?"

Maggie shrugs. "I doubt it. I mean, even if he had an idea that it was true, he would deny it. It's another trait of ours."

"How come you turned out so differently? You don't seem afraid of anything."

Maggie laughs. "Oh, that's another thing about us. Most of us are driven by fear, but we disguise it from everyone by being heroes, of a sort, all those straight A's and medical school, the professional certificates and community awards — but, at the heart of it all is a frightened little girl who was left for a ranch foreman to raise."

"It always comes back to Gib, doesn't it?"

"Yes. And I've been thinking about that a lot, lately. All of us seem to be little satellites to that big body. His pull affects us all, makes our orbits and our lives what they are. He helps define us."

"What happens when he's…gone?" Anisa's voice is small.

"You mean to Jack, don't you?"

"Yes."

"The same thing that will happen to us all — we'll go on." Maggie smiles. "But Gib will never be gone, really, he's too big for that. You see, Nisa, he is genuinely the stuff that myths are made of. He really is larger than life."

"Why is he so different? Where does someone like that come from?"

A moment passes before she answers, "Maybe he came to us from the gods — and only the gods know why."

❄ ❄ ❄

Gib, dehydrated and nearing exhaustion, sinks into the snow to rest. The dry cold air burns his lungs and throat, drawing the moisture from his body as he strides in the bear's tracks. The animal's strides are shortening too, a sign his body is also feeling the effects of the chase. The man looks up and sees the deep snow is thinning out. He can see shards of light through the trees, and hear the winds as they sweep up the tall cliffs above Deer Creek. He rises to his feet.

When he breaks out of the trees, he sees the bear's tracks turn to the left and he follows them, stride for stride. The trail leads out onto a snow laden bowl, a snow cornice poised on a cliff band jutting from the mountain's side. The bear's tracks lead over brush and rocks, then disappear behind a jut of rock in the middle of the steep bowl.

"Got you now!" Gib gasps. If he hurries, he knows he will be able to catch the bear on the open half of the bowl and use the rock to make a steady shot. He forces himself to pick up the pace. He needs to catch the animal before he can disappear into the tree line on the other side. Once into those trees, Gib knows, the animal will be gone for good.

The snow field is steeper than it looked. The sun glances from the white-ness, making his eyes water, but he has no trouble staying in the track. He pushes forward, leaning into the slope, his pace a machine-like, determined slog. His legs feel wooden.

Reaching the middle of the bowl, he welcomes the feel of rock beneath his feet. Another ten yards and he will be able to see the other side of the cirque. Another ten yards and he will have the bear in his sights — then he will only have to make the shot. His heart is pounding. The sound of his breathing is labored, whistling into his lungs as he makes his body obey. He stops in the middle of the rock, flips off the safety, and paused to catch a few breaths. He will need the oxygen in order to steady his hands for the shot.

He takes a half dozen deep breaths, feeling his heart begin to respond to the increased oxygen and reduce the pumping rate as his heart stills itself. He is putting out his foot, to begin his last stride, when a shadow falls over him, blotting out the sun. He looks up and sees the bear, coming out of a crouch in the rocks, a dozen feet above him.

As the animal drops down onto the man, he sees the upturned and startled face. The sun is glancing from the man's silver stubbled cheeks and wide blue eyes. The mouth is open, his hat falling off.

The ambush almost misses as Gib drops to a crouch, but a paw catches him on his shoulder and knocks the wind out of him. He hears his collar bone break, but he feels no pain. His whole being is intent on the fact that he has been knocked onto the steep, wind hardened snow of the alpine cirque.

The man tries to arrest himself with his good hand, but his fingertips only scratch and ratchet as he gains momentum. A protruding rock catches his knee and he bounds into the air. Then he is sliding again, gaining speed as he hurtles toward the edge of the cliff below.

He catches the bear halfway down the slope. They bump into one another, spin until they are, for a fraction, looking into one another's eyes. The huge amber eyes of the animal mirror the great wash of fear Gib feels as their slide accelerates.

Gib sees his rifle go by, passing them both. He hears it clack against the lip of the vertical cliffs and then silence as it flies out into the enormous void over Deer Creek. And then he is airborne too.

Spurring his exhausted horse, Jack breaks into the open just as the bear launches himself from the rocks. He sees them collide, then begin their slide down the steep snow field. He sees Gib bounce into the air. He sees the bear scratching desperately at the slope, breaking away great clods of snow with his claws. Then the two meet, spin apart, vault out over a thousand feet of nothingness. For a moment, they look as if they are embracing, or perhaps reaching out for one another. Then they drift apart, and fall from Jack's sight.

Epilogue

Maggie parks her car in front of the hospital in Cody. She douses the headlights and turns off the key, the engine fluttering and running on for a moment before it dies.

It is cold and dark. The gasping wind catches at her as she makes her way across the rutted, icy street toward the indistinct bulk of the hospital. When she opens the door, the smells and the lighting cause her to smile. This efficient environment had been a major part of her life. She loved it for its sense of quiet order. She walks down the gleaming corridor to the elevators and rides one of the faintly humming machines to the second floor. It is past visiting hours and the staff is busy with their routines, but they all smile and say, "Good evening, Doctor," as she walks to Ole's private room. Inside, another nurse gathers her sphygmometer and stethoscope as Maggie enters.

"How is he doing?"

The nurse, a large woman about Maggie's age, looks at Ole's slight figure on the bed and then looks back at Maggie. She leaves the room without a word, pulling the door softly shut behind her.

Maggie shrugs off her coat, drapes the garment over a chair and goes to Ole's side. She turns the bottle dripping into the shallowly breathing form to read its label, nodding as she deciphers the writing added in magic marker. It tells her a great deal.

She looks down at Ole's face and puts her hand on his cool forehead. She feels the fragile bone vessel lying so close to her palm. All the knowledge of her years as a doctor flow into her touch. The long years of study and their knowledge are as palpable as this dear, familiar form.

Her fingers go to the scrawny throat, covered with stickery white bristles, and she monitors the blood's thready pulse. She listens to Ole's breathing, reading its message also. The faint cadence of it all seems to set up a sympathetic rhythm in Maggie's own body as if her systems were wedded to the old man's.

Faces and rooms come and go — patients, doctors who had taught her, nurses she had loved as friends, fellow students she had loathed, the confetti of a distant city rushing into a rain grate as she waits to cross a thousand streets, bunches of flowers, the feel of dry eyelids and fatigue, the smell of gasses and viscera, lumps of green linen stuck with masking tape, the clatter of a dropped instrument, the bony touch of fingers on her arm...

"Maggie..."

She gives a start and snaps back into the room. "Hello, Ole," she says quietly as she looks down at him.

"I'm dying."

"Yes."

He closes his eyes, his hand still resting lightly on her arm. She sees his eyes moving under their translucent lids. His tongue sticks lightly to the roof of his mouth as he tries to speak. He wets his lips, begins again. "I hat a dog..." He was very, very weak.

"Queenie."

Ole smiles. "No, his name vas Mex — Dan's dogs vas all called Qveenie." He passes his tongue over his lips again. "Some Mexicans give him to me 'cause dey vas leafin de country. He vas vun heckuffa dog, ven he fin'lly learnt English." He gave a transparent chuckle and paused. "You vant to know sometin dat's de trut'?"

"Sure."

"Dat dog knew, efery time, ven you vas talkin 'bout him. He did." Ole nods his chin slightly and smiles. "He vas de smartest dog in dis part of de country, and den some — an' de cows knew it, too."

Maggie smiles and puts her hand on Ole's. "He must have been really something."

"He sure vas. He vas a pistol, alright."

Ole smiles again and opens his eyes, which are a clear, luminous blue. "You vant to know sometink else?"

"You bet," Maggie says, huskily.

"He vas here — yust a coupla minutes ago."

"He was?"

"Ya. And he vas wit somevun who vas sayin' some very nice t'ings to me. Den de nurse come and scairt 'em avay." He closes his eyes and gives a slight nod. His lips move a bit, his chin gives an almost imperceptible tilt. His life is gone.

Maggie crosses the little man's hands, then walks across the room to sit in the lounge chair someone had dragged into the room.

She watches what remains of Ole and listens to the wind blow outside. It reminds her of childhood nights when the great chinooks would shake the very walls of the ranch house. Sometimes she would get up and call down the hall for Gib. He would always call back, "It's OK, try to sleep."

Gib was gone, now Ole. A whole generation passing, right on its schedule. It is sad, in a way, but she understands this is the nature of life. Death is only a natural end to the precious process.

For the first time, she realizes that her biblical generation of twenty years has begun with the death of the men who had served as her father figures for all these years. It leaves her only twenty years to do all that she has planned. Everything which had gone before was only preparation for this moment.

She stands and rings for the nurse, then leans over Ole and kisses him lightly on the forehead. "Thank you," she says, and pulls the sheet over the little Norwegian bachelor whom everyone had loved.

And then something comes to her, something else from the Bible — a verse about being generous, because you never know when you might be entertaining an angel.

❄ ❄ ❄

JC finishes cleaning and inspecting the horse's hoof. "She's bruised the frog in this front one, she won't be going up on the next hunt," he says, straightening to his full 6'1" height. "Turn her out in the pasture and bring in one to replace her." The oldtimer holding the horse's halter takes the horse away.

The tall young man takes off his hat and gauges the cloudless sky overhead. The sun lights his eyes, turning them a colloidal, Caribbean blue. He shakes his head and puts the hat back on.

A high pressure weather system has been sitting squarely over the Big Horn Basin for a full month, giving them flawless weather all that time. It was nice to have a first day in November as fine as this, but it made the hunting business a tough affair. The animals were still hanging in the highest country available, and tracking them was next to impossible. Their success rate has been low, and the hunters all bitched about the poor hunting. More life.

He leaves the corrals and walks toward the main lodge, which sits in the old bull pasture next to the ancestral ranch house. He glances around as he walks, shaking his head at the changes of the last five years. The "Rocking Chair Ranch," as the residents call it, seems to have appeared out of nowhere. But it is real all right. The quilting circle is on the patio, quiet except for snippets of gossip and little titters as they comment on the passing scene of a working ranch. JC waves at Security, who is pushing an old lady in a wheelchair. He waves back and smiles.

JC steps onto the porch and says, "How's it going, Joe?"

Joe Echeverria raises his hand in acknowledgement but, as always, says nothing. Then he turns his attention back to the sky over Carter Mountain, comforted by the enormous LU sheep ranch lying on the other side — one of the few remaining big sheep outfits. He is constantly pleased the business has not died out completely. His heart is on the other side of the mountain. It has been his only consolation since his friend, Red, had died the year before, and his black hair had finally started to turn gray.

JC smiles and thinks, Enjoy yourself, Joe, you paid for the place. And he had. His three hundred thousand dollars of seed money had made the place a reality.

Inside, Dan Williams and Moon are playing Cribbage. "Fourteen two, fourteen four, and a Jack for nobs. I'm out. That's a Crib." Dan smiles wickedly and says, "Beat ya agin."

Moon looks sour and throws his cards down. "Why you old shit, no one can be that lucky."

"I'm good — too durn good to be frittering away my time beating your socks off, day after day. I swear, it's a shameful waste of talent."

"I wouldn't be a damn bit surprised if you haven't been cheating."

"Aw, I been beating you at Crib for more'n fifty years."

"And you probably been cheating for them fifty years, too!"

"Whatsamatter? Yer rheumatiz acting up again?"

"Yeah, and my gout, and I'm bound up tighter'n hell again."

"Yep, your eyes is sticking out — like a bullfrog staring through ice."

"That ain't as funny as you think…look at that kid," he says, thrusting his chin at the passing JC.

"What about 'im?"

"Sometimes it's plain eerie, how much he can remind ya of Gib."

"Well, he'd damn sure going to be as tall. He's growing like a weed."

"It's more than that. Hell, look at that walk. He's Gib all over."

"Well, he's a hand all right. Won it all at the National High School Rodeo last year. It must be something in the water here."

But both old men know the truth, though each isn't sure the other one knows.

"Can you stand another game?"

"Why not? You deal."

Dan scoops up the cards and begins to shuffle. "Gib," he says. "I was just thinking about him last night. Couldn't sleep."

"Mmmm."

Dan chuckles. "It come to me — in life nobody ever could tell him what to do, and even God couldn't tell him when, or how, he was gonna die. Now that's stubborn."

Moon grins. "He was different, all right. Different."

"Sometimes I miss him. A lot."

"Hell," Moon mutters, "I miss him every damn day — boring as hell without him stirring things up." He chuckles. "Heh, heh, remember the night he shot ol' Red's pissbag off?"

Inside Maggie's office, JC waits for his aunt to finish her phone conversation. He smiles as he looks at the sampler hanging on the wall above her desk. It reads: *THEY'RE NUTS.*

She'd had the sewing group make a second one for Doctor Hillyard, down in Evanston. He'd hung the needlepoint motto in his office at home and sent her a picture of him sitting beneath it, a big smile on his face. The picture was on her desk.

Maggie finally puts the phone down and looks up at her nephew. He has no way of knowing what she is thinking, but her eyes soften as she looks up at the tall young man. She is seeing the same things that Dan and Moon had seen in him, minutes before.

"Aunt Maggie, I'm going to town for grub and stuff. I'm going to need a check from the hunting account."

"All right." Maggie reaches into a drawer and takes out a commercial checkbook. "You are getting taller every day, JC."

"Yes, ma'am." JC looks down fondly at his aunt as she bends over the desk and writes the check. "Where's Dad?"

"He and your mom took the baby and went up to the cemetery."

"I been thinking about them all day, myself. November already — strange how they would all die in the same month."

Maggie looks up at JC as she hands him the signed check. "Walk up with me."

"You bet. I'd be glad to."

Up the hill, Jack and Anisa with four-year-old Justine, stand in front of the tombstones. In the center of the fenced square are the large and ornate headstones of Jack's nominal parents, grandparents, and great-grandparents. Anisa puts down the basket she is carrying and takes out the bunches of flowers, the season's very last. She puts them, one by one, on the graves.

Jack stands over them, his lips pursed in thought. Justine runs to the fence, peeks through and laughs at the horses in the pasture below. "Rosses," she says, pointing.

Anisa gathers the last three bunches of flowers and goes to a second row of headstones, these smaller and fashioned from local rock. The names are cut into facets polished on the rock faces.

"One for you, Ole," she says, placing a bunch. "And one for you, too," she says as she places the second bunch on Red's grave. Then she puts the last bunch in Jack's hands and he stoops to put them in front of the one that reads:

Hurley John Gibson

GIB

Jack stands and puts his arms around Anisa's shoulders. "Maybe we should put some dates on the stone. I mean, now that we know when he was born — and when he died."

"Oh, I don't know. I kind of like it this way."

"How so?"

Anisa shrugs. "Well, he never really seemed to belong to any one place, or to any one time." She pauses. "I don't know how to put it, exactly."

"Maybe you mean that he never really belonged to anybody." There is a pained note in Jack's voice.

Anisa puts her hand on his and looks up at his weathering face. He is smaller, and he has his mother's strawberry blonde hair, but the likeness is apparent to anyone with eyes. She says, "He'll never be dead as long as you are alive. He gave you everything he had to give."

She shades her hand over her eyes and looks across the valley at the cloud banner streaming from the east end of Carter Mountain. "Looks like we're finally going to get some weather."

Jack pulls her close. "Let 'er come," he says as he looks toward the ranch. His sister and son are walking up the hill toward them.

Anisa gives a little start and says, "Where's Justine?"

They turn around, about to call the child's name, but stop to stare. The golden-haired child is standing beneath the quaking aspen behind Gib's grave. Despite the breathless mountain day down in the valley, the tree's leaves are glittering and dancing. Their rustling sound is falling down onto the child's charmed and upturned face, like mountain music.

The End